THE BEAST

Baron Hector ~~~~~~ ~~~~~~~ everything that
Leonora detested—a selfish, greedy, lustful brute.
Even worse, he made it plain that he wanted
Leonora for his own.

Leonora vowed that there was no way she would
satisfy his base desires.

But now Burlington gave her the most devilishly
despicable ultimatum. She must submit to his
wishes, or he would reveal the secret that would
ruin her in the eyes of the man she loves.

Never had a young lady been faced with a crueler
choice—or decided on a more daring gamble. . . .

A native of Yorkshire, England, IRENE SAUNDERS
spent a number of years exploring London while working for the U.S. Air Force there. A love of travel
brought her to New York City, where she met her
husband, Ray, then settled in Miami, Florida. She now
lives in Port St. Lucie, Florida, dividing her time between writing, bookkeeping, gardening, needlepoint,
and travel.

LORDS AND LADIES

Laces for a Lady

— by —

Irene Saunders

A SIGNET BOOK

NEW AMERICAN LIBRARY

NAL BOOKS ARE AVAILABLE AT QUANTITY DISCOUNTS WHEN USED TO
PROMOTE PRODUCTS OR SERVICES. FOR INFORMATION PLEASE WRITE
TO PREMIUM MARKETING DIVISION, NEW AMERICAN LIBRARY,
1633 BROADWAY, NEW YORK, NEW YORK 10019.

SIGNET TRADEMARK REG. U.S.PAT. OFF. AND FOREIGN COUNTRIES
REGISTERED TRADEMARK—MARCA REGISTRADA
HECHO EN CHICAGO, U.S.A.

SIGNET, SIGNET CLASSIC, MENTOR, PLUME, MERIDIAN and
NAL BOOKS are published by NAL Penguin Inc.,
1633 Broadway, New York, New York 10019

First Printing, April, 1989

1 2 3 4 5 6 7 8 9

PRINTED IN THE UNITED STATES OF AMERICA

Prologue

Leonora Clairmont, never a slugabed, awoke with a feeling of excitement. Not bothering to reach for a robe, she jumped out of bed and ran barefoot to the window, pulled back the curtains, and smiled, for it was just the kind of day she had hoped for.

The sun gleamed on the water of the bay, and a fair wind sent a few puffy clouds scuttering across the blue sky. It was perfect weather for sailing.

She turned as Millie, her maid, came hurrying in from the dressing room carrying a set of boys' clothes over one arm and a voluminous cloak over the other.

"I should 'ave woke you before now, milady," she said, looking worried. "You'd do better with a bite of breakfast in you, but now there's no time."

"Stop worrying, Millie," Leonora told her as she stepped into the trousers, then pulled the jersey over her head. "I'll get the sloop and bring it to the village jetty while you hurry down and let them know I'm on my way. I would not like them to think me chickenhearted."

They sped swiftly down the back stairs and into the fresh air, parting company as the maid put the cloak over her uniform and headed toward the village while Leonora tucked her hair under a fisherman's knit cap and took the path to the cove.

Some thirty minutes later Leonora brought her sloop alongside the jetty where Joe Turner's slightly larger fishing sloop lay at anchor and a crowd of villagers waited. An enterprising fisherman-turned-bookmaker was busy taking bets on the outcome of the race.

After a brief discussion between the participants, the

two vessels headed toward open water, where they
jockeyed into position beside a buoy lying to the east.

Standing back slightly from the crowd, two well-dressed
gentlemen watched the proceedings with mild interest. "If
I were placing a bet, my money would go on the older man,
I believe," Lord Gerard Sinclair remarked to his friend,
"but it all depends upon how long the race is. If it's short,
then the young lad might just take it, but the older fellow
would have more staying power in a longer race."

"I heard one of the fishermen say they're to go from the
east buoy around the buoy to the west and back twice, then
make for the jetty," his friend, Sir Timothy Torrington,
informed him.

"Well, we may as well stay and watch the finish, as it
appears that no business will be conducted here in the
meantime," Sinclair said with some asperity. "If my
memory serves me, the fellow who is about to signal the
start is the innkeeper I want to question."

A cheer went up from the crowd as the race began and
the two vessels got under way.

There was a hush as the boats appeared to sail side by
side, then a murmuring in the crowd as one of them forged
ahead, rounding the westerly buoy and putting distance
between them.

"Well, I'll be damned if the lad isn't leading," Sinclair
exclaimed. "If he keeps his wits about him, the race will be
his by a mile."

The crowd on the jetty were becoming vociferous,
calling, "Come on, Lady Leo," "Get a move on, Joe,"
though there was little chance that the participants could
hear them at this distance.

Then, as the smaller vessel rounded the easterly buoy for
the second time and headed for home, there were loud
cheers mingled with groans from some who had backed the
other.

"It's a good thing we'd no one here to place a wager
with, for we would surely have lost in this race,"
Torrington said thankfully. "Who would have thought
that the young lad could have pulled it off with such
flair?"

"Well, I'd never have believed it!" Sinclair exclaimed. "That's no young lad, Timothy, it's a girl. Just look at that hair!"

As the victor crossed the agreed finishing line and the crowd started to cheer, she had pulled off the fisherman's cap she wore and exultantly tossed it high, permitting a mass of black hair to tumble around her shoulders and down her back.

The race had been a private wager that had rapidly become public as word had spread among the village folk. Leonora could see several of the house servants on the crowded jetty, and in the rear she noticed two well-dressed gentlemen whom she knew she had never seen before and hoped were not friends of her father's.

This was no time to linger and taste the fruits of victory, for if word of this latest escapade reached Lord Clairmont, he would be in a rare taking and might even forbid her to sail for an indefinite period.

Picking up her cap from where it had fallen, she crammed her hair under it once more, put the sloop hard over, and as she came about, gave a victorious wave to Joe Turner, then sailed out of the harbor.

"Probably the daughter of one of the fishermen," Sir Timothy suggested, "for in villages like this the children learn to sail before they can scarcely walk."

Sinclair shook his head. "That was no working boat," he murmured, "for there were no nets or traps aboard. It looked more like a vessel a gentleman would keep for pleasure, and did you see the name?"

"*Lady Leo*, wasn't it?"

"Yes," he said with a nod, "that was it. It's a pity we don't have time to pursue it further, for it piques my curiosity. However, the innkeeper is returning to his place of business. Let's see what we can find out about this seemingly quiet fishing village. I see some of the winners already hurrying to celebrate."

One hour later, and considerably lighter in the pocket, Lord Sinclair left the inn no wiser as to the villagers' activities than when he went in.

When he had collected his curricle from the stable where

he had left it, and he and Sir Timothy were clear of the village, he told his friend, "That was not as complete a waste of a morning as it appeared. Their unusual skill in evading my questions leads me to believe I am on the right track," he murmured.

"Just what are you trying to find out?" Torrington asked. "I can hardly believe that Perceval wants you to single-handedly put a stop to smuggling. It's been going on since long before Boney threatened any European countries who traded with us."

"And will continue, no doubt, when we're long forgotten. It's no longer a simple evasion of import duties, of course, but a way of procuring goods that can no longer be obtained in legal trade," Sinclair added. "However, I'm not concerned with the goods that are brought into the country. That's up to the Revenuers. What I'm trying to do for the Prime Minister is locate and expose those smuggling gangs who supplement their income by bringing in French spies. I've been fairly successful around Dover and up the East Coast, and now I'm concentrating my efforts on the South Coast."

"I'm not going to ask you how you go about it, for it sounds like a dangerous business to me," Torrington remarked.

Sinclair gave a short, bitter laugh. "Not nearly so dangerous as fighting in Spain with Wellington, I can assure you. But since the old marquess used devious means to prevent my acceptance in the Army, spy-hunting is the next-best thing."

Torrington grunted. "That's a matter of opinion, I would think," he said, "but if you should get into something you can't handle alone, feel free to call on me at any time. Might not be as quick as you, but the spirit's willing, and I can keep a still tongue in my head when necessary."

"Thanks, old chap. I'll remember that—and I may just need a hand one of these days," Sinclair said, touched by his friend's offer. "Now, let's find an inn that serves a good luncheon, for it's been a long time since breakfast."

1

Though the hour was late, the candles had still not been snuffed in the earl's handsome bedchamber, and he seemed disinclined, as yet, to rest in the arms of Morpheus. He had something on his mind that he must discuss before he and his lady, who shared his huge bed, could turn to pleasanter activities.

"I've been giving some thought to that adorable hoyden I have for a daughter," he began. "Since you took her in hand, Adele, I've seen a vast improvement in her dress and deportment, but sailing, swimming, horseback riding, and goodness knows how many other things Geoffrey taught her, are hardly ladylike pursuits.

"Now that her brother's off with Wellington, it's high time we found her a suitable husband, but he'll need to be strong, with a tight hold on the reins to keep her in check. I know I'm to blame, my dear," he conceded, "for she was let run loose too long. But before it's too late, Leonora must be turned into a lady, given a Season in London, and a good match found for her. Do you not agree with me?"

Lord Clairmont, fifth Earl of Bristol, still retained a modicum of his earlier handsome countenance, but had begun, of late, to appear older than his fifty-two years. Now reclining at ease upon the bed, he looked with affection at the kindly gentlewoman he had taken as his second wife just six months before. Her head was nestled against his shoulder and there was something so peaceful and relaxing about her that he wished he had not waited so long, but had married her when first they met.

Instead, he had wasted precious years seeking consolation for the loss of his first wife, by frequenting the gaming hells of London, drinking, gambling and carousing, and, by example, showing his son the fastest way to ruination of health if not estates.

Not that he had ever lost heavily at the tables, for he was an excellent card player, but his liver would never be the same, he was plagued with gout, and he became out of breath from even the slightest exertion.

Adele Clairmont, an attractive woman, though tending to plumpness and with some silver in her softly curling brown hair, was an eminently suitable second wife for the earl. In her early thirties, she was still young enough to remember when she was Leonora's age, yet mature enough to be of no romantic interest to the twenty-one-year-old Geoffrey. A lively sense of humor and an unusual amount of tact and understanding had served her well in adjusting to the earl and his family.

She lifted one of his hands, caressing the soft palm with her fingertips, then holding it against her cheek. "I agree entirely, Roland, but just how do you propose to accomplish this? Your daughter needed little persuasion from me to start behaving in a more ladylike way here in the house; however, she has no experience with suitable young men, and I feel most strongly that she should acquire a deal more polish before being plunged into a London Season."

Lord Clairmont grunted. "I haven't seen her at her needlework of late, and only last week I caught her stealing through the kitchens and out through the back door when Burlington's carriage came up the driveway."

She turned to gaze directly at her husband, noting how pallid and lined his face was becoming, and she earnestly prayed her loving care might heal his ills.

"Now, Roland," she said with a gently reproachful smile, "your daughter has no aptitude for needlework. Why force her to endure pricked fingers and frustration? Tomorrow I will show you some of her watercolors, and you will see where her artistic tendencies truly lie. She is indeed quite accomplished."

"Is she, by Jove?" Lord Clairmont exclaimed. "I'd be glad to see her work and offer her a little encouragement.

My father painted, you know, but had to give it up when the estate took up most of his time."

"You should be ashamed that you did not know of your daughter's talents, my lord," Adele scolded lightly, "but we'll both forgive you if you can devise some way to keep that horrid Lord Burlington away from her. Good gracious, the man's more than twenty years older than she is!"

"I'm almost twenty years older than you, and we have one of the best marriages I've seen in a long time." He chuckled softly. "Have to admit, though, that when I made my offer I'd no notion what a warm, passionate heart lay hidden beneath a somewhat frigid exterior."

Adele smiled. "Not frigid. Restrained, perhaps, for I had not thought to find a love match at this time. We were indeed fortunate, but the situations are not alike. I was not just eighteen years of age, and you were not looking for a good, strong breeder, as I once overheard Burlington telling someone," she said disgustedly. "He should try to find himself a healthy farmer's daughter!"

Roland Clairmont reached for his wife and drew her close once more. "In six months you have worked miracles, my dear. You realized Geoffrey was emulating me with his carousing, wenching, and heaven knows what else, because he was bored. I never saw him happier than when I proposed buying him a commission, for it was apparently what he'd always wanted." He pressed a soft kiss in her ear and marveled when she trembled with delight. "And I'll admit Leonora is a little less tomboyish than she was, and even seems to enjoy dressing up once in a while, though she don't care enough for dancing and female pleasures, to my way of thinking."

Adele sighed. "Leonora loves to dance, but she hates to have young boys still wet behind the ears trample all over her feet. She meets few gentlemen of quality in these parts. I believe we should spend a month in Bath to get her accustomed to being with people her own age and class, before journeying to London. It would probably do you a world of good, also, to sample the waters."

"Just a minute, my lady," Roland protested with a wolfish grin. "I'm not ready to be pushed around in one of those demmed chairs yet. I can still show you a thing or two," he promised, reaching a hand beneath the sheets to stroke her intimately.

Adele Clairmont gasped with delight, and all thoughts of her husband's children were forgotten as he took her to heights of pleasure unknown to her six months ago. Her last thought as she fell asleep in his arms was that she must find for Leonora a husband who could make her as happy as she herself was at this very moment.

Clairmont House was in total darkness, its occupants having retired more than an hour before, when a small figure, dressed in old trousers tucked into heavy socks, and a thick wool jersey, crept silently along the corridors and up the stairs to the attics where the servants were quartered. Pausing but momentarily as the sound of muffled giggles came from behind a closed door, the prowler moved steadily toward the east end of the hall, unlocked the last door on the right, and entered an unused room, carefully sliding the well-greased bolt before crossing to the window.

Only someone familiar with the room by day could have proceeded with such confidence, for the night outside was black as the room itself. This condition prevailed for but a moment, however, for there was a scratching sound, then a flame touched the wick of a candle conveniently placed in the center of the windowsill. It sputtered slightly, then rose to send its warm light over the sparse furnishings and out into the night.

Above her brother's cast-off clothes, the oval face of Leonora Clairmont looked its loveliest in the soft glow, though her mass of black hair was hidden once more under a fisherman's knit cap. A worried frown creased her brow and there was concern in her sapphire-blue eyes. She hastened from the room, carefully locking the door behind her, and stood for a moment until her eyes adjusted again to the darkness.

Hurrying now, she retraced her steps, passing her own bedchamber and taking the back stairs, through the kitchens and to the very end of the wine cellar, where she struggled to roll a barrel out of the way, then pressed a part of the wall firmly, as her brother had taught her.

The door that swung inward was no more than five feet in height, revealing a dark passage and, just inside, where she had placed them earlier in the day, her boots and a lantern. Moving less cautiously now, she quickly donned the boots, lighted the lantern, and hurried down the gradual slope of the passage.

When the lamplight fell on a door in the wall, she sighed with relief, then took several more steps forward until she found what she sought, a deep hole in the face of the rock above her, through which she could feel and smell the salt air. She placed the lantern firmly in the hole, then turned around and went through the door and out into the black night.

She was surefooted despite the darkness, and moved swiftly along a rough footpath until she came to the road that ran through the village. Afraid of meeting anyone, she kept to the rough terrain on one side, stumbling against tufts of coarse grass and gorse that pulled at the threads in her knit socks and jersey as she made her way into the village and down to the jetty where a fishing boat lay alongside.

She hesitated, barely making out several bulky figures and an occasional soft murmur. Then one of the figures moved toward her, and though she could hardly see more than his outline, she realized he knew who she was.

"Let's 'ave you aboard, m'lady." The words were a gruff whisper and she felt a rough hand grasp her arm and pull her toward the boat. "Just keep your eyes and your ears open and your mouth closed. If we need you, I'll tell you," the man said as he guided her along the deck to a spot where she would be out of the way.

She watched the men cast off, recognizing them now, despite the darkness, as local fishermen she had known all her life. As they went about their tasks, she was surprised at their unusual silence, for she had often seen them fishing by day and heard their sometimes crude jokes and shouts of laughter. Then she recalled that French warships were known to frequent these waters at night, capturing any vessels they could. Leonora knew that noise carried a long way over water, so she decided the crew was being cautious.

As the lugger plowed quietly through the dark waters, she thought of Geoffrey, her brother, now fighting Napoleon's army in Spain. He was the reason she was here now. Before leaving, he had asked her to help him and she had been so miserably unhappy at his imminent departure that she had agreed without question.

Her beloved brother Geoffrey was four years her senior. She could not remember a time when he had not been there, teaching her how to swim, to ride, and to sail their sloop, which was now hers. It was he who had discovered the secret passage from the wine cellar and had taken her through it to the cavern, an unusual rock formation at the west side of Clairmont Cove, where their sloop, and even a boat as big as this fishing vessel, could dock and be completely out of sight.

Entrance to the cove itself was hazardous, for there were hidden rocks and sandbars to trap unwary vessels, but at a very early age Geoffrey had taught her how to navigate the deep channels to and from their dock and, when she was a little older, to the cavern on the far side of the cove.

Lulled by the sound of the waves and the rocking of the boat, she was almost asleep and had not seen the signal from the vessel that was now suddenly alongside. There was a murmur of voices, and she strained her ears to catch what they were saying, recognizing French words and heavily accented English ones mingled with the familiar voices of the fishermen.

Holding her breath, she crept to where she could just make out the outline of the other boat, then watched in shocked disbelief as kegs of what could be nothing else but brandy were brought aboard and stowed, along with some other oddly shaped bundles, quite close to where she lay hidden. One thing was suddenly very clear. Her brother must have been part of a local smuggling operation, and now she was also involved!

The French boat slid silently away, and as the lugger turned for home, Leonora found herself nervously scanning the waters, watching in case one of the fast Revenue cutters came into view. Twice she let out a gasp as she thought she saw a sail, and felt her heartbeat quicken with fear, but each time she was mistaken, and the trip back was as quiet as the trip out had been.

When they were once more at the jetty, and the men started to carry the kegs into the nearby shed, Leonora felt strangely elated. She had done nothing yet, but it had been an exciting experience and she could understand why her brother had joined the enterprise, for life at Clairmont House was extremely dull for her, and it must have been much more so for Geoffrey.

Ted Peterson, who seemed to be in charge, came over as she scrambled onto the jetty. "Wait over there, m'lady," he said, almost under his breath, "and as soon as we're done 'ere, I'll walk back with you."

He motioned to the side of the shed, and Leonora readily complied, for there were many questions she wanted answered. First and foremost, why had they taken her with them tonight? She was no longer afraid, for though Revenue men might be close by, waiting to spring out, she knew the surrounding countryside better than even the village people, and could lose them easily in the darkness.

In less than ten minutes the boat was unloaded, its cargo hidden away, and the men had melted silently into the night as Ted came over to where she waited.

"You're likely sorry we didn't need you tonight, m'lady," he said quietly as they started to walk up the village street, "but the rest of us were not, for we don't look for trouble. But with Bob Bowers ailing again, I thought it best to 'ave you aboard."

Leonora was having difficulty keeping up with his long strides. Suddenly she stopped altogether, forcing him to halt and turn around.

"Mr. Peterson—" she began, but was interrupted.

"Ted's enough," he told her, "and I think we'd best call you Leo, as Geoff did. It'll be safer."

"Very well," Leonora said with a sigh, for his interruption had lessened somewhat her determination to set him straight. "Ted it shall be, but I think you had best do a little explaining. Just what exactly did you think you might need me for?"

She couldn't see him clearly, but she could hear the surprise in his voice as he asked, "D'you mean you don't know? Didn't Geoff tell you we might need you to get us to the cavern in Clairmont Cove?"

"In pitch darkness and handling a fishing boat?" It was so ridiculous that Leonora almost laughed, but stopped herself as she realized he was deadly serious. "You have no notion of how fortunate it was you did not need me," she said with a shake of her head, then started to walk up the road again. This time Ted shortened his steps to fit hers.

"But that's what the lights are for. 'E and Bob use them to keep in the channels," Ted explained. "Didn't 'e tell you that, neither?"

"My dear brother, bless him," Leonora said slowly, "asked me to put the lights in place each time I got a note from you, and he told me you might send other instructions if Bob should be indisposed, though he did not say how I was to help." She paused for a moment. "But, Ted, the most important thing he failed to reveal was that you, and he also, are smugglers."

They had almost reached the path leading to the hidden passage, and now it was Ted's turn to stop.

"A fine bloody mess we'd 'ave been in then if Revenuers 'ad got wind of us," he muttered angrily. " 'E was that anxious to get at Frenchy in Spain that 'e clean forgot 'is obligations 'ere."

"But why did he go out with you in the first place?" Leonora asked. "It couldn't have been for the money, for Papa has always given him an ample allowance, or so he told me."

"Young Geoff didn't take money from us, if that's what

you were thinking. 'E did it for the fun of it, 'e told me. 'E liked nothing better than to make a run for the cove with the cutter on 'is tail.''

She looked worried, and he touched her arm. "I know you can't understand 'im taking up with the likes of us, but 'e'd 'ung around us since 'e was a youngster and, with your father away so much, there was nothing 'ere for a young dandy like 'im to do.

"We wouldn't let 'im in at first, but then 'e came up with this idea of using Clairmont Cove when we 'ad to. So 'e come with us, and we tried it, and then 'e showed Bob 'ow to get in and out. 'E always put lights up, but 'e didn't come with us every time, just when 'e felt like it, or when Bob was feeling bad.''

Leonora made a quick decision. "Don't worry, Ted," she said firmly. "I know now, and I'll practice in my sloop until I can come in blindfold—or almost."

"And you're still willing to 'old yer tongue and take the risks with us?" he asked in surprise. "Geoff said you were a game one, but I never for a minute thought you knew nothing about it.''

"By the time you're ready to go out again, I'll be as competent as my brother was," Leonora bragged, though inwardly she quaked a little.

The fisherman grinned. "You might even be better, for 'e said you were as good as 'im, and you didn't take damn fool chances the way 'e did when 'e'd a drink or two in 'im,'' he said dryly. "Only thing is, do you 'ave the nerve? You'll only be taking us in that way if a Revenue cutter's right behind us.''

"I'm afraid I can't answer that until I've been through it, Ted," she told him quietly. "Tell me what you usually do under such circumstances.''

Ted had begun to have doubts again, and he shook his head as he started to explain. "If we pick up the Revenuers, we don't come into our jetty, but make for Clairmont Cove instead. If it's a cutter that's been there before, it'll turn back unless it can catch us in open water, but we can't go back, as it'll be sitting out there waiting for us.''

Leonora nodded slowly, for she knew how easy it was for a boat to founder on the rocks at the entrance. She had heard that some of her less-pleasant ancestors used to wait for boats to run onto the rocks, even guiding them there with lights sometimes, then claimed whatever they could salvage off the sands and out of the water as their own.

"Then what we need is a good 'ead and a steady 'and to take us through the channels and into the cavern. Once inside, we 'ave the rest of the night to unload and bring it up the steps and along the passage to 'ere." He gestured toward the bushes they had now reached, which concealed the door to the passage. "Do you think you'll be able to 'andle it?"

"I think so, for I won't have much choice, will I? I dare not think of what would happen if we were caught," she whispered.

Ted nodded, seemingly satisfied by her answer.

Leonora hadn't noticed in the darkness that Ted was carrying anything, but now he thrust a package into her hands.

"This is a little something for yourself for coming tonight," he said gruffly. "Geoff used to take a bit of brandy when 'e felt like it, but there's no use in giving you that, for the earl always gets 'is regular deliveries from us, but I think this will suit you better. It's laces for a lady. Good night now, Leo."

He touched a finger to his cap in salute and disappeared into the night as Leonora entered the passage, took down the lantern, and made her way back to the wine cellar.

Creeping stealthily through the kitchen and up the back stairs, she reached her bedchamber without incident. Suddenly she felt exhausted and a little shaky, so that it was a tremendous effort to remove the heavy garments she used for fishing and slip into her warm flannel nightgown.

But, tired though she was, when her eye fell on the package Ted had given her, lying where she had dropped it, she could not resist opening it right away. As she tore off the wrapping, yard upon yard of the most beautiful pure white wide lace edging spilled out.

She held it before her mirror and, dreaming how lovely it would look edging the neckline and hem of a ball gown, clutched it to her bosom as she started to execute the steps of the waltz, the wicked new dance that Adele, her stepmother, had insisted she learn.

Still hugging the lace, but feeling a little dizzy from twirling about, she sat down abruptly on the edge of the bed. She was not at all sure she wanted to be a part of a smuggling operation, and she had taken no part in the activities last night, so she could hardly be labeled "smuggler" yet. But she doubted seriously that Ted and the other men would allow her to back out of her brother's agreement. There was nothing they could do to her, but they might be able to harm her brother if they chose. What if he was discharged from the army, brought back to stand trial, and hanged?

Her eyes fell on the lace once more. If Papa could have French brandy, she could have French lace, she decided, but there was one thing she drew the line at. If they should ever bring in spies, she would have nothing further to do with them, and she must make sure that Ted realized how she felt.

Carefully refolding the lace, she hid it in the bottom drawer of her armoire, then climbed into bed and fell into a deep, dreamless sleep.

2

Clairmont House had belonged to the family since the fifteenth century, and there still remained some of the original Tudor and Stuart portions around which the present mansion had been built in the eighteenth century by Roland Clairmont's grandfather, a man of enormous wealth and ambition.

Robert Adam had designed the elaborate dining room where dinner was served each evening, but breakfast was a much less formal meal partaken of in a smaller room overlooking the rose garden. The sideboard invariably held a dozen or more hot dishes, and either Smathers, the butler, or one of the footmen assisted the family.

Before finally closing her eyes last night, Lady Clairmont had persuaded her husband to sleep late this morning. She had hoped to have a few private words with her stepdaughter, but when Leonora had not appeared within twenty minutes, she had resigned herself to dining alone. Then she heard a tap-tapping in the hall, and Lady Davenport, the earl's elderly aunt, slowly entered the room, leaning heavily on her brass-handled cane.

At the age of seventy, she had lost the straight carriage of which she had been so proud, and her parchment-colored skin was wrinkled, her cheeks sagging, and her eyelids drooping, but beneath them still sparkled a pair of bright blue eyes.

As always, her maid had rouged her cheeks and lips, and today she had dressed her in a purple morning gown that would have been fashionable some thirty or more years ago, with a fitted bodice, small waist, and billowing skirt over a bustle, ending in a flounce. On her head was a powdered hedgehog wig, and it was assumed she had several identical ones, for she had not been seen without it for years. Topping it off was a white cap trimmed with lace and ribbons. She abhorred the current, simpler styles and refused to wear them.

Smathers moved quickly to assist her and settle her in a chair close to his mistress, for he knew the older lady to be a little hard of hearing.

"Good morning, Adele," she said loudly as Smathers filled a plate for her. "Has Leonora already had breakfast?"

"I don't believe so, Charlotte, though I'll grant you it's rare for her to lie abed. Perhaps she went for an early-morning ride." Lady Clairmont looked at Smathers, who shook his head.

"In my day ladies never rose early," the old lady declared. "Couldn't, for we were out dancing to the small hours of every morning." She paused, craning her head to see what Smathers was getting for her at the sideboard. "Don't give me any of that soft stuff, you rascal. I'll have bacon and kidneys and a couple of those sausages," she shouted, pointing a bony finger while the ruffles on her sleeve trailed through the dish of strawberry jam on the table.

She turned back to Lady Clairmont as though there had been no interruption. "It's high time the little gal had some excitement in her life. Mansions such as Clairmont weren't meant to be lived in year-round, but to repair to for a well-earned rest, or to bring another young 'un into the world."

"My sentiments exactly," Lady Clairmont said with a twinkle, for she was fond of her husband's eccentric old aunt. "I believe I have succeeded in persuading Roland to spend a month in Bath, so all I have to do now is talk Leonora into joining us."

The old lady gave her a sly look. "She'll have to. No question about it, for she can't stay here alone, and I'm coming with you. Be sure to tell Roland to get a house that's big enough, for I can't abide being crowded," she said gleefully, then added a little hesitantly, "You needn't think I'll be a bother to you, for I have lots of old friends there that I haven't seen in years.''

Lady Clairmont felt guilty. How could she have forgotten Roland's Aunt Charlotte when making her plans? "But of course you're coming with us, Charlotte,'' she said quickly. "You couldn't possibly stay here by yourself. We'll be taking two carriages, and I'll coax Roland into joining us in the larger one, for I don't believe he's well enough to ride alongside.''

"He has only himself to blame for that, Adele,'' Lady Davenport said bluntly. "When I first arrived here seven years ago, after my dear Edward died, there was only a governess to look after the bairns. And a sorry sort she was, too, spending all her time drinking Roland's port while Geoffrey led little Leonora into all sorts of mischief. It's a pity Roland didn't meet you years ago.''

Lady Clairmont glanced around the room to make sure Smathers had left, then said, "We met many years ago, my dear, but I was wed to Sir Gilbert Foster at the time, and in any case, Roland did not consort with ladies of the *ton* in those days. He had a wild streak in him that I'm afraid Geoffrey may have inherited.''

The older lady nodded, scowling fiercely. "Mayhap the army will rid him of it and he'll be ready to settle down when he comes back. I disremember the number of times I tried to tell Roland of the harm he was doing to his youngsters, but not a bit of notice would he take. It wasn't until he saw Leonora all dressed up for her sixteenth birthday that he came to his senses.''

Lady Clairmont nodded, having heard the same story many times before, but never doubting the truth of it. "Fortunately, it's not too late. Leonora is a very lovely young lady and is bound to make an excellent match,'' she said, then rose. "If you'll excuse me, my dear, I think I'll go to her chamber and make sure all is well with her.''

The old lady muttered something unintelligible as she stared at her half-empty plate, then bellowed, "Send that rascal Smathers back here, will you, Adele? He didn't give me enough to keep a bird alive!''

Lady Clairmont was smiling as she gracefully ascended
the great stairs and moved along the corridor to her stepdaughter's room, for she could still hear Charlotte engaged
in her favorite occupation of berating Smathers. The
butler was extremely fond of the old lady and would have
been most concerned and afraid that she was not feeling
well had she behaved in any other way.

Tapping lightly on Leonora's door, Adele heard a sleepy
voice call, "Come in," then entered the bedchamber and
crossed the room to the large carved mahogany four-poster
bed in which her stepdaughter lay lazily stretching her arms
and yawning, having quite obviously only just awakened.

"I had become concerned about you, my dear," Lady
Clairmont explained, "for it's most unusual for you to
sleep this late. You're not feeling out of sorts, are you?"

Leonora smiled. "It's nice of you to worry, but I feel
wonderful, as usual, though I did stay up reading rather
late last night. I wonder where Millie got to."

"She probably peeked in, found you sound asleep, and
did not have the heart to waken you." Lady Clairmont
tugged on the bell rope, then sat down in a chair a little
distance away, thoughtfully fingering the cover, which
matched the intricate needlework hangings of the canopy
and bed curtains. "This is a delightful room, Leonora, and
must, I suppose, date back to the time of your great-grand-
father."

"Yes, it does. I've always loved it, so I begged Papa to
let me have it when I came out of the nursery." Leonora's
eyes sparkled. "But I seriously doubt that you're sitting
here waiting to discuss the furnishings. Did you wish me to
join you for breakfast downstairs?"

Her stepmother laughed. "No, I had mine already, and
came to save you from Aunt Charlotte's tongue. She is
happily haranguing Smathers in the breakfast room, so I
think you might prefer to have yours in here."

As Leonora groaned and pulled a face, Millie entered
with a cup of hot chocolate, promising to be "back in a
jiffy" with something more substantial.

"What I really wanted to talk to you about privately is

the prospect of our all spending a month in Bath," Lady Clairmont told her.

"To what end, Adele?" Leonora asked cautiously.

Her stepdaughter was nothing if not forthright, Lady Clairmont thought, and it would be best for her to be the same. "From my point of view, for a change from the deadly quiet of Clairmont House; then, I think your father's health might improve considerably if he could be persuaded to see one of the eminent doctors there and perhaps try the waters."

"And for me?"

Adele sighed. "You have to marry sometime, my dear, for you're far too lovely to remain a spinster," she said frankly. "You might quite possibly find a month in Bath, attending the assemblies, visiting the theater, and going to routs, not only tolerable but perhaps even enjoyable. You would meet people of your own age, and we would, of course, have gowns made for you in the very latest fashion. You know, there's something particularly delightful about knowing you're dressed just right for the occasion and that everyone's looking at you, the men with admiration and the women with just a little touch of envy."

There was a pause while Millie brought in a breakfast tray and set it on the bed beside Leonora, then left the chamber.

"If I agree to go to Bath, will I still have to have the Season in London that Papa keeps talking about, or will the one visit be enough?" Leonora asked as she liberally spread a piece of toast with butter and jam.

Lady Clairmont shook her head. "It won't take the place of London, my dear—that I cannot promise you—but it might make you more reconciled to going there later. It would give you the polish, the town bronze which would make the Season in London much easier for you. And you would meet other young ladies who will be coming out in London with you, and not feel so alone in the big city."

"Why don't you and Papa go together, and I'll stay here with Aunt Charlotte, for someone has to stay with her,"

Leonora suggested slyly, and was surprised when Lady Clairmont started to laugh. "Now what did I say?"

"For some reason, I had completely forgotten about your Aunt Charlotte, and was telling her of our plan, when she immediately decided it was precisely what she wanted to do, and told me to be sure we rent a house big enough, in fact."

Leonora gave a helpless shrug. "Then I suppose it's settled, but it was nice of you to come and divulge your plans to me instead of allowing Papa to break it to me suddenly at dinner. I only wish Geoffrey was going with us," she said sadly.

Lady Clairmont went over to the bed and placed a hand over Leonora's smaller one. "I know you miss him terribly, but he's doing something he apparently always wanted to do. It will be a change for you to get away from here, and I have a feeling you'll enjoy yourself much more than you think."

She had almost reached the door when Leonora asked, "When will we be leaving?"

"That depends on when your papa can get us a house to rent, but I should think it will be in about a month," she replied, then left her suddenly thoughtful stepdaughter to dress.

Leonora spent as much time as she could during the next couple of weeks sailing her small sloop in and out of Clairmont Cove. But soon there was little time for sailing, as Lady Clairmont had arranged for a modiste to stay at the house and fashion gowns for them. She brought with her many bolts of cloth, and trimmings, though none were as lovely as the lace edging Ted had given Leonora, and when she crossed her fingers behind her back and said it had been in one of her mama's boxes, no one thought to question her further.

Her father had contrived to rent one of the houses on the Crescent, quite an accomplishment at such short notice, and she was becoming somewhat more reconciled to the visit as her wardrobe seemed to grow larger by the hour.

A few days before they were to start out for Bath, a note came from Ted, with the word "Wednesday" printed on it. Then, on the afternoon before their departure, another note came telling her to be at the jetty at midnight. Presumably Bob was sick again.

Leonora was secretly pleased, for she had wanted to try out her navigating skills at night, though she could have wished it had been a little earlier. She shrugged. It was really of little consequence, for she could sleep most of tomorrow in the carriage, as Aunt Charlotte would most certainly do.

By the time she retired to her bedchamber that evening, supposedly to get a good night's rest before the journey, her luggage was packed and all she needed to do in the morning was get up, get dressed, and step into the coach.

As before, once the house was quiet, she set out the lights and made her way down to the jetty. At first, everything went smoothly. They had kept their rendezvous and were on their way back, so she stretched out in a quiet spot and even closed her eyes for a few minutes.

When Ted's rough hand jerked her shoulder, she was awake in an instant and racing to take the helmsman's place. They were not far from the cove, but as she looked over her shoulder she could clearly see the Revenue cutter on the horizon. Like them, it was sailing without lights, but its outline was growing bigger by the minute, and she felt a twinge of both fear and excitement as she saw how rapidly it was gaining upon them.

She peered at the coastline, trying to make out the outlines of rocks she knew so well by day. They were very different in the dark of the night. She sensed rather than saw the eyes of the crew watching her, and knew she must not make any mistakes.

Then, while still not quite in range, the cutter started to fire its cannons, and though the balls fell short, Leonora felt her heart beat faster and knew a moment of sheer panic followed by profound relief as she reached the entrance to the cove.

She strained her eyes, scanning the cliff face till she saw

the light she had set there, and was surprised to see quite a number of lights in the attic of the house. This was all to the good, however, for only she knew which was her marker. Now there was no time to look back. She closed her ears to the cannon fire as she guided the craft through the dark waters with Ted at her elbow, encouraging her and telling her when their pursuer gave up the chase.

Suddenly everything felt right as she sailed the familiar waters, tacking back and forth, feeling the tiller in her hand and the tug as the sails filled in response. When she swung toward the cavern entrance, two of the crew jumped onto the rocks and helped pull the vessel inside, and within minutes she was secured and the crew were busy unloading her.

Now Leonora was exultant and just a little gleeful, secretly hoping that Bob would be sick quite often. One thing puzzled her, however, and she asked Ted, "How will you get the lugger out of the cove, for surely that cutter will stay there watching for it?"

"We'll take the fishing fleet out tomorrow or the next day, and as we pass 'ere Bob will slip 'er in and no one will be the wiser," he told her with a grin.

There was no need for him to walk partway with her this time, but he did come up the steps, and when they reached the spot where the lantern still burned, he took it down and handed it to her to light the rest of her way.

She had told him earlier that they were leaving in the morning for a month in Bath, but would probably be back before the men went out again.

"My thanks to you, Leo. I thought we were done for when the cannons were coming close, but even Geoff couldn't 'ave done better." He gave her the package he had been carrying. "You earned this and a lot more tonight. Fine French laces for a lady we're all proud of. Enjoy your 'oliday and 'appens you'll be back before we go out again. All depends on the moon and tides."

By the time she reached her chamber, she was almost too tired to open the package, but her curiosity prevailed. Inside was a whole bolt of delicate lace in the palest shade of ice blue—enough to make a magnificent ball gown, with yards to spare.

When Leonora saw the house her father had rented, she did not need Aunt Charlotte's grunts of approval to realize how fortunate they were. The Crescent was a row of the finest houses in Bath, and she heard that the Duke of York, brother to the Prince of Wales, who had only months before been named Regent, was actually in residence just a few doors away.

They were all too weary to think of anything save their beds on the first night, but Lady Clairmont had written from Devon to several friends telling them when they would be there, and she had Cook prepare special tarts and pastries in case any of them should call the next afternoon.

The first caller, however, was not one of her friends, but a gentleman to see Lord Clairmont, with whom he was closeted for some time.

Leonora had been peeking over the banister as Smathers had admitted him, and when he was shown into the study to see her papa, she hurried to Lady Clairmont's chamber, where Adele's maid was putting final touches to her ladyship's appearance.

"I've never seen anyone so elegant, Adele," Leonora said with a sigh, "and you must know who he is, for he said Papa was expecting him."

"Good gracious, Leonora," Lady Clairmont scolded lightly, "you've seen well-dressed young men before. Was he possibly one of the dandies, with a fancy waistcoat, padded calves, and corsets pulling him in?"

"No, he wasn't, my dear stepmama." Leonora gurgled at the very idea of such ludicrous dress. "His clothes were the kind of thing Geoffrey wore when he was dressed up, only they fitted Papa's visitor much better, and his cravat was like a snowy waterfall. From above I couldn't quite see his face, but he had the light coloring that goes with sandy hair and, when I think of it, his hair was a little unruly."

"Many young men wear it that way for effect," Lady Clairmont told her, "and there is an actual way of arranging a cravat called a waterfall. But it's a wonder you didn't fall over the banister, spying on a guest like that. I don't know what has come over you. Are you sure he didn't see you?''

"Of course he didn't, Adele. You know I wouldn't let someone see me staring so.'' Leonora was a little put out, for she had been sure her stepmother would know who such an interesting gentleman was.

Adele put her arm around her shoulders and started toward the door. "I was only teasing, my pet, for I know you wouldn't be so rude. You're going to meet so many young men these next few days that this one will seem quite ordinary. But I'm glad to see you're more excited than I've ever known you since I came to Clairmont House. I believe you're going to enjoy your stay here very much indeed.''

While Adele spoke, Leonora allowed herself to be guided down the stairs and into the drawing room, a richly decorated chamber on the first floor, its walls hung with a soft gold silk and cotton damask that had been dyed to match the Wilton carpet.

A table in front of the Hepplewhite sofa already held a silver tea service, and the finest china was set on the side, awaiting guests as the fashionable hour for paying calls approached.

Despite what Adele had said, Leonora knew that she would never think her papa's visitor ordinary, for there had been nothing ordinary about him, from his tight buckskin breeches, to his tailored light gray coat with brass buttons, which fitted him like a second skin, to his pale yellow waistcoat and snowy cravat. But it was not so much his clothes as the way he wore them, as though he was not dressed up at all, but always looked that way.

The first to arrive for tea were three of Lady Clairmont's friends, with a total of four daughters and two sons, and before long the young ladies left their mamas and drifted toward Leonora, for the gentlemen had instantly been drawn to her like bees to honey.

Lady Dexter had brought along her twin daughters, Julia and Jennifer, pretty blond girls with pouting mouths who wore identical gowns, and had hardly a brain between them but were harmless, or so Leonora decided at first glance.

They both appeared to be extremely interested in Lord Alexander Burton, a tall, well-dressed gentleman who affected an air of detached boredom and had, on entering, raised his quizzing glass to gaze at Leonora across the room before going over to get a closer look. She had found difficulty in suppressing a giggle, and had turned her head toward the window until the urge had passed.

His sister, Miss Andrea Burton, was also tall, but more willowy than her brother, and she paid little attention to the other young ladies, concentrating her efforts on Sir Henry Wallace, who replied to her numerous questions in monosyllables. He appeared more interested in the conversation between his sister Genevieve and Leonora.

"No, I have never been to Bath before," Leonora was saying, "and though it looked to be a most interesting city as we entered yesterday, I have not been able to put so much as my nose out of the door as yet."

"You must permit me to remedy that situation, my dear," Lord Alexander Burton drawled. "I have been here times without number, and have seen and done everything there is to do here, of course, but would be delighted to show you around. Perhaps I could take you for a drive tomorrow afternoon?"

Leonora forced a smile. She could imagine how very dull an afternoon drive would be with this tedious young man. "Thank you, sir, but I'm afraid I do not know what plans my papa and stepmama have for tomorrow. Perhaps after we have had a chance to settle in?"

Sir Henry Wallace raised bushy eyebrows and grinned broadly. "Don't rush the gel, Alex. When she's ready, I'll be more than happy to show her the sights myself," he said, giving Leonora a sly wink.

His sister, Miss Genevieve Wallace, who was standing at the other side of him, gave his knuckles a sharp rap with her fan. "Behave yourself, Henry," she scolded. "Lady Leonora is obviously unused to such forward ways."

She need not have worried, however, for Leonora had forgotten all about Sir Henry. Her father had just entered the room, and with him was his guest, who looked even more distinguished from her seat on the sofa than he had from the top of the stairs, but she had a strange feeling she had seen him somewhere before. She watched as he was introduced to Lady Clairmont and her friends, a smile of anticipation twitching at the corners of her mouth. Then her papa brought the gentleman across the room toward her.

Excusing herself to the others, she went to meet Lord Clairmont, who appeared to be in the best of humors and completely recovered from their journey.

"Leonora, I would like to present Lord Gerard Sinclair, who is a distant relative of ours. Sinclair, meet my daughter, Lady Leonora," he said, beaming with pride. "And now I'll leave you to introduce him to your friends here while I get back to my work."

Leonora sank into a demure curtsy, then looked up at him as he raised her hand to his lips. She saw eyes as silver as a moorland stream that met hers and held them like a magnet, awakening an emotion inside her that she didn't quite understand. His eyelashes, thick and dark like his eyebrows, were in sharp contrast to his sandy hair. She was just admiring the cleft in his chin when the lips above it parted in a wide grin and she flushed as she realized she had been staring at him much too long.

"I beg your pardon, my lord, but," she hastened to explain, "I thought for a moment that I had seen you somewhere before. I must have been mistaken, however."

"I know I have never seen you before, my lady," Lord Sinclair assured her, "for I could not possibly have forgotten the occasion."

Adele would have been proud of the way Leonora made the introductions, for she did not forget a single name. When she was finished she brought Lord Sinclair a cup of tea, then sat with Genevieve Wallace some distance away, covertly watching him as he conversed with one of Lady Clairmont's friends. His face when in repose revealed something a little fierce and frightening about him, but at the same time vastly intriguing.

When Genevieve and Sir Henry had left and she was alone for a moment, he came over to where she sat. "May I?" he asked, indicating the seat Genevieve had vacated.

"Of course, my lord," she said readily. "Are you staying in Bath long?"

His smile was wide and his eyes warm and friendly. "I'll be here for the month," he told her, "and am looking forward to the pleasure of escorting you and your stepmama on occasion. After all, we are family, and, while I think about it, it is quite permissible for cousins to be on a first-name basis—Leonora."

3

"The first thing we must do is become subscribers, so that we can attend the various entertainments at the Assembly Rooms. The master of ceremonies, Mr. King, keeps a book in which we must put our names for this purpose," Lady Clairmont explained to Leonora as they alighted from their carriage. "After that we'll stroll along Milsom Street and look in the shop windows, unless there is something you would particularly like to purchase."

For all the notice Leonora took, Lady Clairmont might have been talking to herself, for her stepdaughter was intently gazing at the hustle and bustle in the streets, which teamed with carriages, sedan chairs, and people of every sort, from shop girls to duchesses.

Although Geoffrey had occasionally gone away for several days, and her father had spent most of his time in London, neither of them thought to tell her what cities were really like. Surely London could not be any busier than Bath, she decided.

Suddenly she realized her stepmama was addressing her, and she looked embarrassed. "Adele, I'm sorry. I was busy looking everywhere at once and did not hear what you said."

"It was nothing of worth, my love," Adele assured her. "We have an hour or so to look around before we must collect your Aunt Charlotte from her friend's home. This afternoon we'll call on some of my old acquaintances, so that when we attend the ball tonight you will know quite a number of young people to talk to."

"Do you think Gerard will be there?" Leonora tried to sound casual.

"Yes, I think he probably will, but which of your governesses said you could address by their first names gentlemen to whom you have just been introduced, for it certainly was not I?" Adele asked.

"The gentleman in question assured me it was perfectly correct since we are distant cousins." Leonora sounded a little belligerent.

"Oh, yes. Your father did mention as much last night. Something about one branch of the Clair family taking the name of Sinclair and the other Clairmont," Adele murmured thoughtfully, but she did not tell Leonora that her father liked the young man very much and was contemplating a little matchmaking. "Have you decided what you will wear this evening?"

"Do you think the blue gauze over white satin would be suitable?" It was the one trimmed with the first piece of lace Ted had given her, and just about her favorite gown.

"Most suitable"—Adele nodded in agreement—"and if you glance over there at that flower seller, you'll see some bunches of forget-me-nots that would look lovely in your hair."

They made their purchase, visited Mr. King, and continued walking along until they reached the Grand Pump Room.

"I hope I can persuade Lord Clairmont to try the waters while we're here," Adele said, "but I know they are not at all palatable, and the baths are always crowded with ailing people many years older than your papa."

Leonora doubted if even Adele could talk her father into either drinking or bathing in the waters, so she smiled vaguely and turned to look closer at the unusual embellishments of the turrets on the west front of the Abbey Church, where angels ascended and descended a ladder. She just had to go inside and see more of the magnificent old church, and by the time they came out, much to her disappointment, their carriage was waiting.

"If there were just the two of us, we could look around a little longer, but we must not keep Aunt Charlotte waiting. An hour may not be long enough for a visit after all these years but, on the other hand, if they've both changed drastically, it might be far too long," Lady Clairmont said with a chuckle.

Lady Davenport had gone to call on someone who had been a bosom bow when they had made their come-outs more than half a century ago, and she was eager to see how the years had changed her friend. She herself had been an Incomparable, and when she straightened her shoulders and looked in her mirror, she still saw the delicate features and the tiny waist, though her wig was nowhere near as magnificent as her raven-black hair had been. When she had first married Lord Davenport, he had marveled at its length, for she could easily sit on it, and he had enjoyed taking her brush and running it through the lustrous strands. That did not last long, however, for once it became obvious that she could not conceive, his interest faded and he took his pleasures elsewhere.

Her friend lived at an excellent address, for her husband had purchased a house in the Circus, a circle of grand attached homes built of the same golden stone as the Crescent, and considered to be a masterpiece when completed some sixty years ago.

Though it was not far from Abbey Church, the carriage could make but sluggish progress through the crowded streets, and it was almost fifteen minutes before it drew up in front of the house. Jim, the coachman, knocked on the door and offered his arm to the waiting Lady Davenport, then assisted her into the carriage.

From the glint in the old lady's eyes, Leonora could not quite tell whether her aunt had enjoyed or hated her visit, but of one thing she was certain: she had not been bored.

"Did you have a nice visit, Aunt Charlotte?" she asked, then mischievously added, knowing the old lady was almost bursting to say something, "Or are you perhaps too tired to tell us about it just now?"

"I'm not the one that's tired," she said, looking from one to the other, "though you two may be after traipsing about crowded streets and dodging carriages and sedan chairs. It wasn't like this in my day. Nowhere near as many people came then, and the lower classes walked in the road, where they belong, and left the pavement for their betters.''

She paused to catch her breath, and Lady Clairmont wisely said nothing, though she knew that Bath had been in its heyday when Charlotte was a young woman, and had, in fact, declined somewhat in recent years.

"But poor Louisa, Lady Sherwood, is in sad shape." Lady Davenport dramatically closed her eyes and slowly shook her head. "Her face is a mass of wrinkles from the top of her forehead to below her chin, and I told her, in a kindly way, of course, that she should wear a ruff around her throat, for I've not seen such a scraggy neck since the cook showed me a fresh-plucked hen."

There was a muffled sound as Leonora tried to prevent a determined gurgle, and she turned her head into the corner of the carriage and started to cough.

Lady Clairmont passed her a handkerchief, then turned back to Aunt Charlotte. "How is her health? Is she able to get out much?"

Lady Davenport shook her head once more. "The poor thing could scarcely walk, bent in half nearly, though there was nothing wrong with her voice. Never was, if I recall," she said sharply. "I couldn't get a word in edgewise. Her memory is certainly failing, no doubt about it. We talked of when we were both young things, and danced the nights away, but she disremembers quite a bit, for I was the one who had all the beaux. She married the first man who looked at her twice. To hear her tell it, you'd swear it was the other way around."

Leonora had recovered her composure and now said, "I'm sorry you had such a disappointing visit, Aunt Charlotte. I suppose you'll not be calling on her again."

Lady Davenport's bright blue eyes flashed. "Do you think I don't know my duty, young lady? Of course I'll call on the poor thing and try to cheer her up a little. Promised to be there next week, in fact, and tomorrow I'm going to take a look . . . to call on Bertha Owens. I've not seen her for nigh on forty years."

Looking very pleased with herself, Lady Davenport allowed Jim to help her out of the carriage, and Leonora took her arm as the three ladies walked up the few steps and entered the house. It had been a most successful first morning in Bath.

From the outside the Assembly Rooms were not very imposing, but when they reached the Upper Rooms Leonora was more favorably impressed, having only been in ballrooms of private homes before.

"I believe we shall join Lady Wallace and her children," Lady Clairmont said, catching sight of them on the other side of the room. "Didn't you say that Genevieve was a rather amiable young lady?"

"She's the most sensible young lady I have met so far," Leonora confirmed, for the two of them had found they had much in common, such as riding and sailing, "but her brother is nothing but an arrogant buffoon who says things I don't quite understand and then laughs and winks. Genevieve seems to be able to keep him in hand, however, for she raps his knuckles with her fan."

"Oh, dear, do try not to give him the slightest encouragement, my love, and make sure never to be alone with him," Lady Clairmont advised cautiously, for she recalled many such young scamps from her own come-out. "Lady Wallace and I will probably sit behind with Lady Dexter and the chaperons. Should anyone whom you have not already met, ask you to dance, send him to me. Or if anyone says he has my consent, look across to me and I'll either nod or shake my head. You can't be too careful, for there are a great many upstarts in Bath these days who would never be allowed in Almack's in London."

Genevieve greeted Leonora in a friendly fashion, and her brother bowed low. They were quickly joined by other young people she had met, including the Burtons and the Dexter twins. Lord Alexander begged for the first dance, and immediately when it came to an end, Sir Henry asked her for the next. She was, of course, unable to decline. He danced exactly the way she expected, jumping around a great deal, and she had to be very nimble to avoid feeling the weight of his large feet on her slippered toes.

He returned her to the area where the older ladies were seated and asked, "Are you ready to take that ride around Bath yet, my dear?"

She looked across the room, wondering just how she could politely avoid answering, and saw Gerard Sinclair coming directly toward her. "I will have to talk with my stepmama, for I believe we have plans for the entire week," she said, and turned to give her cousin a bright smile and a rather breathless greeting.

"May I have the pleasure of the next dance?" he asked, and at her slight nod he took her hand and guided her to where a new set was forming.

He noted her shining eyes and flushed cheeks, and remembered that her father had told him she had never attended a public assembly before, and only a few private balls. "Allow me to tell you how lovely you look, Leonora," he said quietly. "I am sorry that convention will not allow me to have more than two dances with you, but will you make me the happiest of men by permitting me to also take you in to supper?"

"But this is only the first dance," she said, thinking he must somehow have miscounted.

He grinned, his gray eyes twinkling merrily. "Of course it is, and I am now debating whether to request my second one before supper, and then leave immediately afterward, or prolong the anticipation, and also the torture, by waiting until after supper for that second dance."

Leonora was quite unused to flattery and asked, "Torture, my lord? How could that be?"

"Being compelled to watch you in the arms of others is torture indeed, my lady," he said in a softly teasing voice.

Feeling as if she had walked into a trap with her eyes wide open, Leonora knew she was out of her depth. "Gerard, I know you're saying a lot of things you don't mean, as apparently everyone does here, but could you, as my cousin, stop the flummery, please."

Gerard looked taken aback for a moment; then his perfectly formed lips quivered and a ghost of a smile touched his mouth. "What a surprise you are, Leonora," he said with a chuckle. "I'll wager by the time you've had a Season in London you'll think a gentleman strange if he does not flatter you."

"I'm not at all sure I want to have a Season in London, Gerard, and hearing gentlemen say things to me that they don't mean makes me even more reluctant."

She looked bewildered, and he could clearly see the vulnerability in her eyes, so he hastened to make amends. "But I did mean what I said, my dear, though I may have said it in too flowery a form for your taste. I would like to dance every dance with you, and so of course I dislike seeing others do so. Is that better?" he asked gently.

It was very much better, but she did not trust herself to put it into words, for he had a way of making her say things she did not mean, so she gave him a grateful smile and a nod.

When the dance came to an end, he escorted her back to her place, then murmured, "I am looking forward to your company at supper. I'll also come and capture you for the dance before, if I may, but now I want you to meet a very good friend of mine." He waved to someone standing not too far away, a man about his own age, but a little shorter and stockier built, though not exactly heavy, who smiled and came toward them.

"Leonora, may I present Sir Timothy Torrington. Timothy, this is Lady Leonora Clairmont, a rather distant relative of mine." He bowed before leaving her with his friend, then went over to Lady Clairmont to get her permission on Timothy's behalf.

"If you vouch for him, then of course Leonora may dance with him, my lord," Lady Clairmont agreed immediately. "My husband thinks most highly of you."

Gerard grinned. "That's good news, at any rate, in view of the other requests I am about to make."

Lady Clairmont looked amused and raised questioning eyebrows.

"I wish to take Lady Leonora in to supper, and I would

also like to take her for a drive around Bath tomorrow afternoon," he informed her, "but I heard her tell Wallace that you and she had plans for the whole week."

"I think our plans can be changed for you, sir," Lady Clairmont said graciously, smiling as she recalled Leonora's very natural reaction when first she had seen this young man, for he was indeed unusually elegant and handsome. Very sure of himself also, she decided, and added, "But did you not ask her yourself?"

"Not yet, but I will, you may be sure." He smiled, bowed, and walked away, and Lady Clairmont could not help but notice how the eyes of a great many young ladies and their mamas followed him as he crossed the room. From their two brief conversations she realized he was a man who made his own decisions, and she hoped that her husband would not be too obvious in his plans.

She watched Leonora dance by with Sinclair's friend. There was something solid and reliable about him, and her stepdaughter appeared to be more at ease conversing with him than she had been with Lord Sinclair.

"Is your family staying in Bath at the moment, Sir Timothy?" Leonora was asking him.

"No, I just came along with Gerard because he had business here," he said. "Thought I'd keep him company, you know. We sort of grew up together, in the same neighborhood, and have been friends ever since."

"Whereabouts was that?"

"Not too far from here, as a matter of fact. Just the other side of Bristol," he told her, then asked, "And where is your home, my lady?"

"In Devon, sir, on the South Coast. Clairmont House is not too far from Dartmouth," she replied with a smile.

Leonora enjoyed her dance with him, for he had nice, kindly eyes, and though he was not much of a conversationalist, nor a flatterer, he had a most pleasant disposition.

He danced with her again a little later, and then Gerard came over for his second dance.

"You look as if you're enjoying yourself, Leonora. Did

you like my friend, Sir Timothy?" he asked as they danced.

"Very much. I felt comfortable with him, as though I'd known him all my life," she explained innocently.

"Although most men would not like to arouse those feelings, I believe old Timothy would. You make him sound like a big brother," Gerard said with amusement.

Leonora put her head on one side and thought about it. "I suppose that's the way I did feel about him, but yet he's not a bit like Geoffrey."

"Your father told me that you are very close to your brother, and that he's now serving in Spain. I'm sure you must miss him a great deal." He smiled sympathetically.

"It was terrible at first, because we had always been so close, and we had only each other for such a long time." Feeling further explanation was necessary, she continued, "You see, until Papa married again, less than a year ago, he spent almost all of his time in London, and only occasionally came to Devon to hire a new governess or something like that."

"And you were brought up as a little boy instead of a girl?" he suggested knowingly.

There was a hint of mischief in her smile. "I had really no choice, my lord, for Geoffrey was quite adamant that he would not play girls' games," she told him.

"I cannot imagine why," Gerard said, straight-faced but with laughter dancing in his eyes.

Leonora attempted to school her own features but was less than successful. "He taught me almost everything my governesses did not," she said with a grin. "To ride sidesaddle, astride, and bareback, to climb the cliffs near our home, to swim, and to sail the sloop that Papa had bought for us. We have our own cove, named after the family," she added.

"Oh, yes," Gerard said, frowning slightly as he tried to recall some forgotten incident connected with a recent trip, "you're on the Devonshire coast. I was staying with friends a little while ago not twenty miles from where you live, and I thought of visiting, as a matter of fact, but my friends assured me that Lord Clairmont was seldom home.''

So that was where she had seen him before! He and another man, who could easily have been Sir Timothy, had been at the back of the crowd watching her race against Joe Turner. Her sudden flush of embarrassment, and the guilt written all over her face, suddenly triggered Gerard's memory.

His eyebrows rose. "You've remembered also, I see, where we saw each other before, haven't you?" he asked a trifle grimly.

She bit her lower lip and nodded. "Are you going to tell Papa?" she asked.

"I've never cared much for tattling," he said, "so you're safe as far as I am concerned. Do you make a practice of challenging the local fishermen to races?"

He had become quite stern, and she instinctively resented his tone. "No, and I didn't challenge him," she snapped. "He challenged me and I thought it would be just a private race when no one was around. I didn't know he'd told everyone, until one of the footmen mentioned it to me, and then it was too late."

A smile twitched at the corners of his mouth. "You're a fine sailor, my dear, if a little indiscreet. And your secret is safe with me and, I am sure, with Sir Timothy, who was with me that day. Let's say no more about it." He grinned. "If you hadn't been so excited when you won, and thrown your cap in the air, we would never have known you were anything but a fishing lad."

The dance ended then and he escorted her into the supper room, where, to Leonora's relief, private conversation was completely impossible. She had a reason for not wanting to discuss the matter that was far more important than that of incurring her father's wrath. Millie had noticed Gerard and Sir Timothy going into the inn, where apparently they had asked a lot of questions regarding wines and brandies. It had been assumed by the locals that they were in some way connected with the Revenue authorities.

Gerard seated her at the table, then went off to procure lemonade and biscuits for her, but their table was soon shared with Lady Clairmont, Lady Wallace, Genevieve, and, to Leonora's distress, Sir Henry, who sat himself down next to her in Gerard's seat. When the latter returned with refreshments, Wallace showed no signs of relinquishing the seat and had, in fact, pulled his chair closer to Leonora.

"How delightful," Gerard said with an air of imperturbability. "I see I must take Lady Leonora to a more secluded table. Come, my dear."

Leonora got up immediately, but at a sharp rebuke from Lady Wallace, her son rose reluctantly, muttering, "You may sit here, as I am joining friends elsewhere," and went to another table, from which he proceeded to glare at everyone except Leonora.

Gerard and Sir Timothy left shortly after supper, but not before Gerard had asked Leonora if he might take her for a drive the following afternoon. He was to come for her at two o'clock.

"I believe you enjoyed yourself tonight, didn't you, my dear?" Lady Clairmont asked as they entered their carriage and started back to the Crescent.

"Oh, yes," a sleepy Leonora, who had completely forgotten her embarrassment with Gerard, replied. "It was far more pleasurable than anything I could have dreamed of, and tomorrow afternoon Gerard is taking me for a drive."

Her stepmama did not miss the change from sleepiness to a note of eager anticipation in Leonora's voice. "I know," she told her, "for he very properly asked my permission first. He is certainly a charming young man and I am sure your realize you were the envy of all the young ladies there."

"Yes, I did notice," Leonora said softly, "and I couldn't help but feel sorry for the ones who danced only when partners were found for them. I didn't know I was pretty until you told me, for Geoffrey never said anything of the sort, but now I'm very glad that I am."

"You're more than pretty, Leonora. You have good bone structure and a loveliness that will last, I believe, throughout your life," Lady Clairmont assured her. "You are most fortunate."

"You mean I'll never be a mass of wrinkles from my forehead to below my chin, and I won't have a neck like a plucked hen's?" Leonora giggled, then said, "Poor Aunt Charlotte, she takes such pleasure out of thinking she looks younger than her contemporaries. At her age you'd think she'd be happy just to be alive, and not care about how she looks."

"That, my dear, is one of the grossest misconceptions of the young," Lady Clairmont said emphatically as the carriage stopped and they went into the house. "Sleep late in the morning so that you'll be completely refreshed for your afternoon drive. I'll go and see if your papa has fallen asleep in the study, as is his wont when we're away from home."

4

When Gerard arrived, Leonora was waiting for him, and trying hard to conceal her impatience. She looked particularly charming in an apricot-colored jaconet muslin gown trimmed with beige lace at the throat, a matching large-brimmed hat, and beige-colored gloves. A parasol in a slightly deeper shade than her gown completed her outfit.

"Now, you will take good care of my stepdaughter, won't you, Lord Sinclair?" Adele asked cautiously, having seen his curricle through the window as he arrived. "Are you sure that two-wheeled contraption is safe?"

Gerard looked amused. "Perfectly safe, my lady, as long as I am driving. But my horses are fresh and I would not like to keep them waiting too long, so perhaps we had best leave now. I promise to bring Leonora back in one piece and with roses in her cheeks."

He held out his arm, and Leonora took it and allowed him to help her down the steps and then up into the curricle, though she could easily have climbed into the carriage without assistance. Adele had, however, gone to great lengths to explain that a lady always waited for a gentleman's aid, and would insult him if she did not.

The matched chestnuts were anxious to be off, so Gerard took the reins from his tiger and paused while the young lad jumped on the back, then swept around the curve and along Marlborough Lane to the Bristol Road.

"Where are you taking me?" Leonora asked, as they seemed to be heading away from the city.

"Oh, I'll not run away with you this time, if that's what you're worried about," Gerard said in a teasing tone, though he kept his eyes on the road ahead. "I thought we'd go over to the Pulteney Bridge to the Sydney Gardens, if you've not been there as yet. They have bowling greens and a labyrinth and are quite pleasing to stroll through on a sunny afternoon."

"Won't the horses get restless if they have to wait for us?" She could not control the little twitch at the corners of her mouth, and the hint of mischief in her eyes, and as he turned his head toward her he grinned.

"Not if we give them enough exercise first. If it's all the same to you, we'll pass the gardens and go into the country, and then come back this way a little later and stroll around."

Leonora did not at all mind seeing something of the countryside, but found the Pulteney Bridge they were crossing most unusual.

"Had you not told me in advance, I would never have realized we were on a bridge, but thought it to be a very pretty street of shops," she said. "I must ask Adele to come here with me one day so that I can get a closer look."

"Ah, yes," he teased. "Shopping is, after all, the favorite occupation of ladies both young and old."

Leonora ignored him while she counted the number of elegant gentlemen gazing into the shop windows, and then she turned around to look at Gerard triumphantly.

"I'll have you know, sir, that there are at least two more gentlemen than there are ladies peering into those shop windows," she asserted, "so shopping must also be their favorite occupation."

Gerard frowned and shook his head decisively. "But did you look inside the shops?" he asked, a wicked gleam in his eyes. "I would wager a shilling that they were filled with women. The gentlemen were merely waiting outside to escort their ladies from shop to shop."

Leonora knew he was probably right but could not prove it. "Fiddlesticks!" she said firmly.

Gerard chuckled. "I'll give you fiddlesticks, young lady," he said. "One day I'll escort you to a street like that one and make you eat your words, or at least the paper on which you record our wager."

Leonora's infectious laugh rang out. "You would not be so cruel, sir, would you?"

He grinned and shook his head, then became aware of a farm cart just ahead and concentrated on getting around it without scraping his curricle.

When they had the lane to themselves once more, he told her, "There are gardens just to the south of the bridge, from which you can look up the river and see it at its best, set as it is above a particularly attractive weir." He glanced toward her. "May I hope to have the pleasure of taking you there one afternoon?"

His look was so warm that Leonora felt her cheeks flush. "You are very kind, my lord," she said a little shyly. "I would like it very much."

"You know, Leonora, it is most refreshing to find a young lady who has never really been in a small town, let alone a city. I know, of course, that your knowledge of shops and shopping is limited to your village store, but you spoke up well in defense of your sex. I am indeed most happy that your father requested my presence here at this time," he said with a note of sincerity in his voice.

"Then your call the day after we arrived was not just a casual social call? Why did Papa send for you?"

"I'm not sure that I know," Gerard said thoughtfully. "He said that, as I was next of kin after your brother, he felt the desire to see what kind of a man I'd grown into. I must have passed muster, for he asked me to pay a visit to Clairmont House after your return."

"He probably just feels the need of male company, for it must be tedious in the extreme to have only three females to converse with now that Geoffrey is away," Leonora said airily.

"If that was intended to bring me down a peg or two, it was successful," he told her with a grim little smile.

"Oh, dear, I've said the wrong thing again, haven't I?" Leonora wailed, but her eyes twinkled with mischief. "I really did not mean to imply that any male would do."

He raised an eyebrow, then said in an amused tone, "I'm not too sure of that, for you have an impish look about you, but we'll let it go for now."

After reaching the Sydney Gardens they turned south down Pulteney Road and were approaching Widcombe Prior Park, the grounds of a stately mansion which could be glimpsed on a rise of land in the distance. "It looks like a Greek palace," Leonora said, looking at the huge portico of Corinthian columns. "Does anyone live there?"

"I don't believe so at the moment, for the man who built it died and it has passed into the hands of a number of distant relatives in recent years," he told her. "A pity, for it was a grand place in its time."

He swung the curricle around and headed back to Bath and, on reaching Sydney Gardens once more, alighted, handed the reins to his tiger, and lifted Leonora down. She took his arm and together they entered the gardens, walking slowly down the sunlit footpaths, occasionally stopping to admire a flower or a statue.

As they returned to the Crescent, Leonora came to the momentous conclusion that she liked Gerard Sinclair despite the disturbing way he had of teasing her one minute, and making her feel tongue-tied the next—and she might like him even more if only he were not connected with the Revenuers.

Before leaving her at the door, Gerard had asked if he might take her for a drive on the following day, and she had happily consented. Lady Clairmont, however, had some misgivings.

"I like Lord Sinclair very much, for his manners are exemplary, my dear, but I wonder if perhaps you should see a little less of him and a little more of some of the other quite eligible young men who have begged to escort you," she suggested. "You will meet many different kinds of young men when you are in London, and I would like you to have experience in dealing with them all, if it is possible."

"But I thought Papa preferred my cousin to escort me, Adele," Leonora said. "Surely he introduced him for that purpose, did he not?"

Adele sighed heavily. "In a way, I suppose he did, but I am sure he would agree with me that you should enjoy the company of a number of young gentlemen, so that when a decision is finally made it is more likely to be a happy one."

She and Leonora were waiting in the drawing room when Gerard arrived promptly at two o'clock, with an invitation she could not decline, for it included the entire family.

"I have a box reserved at the Theatre Royal tomorrow evening, Lady Clairmont, and it is my hope that you might all be able to join me and Sir Timothy Torrington," he explained.

"All of us, my lord?" Lady Clairmont was surprised at his thoughtfulness. "I do believe my husband enjoys the theater, though I'm not sure what Aunt Charlotte would do. I should not like to leave her alone."

"Nor would I wish you to," Gerard said with a smile. "Lady Davenport is, of course, included in the invitation."

Adele was quite delighted, for since her marriage she had been cloistered at Clairmont House and sadly missed all the forms of entertainment to which she had been accustomed. "Then I accept for all of us with the greatest of pleasure, and in turn would ask that you and Sir Timothy join us here for supper beforehand."

"Thank you indeed, my lady. I am happy to accept for both of us. And now may I have your permission to steal Leonora for a few hours?" he asked politely, though he would have been shocked had she declined.

"Most certainly, sir, as long as you will take good care of her." She turned to her stepdaughter, however, and said rather pointedly, "Make the most of this outing, Leonora, for tomorrow afternoon I must insist on your staying home to help me entertain callers."

She watched them as they went down the steps to the curricle, thinking what a handsome couple they made, but determined that, despite her husband's quite obvious encouragement, Leonora should have a chance to meet a few more young men with whom to compare the indubitably charming Gerard Sinclair.

* * *

Leonora was unusually silent, for she felt somewhat guilty that Adele had needed to ask for help. She looked a little crestfallen.

"Where would you like me to take you on such a lovely afternoon?" Gerard asked, a benign expression on his handsome face. "If you must stay home tomorrow, I think you should go wherever you please today. Some spot that will take away that solemn face, for I'm sure Lady Clairmont could handle a hundred callers with ease, but is only looking after your interests and anxious that I not monopolize you so soon."

"Oh, of course," she said with a look of relief. "I remember she did say something of the sort a little before you arrived. Do you think we might walk in those gardens you spoke of yesterday? It sounded to be a lovely place and, to be truthful, I miss the walking and climbing to which I am accustomed at home."

"Climbing?" Gerard asked as he carefully guided the curricle past a rather overcrowded coach. Then he realized what she meant. "Of course. I had forgotten that your home is atop the cliffs. You don't, by any chance, go bird nesting, do you?"

Though she knew he was teasing, she could not help herself. "Of course not," she said rather scornfully, "but I go almost daily up and down the very steep cliff path that leads to our cove and the dock where we keep the small sloop."

"Do you, indeed? I know you to be an excellent sailor, and I assume you are a redoubtable climber," he remarked. "But does your father approve of your taking the sloop out on your own?"

Leonora stared at him, thinking he must be about in the head. "He has never said I should not, and whom else would I go with? I doubt that Aunt Charlotte would enjoy sailing in the sometimes rough water," she said with a touch of asperity. "The sloop really belongs to both my brother and me, but once Geoffrey taught me how to handle it, I used it far more than he did."

She waited for his response, quite prepared to tell him what to do with his crackbrained notions should he dare to suggest she not go out sailing alone.

To her surprise, however, he appeared to have no desire to pursue the matter, and as they reached the gardens he gave the reins to his tiger and jumped down. Ignoring Leonora's proffered hand, he placed one of his large ones on each side of her slender waist and lifted her onto the path.

For a long moment he left his hands there, and Leonora could distinctly feel a burning sensation through her thin garments. Then, carefully placing her hand on his arm, he escorted her along the paths between the trees to a spot where the triple arches of the Pulteney Bridge, and the weir beneath it, could be clearly seen. It was an artist's delight, and Leonora regretted leaving her sketching pad at home, acknowledging to herself, however, that she could hardly expect her cousin to sit around waiting while she set down a likeness.

"It is quite distinctive. I heard somewhere that it was a variation of a design for a bridge in Venice that was never built," Gerard informed her, and as she leaned forward to see more clearly, he placed a tentative arm around her waist.

Leonora was unsure if he was merely trying to prevent her falling or checking, for the second time today, her reaction to his touch. They were quite alone, and though she admitted to herself that she did indeed enjoy the warmth of his touch, she did not wish him to think her forward, so she moved away from the edge. Though he immediately removed his hand, the deliciously warm feeling lingered still.

Gerard's gesture had been an initially protective one on his part, but when he felt the warmth of her skin through the thin muslin, he hoped she would continue to lean dangerously forward a little longer and thus give him an excuse for holding her. He was extremely disappointed when she moved away so soon, for he was quite un-accustomed to having his advances rejected.

As they strolled along the path a foot or so apart, he glanced at her slightly averted face, and was unaccountably pleased to note that her cheeks were considerably more flushed than they had been earlier.

The walk had been enjoyable, and Leonora was soon back in her usual high spirits, but when they returned to the Crescent she could not help but see through the drawing-room windows that they had visitors. Studiedly casual, she asked, "Would you care to come in for tea, my lord? It would seem there are already a number of callers, though I did not know my stepmama was receiving today."

"Just for a few minutes," he agreed, strangely unwilling to let her go until he had seen who might be inside.

With a cheerful smile, she walked ahead of him into the drawing room. Her expression changed markedly, and he was immediately curious as to which of the guests was responsible.

There were two or three older ladies, two younger ones about Leonora's age, and three gentlemen present, and it seemed as though they all looked toward the door as the pair entered the room.

Lady Clairmont rose quickly and took Gerard around to make the introductions while Leonora helped herself to a cup of tea. It did not take him long to realize that the eldest of the three gentlemen, Lord Burlington, a man approaching middle age, was the cause of Leonora's discomfort. He had met the man once in London, and taken an instant dislike to him. It was deuced odd to see a man of Burlington's highly dubious background in Lady Clairmont's drawing room, and he wondered how he and Leonora had come to be acquainted.

When Burlington moved to her side, Gerard quickly joined them in time to hear the older man say, "I know you've been avoiding me, Leonora, and I won't have it. Do you hear me?"

He was broad-shouldered but of only medium height, and his love of rich foods and wine showed in the bags under his small black eyes and in a well-rounded paunch.

"Gerard, have you met Lord Burlington? My lord, this is Lord Gerard Sinclair from—" she began, when Burlington interrupted.

"We've met," he said abruptly, "and I'd like to know why you use his first name, while you refuse to use mine even though we've been neighbors since you were in leading strings."

"That is precisely why I use the more respectful form of address, my lord, for you are old enough to be my father. However, Lord Sinclair is a distant cousin," Leonora explained frostily.

Burlington took a sip of his tea, the delicate china cup looking awkward in his large red hand, and as he sought to replace it in the saucer, the cup overturned, spilling the remaining liquid down his yellow waistcoat.

Leonora spun around, trying desperately to control her urge to laugh before Burlington noticed. Swallowing hard, she signaled to a nearby footman, who removed the cup but was unable to do anything about the stain that was rapidly turning the yellow to a dull brown.

"Can I get you another cup, my lord," Leonora asked once she had herself under control, but an angry Burlington shook his head.

"Never did like this habit of stopping for tea each afternoon, and sipping the stuff out of cups no bigger than thimbles," he snarled. "Should give a man a glass of ale or wine, I've always contended. I'll call tomorrow afternoon and take you for a drive, Leonora. We've much to talk about and it'll do you more good than sitting indoors gossiping with a lot of women who've nothing better to do."

Leonora could afford to smile now, for she felt safe. "I'm sorry, sir, but I've promised to help my dear stepmama entertain tomorrow afternoon," she said.

"And the following afternoon she's already promised to go for a drive with me, I'm afraid. So sorry, Burlington," Gerard said with exaggerated courtesy, hoping Leonora would back him up if necessary.

Burlington's bulbous nose went even redder, and his

heavy brows drew together, but then he seemed to collect himself, and forced a thin smile. "Then we'll make it another day. I've waited a long time for you, my dear, so what are a few more days?"

Though her eyes sparked at the man's unwarranted possessiveness, she carefully controlled herself, for there was nothing to be gained by making a scene that might put Gerard in disgust of her. Fortunately, Burlington was finally leaving, having been there more than a half-hour already.

"How does he know you?" Gerard asked quietly.

"He's just a neighbor in Devon, that's all. He is a widower and owns the property to the east of ours," Leonora explained. "He has a skin as thick as cowhide, for I never fail to repulse him. Now even my sweet stepmama has started to do the same thing, for he's forever calling on us at Clairmont House without invitation. It's been worse, though, since Geoffrey left."

Gerard glanced at the clock on the mantelpiece. "I fear I must also take my leave, Leonora, but Sir Timothy and I will be here tomorrow for dinner. Is seven o'clock all right?"

"Perfect, for we'll be having sherry in here first, I'm sure. You've no idea how much I'm looking forward to seeing my first play, but I'm afraid Sir Timothy will find Aunt Charlotte a little trying." She smiled ruefully at the thought of such an odd pairing. "Have you told him yet?"

"Not yet, but he's a kind soul and will make her very comfortable, I promise you. He's particularly good with elderly people and children." He took her hand and touched it lightly with his lips. "Until tomorrow, my dear," he whispered, then went to say good-bye to Lady Clairmont before leaving.

5

Gerard did not call at the house in the Crescent the next afternoon, as he believed Lady Clairmont had been trying to give him a hint. Instead he went to Sir Timothy's rooms, but was irritated to find that he had stepped out for a moment.

While awaiting his friend's return, he paced back and forth as he thought of the clumsy Burlington sipping tea and conversing with Leonora, then cursed himself for being a fool. She had made it quite clear that she loathed the man, and had appeared completely capable of putting him in his place. And, of course, Lady Clairmont would be keeping a careful eye on him also.

"I say, old fellow, that carpet's threadbare already. Are you seeking to make a hole in it?" Sir Timothy asked as he entered the room. "Is something troubling you?"

"Not really, Timothy, or at least, if it is, then I'm being foolish. Do you remember meeting a fellow by the name of Burlington? I was on a winning streak at one of those houses off Curzon Street, as I recall, and he started to handle one of the girls there pretty roughly." He frowned as the ugly scene came back to him.

Sir Timothy nodded. "He tried to say she stole a ruby pin that was in his cravat when he came in, but old Charlie was too smart for that and had it out of his pocket in a flash. Bad *ton*, that one. Ugly, too, but then, who am I to talk?" he asked with a shrug.

"Compared to Burlington you're an Adonis!" Gerard said sharply. "That was one gaming house where he'll not get past the door again. But he's here in Bath, and he knows the Clairmonts well enough to call."

"Does he, by Jove! Can't you drop a hint to Lady Clairmont? Let her know what a bounder he is?"

Gerard shook his head. "It's not quite so easy. You see, he's their neighbor in Devon, and it's more than possible that he's careful to hide his less-desirable traits from the locals." He unthinkingly tapped his whip against his boot as he considered the matter. "I think in this case it would be better to just keep an eye on him. They don't like him, but they do the polite because he lives close by. Leonora is more spirited than she at first appears, however, so if I get the chance, I may warn her to watch her tongue. I'd hate her to antagonize him, for he is the type who would not hesitate to retaliate against a woman. I'd take good care of him if he did, of course, but by then it would be a little too late."

Sir Timothy nodded. "Lady Leonora is most spirited, I would say. You do realize that we saw her once before, don't you?"

Gerard's eyes twinkled and he smiled. "She's a little minx, but a charming one. I promised that we would not tell her father."

"Good. But to get back to Burlington, is he just paying neighborly calls, Gerard, or is there something else?" Sir Timothy asked thoughtfully.

"She did not actually say as much, but from the way Leonora behaved, I think he must be more than a little interested in pursuing her." He laughed shortly. "She did tell him he was old enough to be her father, though, so I suppose he is being discouraged by the whole family."

"I would hope so. I've not yet met Lord Clairmont, but it would be difficult to imagine any father wishing his daughter to marry such a one. That is, of course, if he were a good judge of character, and not short of funds or dicked in the nob."

"That's right, you've not met Lord Clairmont, nor have you met your dinner partner for this evening." Gerard grinned. "Lord Clairmont's Aunt Charlotte will be with us, and I understand from Leonora that she is a bit of a character, though the girl is obviously very fond of her.

She'll probably wear a much-outmoded gown and make outrageous comments."

Gerard knew what a tender heart Sir Timothy possessed, and was not at all surprised when his friend looked pleased and said, "I'll take good care of her, for she sounds very much like a favorite aunt of mine. She tries to rule her family like a drum major, but when you pay her a little attention she's delighted and becomes as gentle as a lamb. What time are we expected?"

"Seven o'clock. I'll come for you at a quarter to the hour, if that's all right." Gerard rose. "Thank you for your kind ear, my friend."

Some two hours later he picked up Sir Timothy, and the pair arrived exactly on the hour at the Clairmonts' door. They were shown into the drawing room, where Lord Clairmont and his lady were drinking sherry, and in less than five minutes Leonora entered, dressed in a pale green silk gown with a silver net overskirt caught up in knots of silver ribbon. More silver ribbon was twined through her glossy black hair, which was braided and piled high on her head, with just a few trailing curls softly framing her face.

With a look of frank admiration, Gerard stepped toward her. She curtsied demurely, though her eyes sparkled and she could not help a happy smile, for she had started to enjoy being dressed up and the center of attention.

She had just curtsied to Sir Timothy when Aunt Charlotte entered the room, leaning heavily on Smathers' arm, for she was having a bad day with her rheumatism. "You always look lovely, my dear, but tonight you positively glow," Sir Timothy said to Leonora. "Would you please present me to your aunt, for I believe she is my dinner partner."

Taking his hand, Leonora brought him to her Aunt Charlotte. "I want to present Sir Timothy Torrington, Aunt Charlotte. Sir Timothy, this is my aunt, Lady Davenport."

Sir Timothy bowed low over her hand. Tonight Lady Davenport was dressed in a bright green silk gown, in the style of her youth, and on top of her powdered wig she wore a confection of beads, feathers, and flowers.

"Sit down, young man," the old lady said a little loudly. "What a blessing it is that I've got too old for curtsying. Up and down, it used to be, up and down every time someone of rank came into a room. What did she say your name was?"

"Timothy Torrington, my lady."

"Yes, I remember now. Are you one of the Torringtons from Bristol way? There was a good-looking young earl in my day called Torrington—Edward, I believe it was. Yes, Edward Torrington, Earl of Edgeworth," she repeated with a nod of her head that threatened to dislodge her wig.

"My grandfather," Sir Timothy said with a warm smile. "When next I see him I'll tell him I met you. I know he will be delighted."

Lady Davenport's eyes opened wide in amazement. "You mean he's still alive? My goodness, he must be eighty if he's a day. He was a handsome man, and a regular one for the ladies, but he must have changed greatly in all these years. Is he full of rheumatism like me?" she asked gruffly.

"He does not carry his age as well as you do, my lady," Sir Timothy said tactfully, "and he rarely leaves the house these days. He does have a touch of rheumatism, and suffers from gout also, but he is still up and around each day, and lets us know it in no uncertain terms."

She called out to her nephew, who was in conversation with Gerard, "Roland, did you know that this young man is Edward Torrington's grandson, and that he's still alive?"

Lord Clairmont excused himself and came over to where she was sitting.

"Was he one of your beaux, Aunt Charlotte?" he asked with a chuckle. "I remember him, of course, but I was just a youngster myself when he was in his prime. I trust he's well, sir?"

"Considering everything, he enjoys reasonably good health, my lord. He resides on the estate just outside

Bristol and rarely visits Bath these days, let alone London,'' Sir Timothy told him.

"Pleased to hear about him,'' Lord Clairmont said, patting the younger man on the shoulder, "and very proud of you he must be.''

"Does he have a lot of grandchildren?'' Lady Davenport asked.

"Not really, my lady. There are only four of us, and we had ten cousins at last count. My father was the only one of his sons to reach maturity, and I have two sisters and a younger brother.'' Aware of the direction the questions were leading, Sir Timothy had no objection to supplying the information, but added, "However, my father is a comparatively young man and is in the best of health, I am very happy to say.''

"Glad to hear you say so,'' Lord Clairmont said warmly, "and now I believe my lady is anxious for us to go into dinner.''

Sir Timothy carefully helped Lady Davenport out of her chair, placed her stick in her right hand, and took a firm hold of her left arm. She gave him an approving nod. "You've helped old ladies before,'' she said gruffly.

Once they were seated at the table, with Sir Timothy to her left and Gerard to her right, Lady Clairmont asked with a twinkle, "Aunt Charlotte, are you going to monopolize this nice young man all evening?''

"I most certainly am.'' The old lady chuckled. "It's been a long time since I had one as young and handsome as him and I intend to make the most of it.''

Not at all embarrassed, Sir Timothy laughed and gently patted the spotted and wrinkled hand that lay on the table.

"Will Robert Coates be performing tonight?'' Lady Clairmont asked Gerard.

"I do not believe so, my lady,'' he replied, "and I doubt we will have such an interesting performance as occurred here just over a year ago. I happened to be there, and it was extremely amusing, if somewhat ludicrous.''

"I heard something about it, but I doubt that anyone else, with the exception of Sir Timothy, has done so.

Would you mind telling us what really happened?'' Lady Clairmont requested.

As the others looked up expectantly, Gerard had little option but to describe the incident.

"Robert Coates, who resides in Bath and is an amateur actor, played Romeo wearing a spangled cloak of blue silk, over a white vest, red pantaloons that were far too tight for him, a wig that Charles II might have worn, and an opera hat,'' he began. "When a seam in an inexpressible part of his costume split and white linen extruded through the red rents, the audience roared with laughter.

"Then, in the midst of one of Juliet's impassioned speeches, he took a pinch of snuff from his snuffbox, walked to the edge of the stage, and proceeded to offer some to the occupants of the side boxes—of which I was one.''

"How very extraordinary,'' Lady Clairmont exclaimed. "Was he perhaps a little drunk?''

"Only with his own personality, I'm afraid, but that was not all. He apparently wanted to die at the end in some degree of comfort, for he first wiped the floor with a handkerchief, then put down his opera hat for a pillow, and lay down, shuffling around to get into a more comfortable position. By this time the house was in an uproar and they shouted, 'Die again, Romeo,' so he proceeded to go through the whole rigmarole twice more.

"I suppose Juliet, who was in her tomb, grew tired of lying there waiting for Coates to stop repeating his extraordinary death scene, for she rose and gracefully put an end to the idiocy by walking to the center of the stage and aptly applying a misquotation of Shakespeare: 'Dying is such sweet sorrow, that he will die again tomorrow.' ''

"It's a very odd story, Gerard, and I do not doubt for a moment its authenticity,'' Leonora said hurriedly, "but how was such a man—you said he was an amateur—allowed to perform on the stage of the Theatre Royal in Bath? Surely only professionals are permitted to do so.''

"I hate to disillusion you, my dear, but money can buy most things,'' Gerard said kindly, glancing at her father, who nodded in agreement, "including the principal part on the stage. If the company is running out of funds to pay the performers, no one, least among them the actors, will protest when an amateur is willing to pay for the privilege of making a fool of himself."

"After that, tonight's performance may fall very flat, for I believe it is to be *Romeo and Juliet* this evening also," Lady Clairmont remarked.

"As it will be the first play I have ever seen, it couldn't possibly be a disappointment for me," Leonora declared emphatically, for she had been looking forward to going to the theater ever since Gerard had extended his invitation.

"You may wish to see the play, but I'll wager half the audience will spend more time watching you, my dear, for you are looking lovelier than ever this evening," Gerard murmured for her ears alone, causing Leonora's cheeks to turn a deep pink.

"If we wish to see the whole, we'd best leave very soon," said Lady Clairmont, rising from her chair. "That is, unless you gentlemen wish to have port?"

"No, we'll not delay you, my love," Lord Clairmont said agreeably. "You ladies can have your tea in the interval between acts while we stretch our legs a little."

When Leonora looked back on that night, she could not remember when she had spent such an enjoyable evening. The company had been delightful to be with, for even Aunt Charlotte, receiving the full attention of the thoroughly nice Sir Timothy Torrington, had not complained once. In fact, her aunt had been in high alt, for that young man had agreed to take her to see his grandfather one day before they removed to Devon. Leonora could not judge whether the play was good or bad, for she had nothing with which to compare it, but it had been exciting to watch professional actors performing.

And Gerard had been right, for when she had peeped above her fan on several occasions, she had seen any number of eyes upon her, making her feel more like a

queen than the unpolished young lady who had arrived in
Bath only the week before.

But the continuous round of social events made Leonora
feel restless, and when one morning about a week later,
Millie came in earlier than usual with her hot chocolate,
she had an idea.

"How would you like to join me in an adventure,
Millie?" she asked eagerly.

"Now, milady," Millie began, "you don't really want to
get up to any mischief 'ere, do you?"

"It's not exactly mischief that I had in mind, Millie. I
saw a pretty scene one day that I'd love to paint, but I
could hardly ask Lord Sinclair to wait around while I
fetched my paints and made a likeness, could I?" she
asked. "Besides, he would have made me too nervous to
paint."

Millie knew her mistress well and felt most apprehensive.

"We're the same size, so you could lend me one of your
cotton dresses, and the two of us could easily walk down to
the spot where there is a bridge with a lovely weir beneath.
I could put up my easel and start to paint, and you could
keep a lookout for me. That's not really very much to ask,
is it?" Leonora suggested.

"Why can't you dress properly and go with her ladyship?" Millie asked.

"Because it wouldn't be anywhere near as much fun that
way, silly. We could leave our hair loose, unbutton our
dresses a little at the neckline, and go barefoot like a pair
of vagabonds. I could pretend to be a poor, starving artist
while you go around with a hat taking pennies," Leonora
suggested. "Do let's try it just for the fun, for we'll be
leaving here in less than a fortnight now, and you won't
have anything to remember it by."

"We'd 'ave to put some paint on our faces, in case
someone recognized you," Millie warned.

Leonora smiled, for she realized she had talked Millie
into going along with her. Half an hour later, they were
trudging down to the center of the city, Leonora carrying

the easel and Millie the paints and pad and an old straw hat that Leonora had discovered in the attic of the rented house.

Leonora had no difficulty in finding the gardens again, and they walked to the spot which had the best view. She set up the easel and got out her paints. Millie refused to hold the hat out to passersby, so Leonora placed it conspicuously on the ground while her maid stayed close by.

As usual, she became absorbed, and it was more than an hour later that Leonora realized Millie was no longer at her side. The hat was also not where she had placed it. Looking around, she saw Millie some distance away with a couple of rough-looking men who appeared to be trying to persuade her to go with them. One of them held the hat out to the maid, then drew it quickly back as she reached for it.

Placing her painting block on the ground with the paints, Leonora quickly grabbed the easel and ran to Millie's aid. The maid was now trying to get away from them, but one man had a tight hold on Millie's arm while the other was talking to her.

Leonora swung the easel up in the air and brought it crashing down on the arm of the man holding Millie. With a curse, he let go and reached for his arm, which, if not broken, was badly bruised. She had swung the easel high once more and was just about to attack the second man with it, when she felt the weapon lifted from her hands from behind and heard a slightly familiar chuckle.

She turned quickly around to find Sir Timothy Torrington holding her easel. The two men had dropped the hat and taken to their heels.

"That was good timing, Sir Timothy," she said, then looked at Millie. "Are you all right?"

"Yes, m'lady," Millie assured her. "You were so busy, you didn't see them grab the 'at, but I did, and went after them."

"You should have let them keep it, Millie, for it's of no value and certainly not worth your being injured," Leonora said.

"There was three shillings in it, m'lady," Millie

protested. "You didn't even see 'ow people kept looking at your painting and putting coins in.''

Sir Timothy shook his head. "You were painting, dressed like this, Lady Leonora?" he asked.

Her eyes sparkled with mischief. "I'm afraid so, my lord. You see, I wanted to paint the picture and have some fun at the same time, so I persuaded my rather reluctant maid to come along with me."

They walked back to where she had left her paints and the finished painting, and Leonora held it up for inspection.

"Excellent, my dear," Sir Timothy said, "but don't you think it would be a good idea if I took you both back to the Crescent before you get into any more mischief?" He was quite obviously amused, but more than a little concerned for their safety.

"Dare you be seen with two such vagabonds?" Leonora asked with a grin.

"You'll be concealed in my carriage," he told her with a laugh, "and I trust you have some footwear to cover those none-too-clean feet."

Reaching into the voluminous skirt of the gown Millie had lent her, she produced a pair of slippers, and when Millie had found hers also, they stepped into Sir Timothy's closed conveyance.

Sir Timothy was amused at her antics but had a sister about Leonora's age, and knew that if he had not come across her at just the right moment, she might have suffered injury at the hands of the two ruffians she was attacking.

"I imagine you would rather no one heard of this little escapade," he said with a half-smile, and when Leonora nodded, he continued more seriously, "and I will agree, provided I have your promise that you will not try anything so foolhardy again. Those men you attacked could have done you serious injury, you know."

"But they were attacking Millie and trying to take her with them," Leonora protested. "I couldn't let them do that."

"I know," he said with a twinkle. "But had you requested that Lady Clairmont, or even Lord Sinclair, escort you so that you could make a likeness of the scene, one of them would have been glad to do so, I am sure. Provided, of course, that you wore conventional attire."

Leonora tried to look properly chastened, but did not quite succeed.

"I assume you would like to alight close to the back door?" Sir Timothy asked with a rueful grin.

"Thank you, sir," Leonora said sincerely. "You are very kind and I promise not to repeat this prank while we are in Bath. Or anywhere else," she added when he gave her a reproachful look.

He alighted in the back street and handed first Millie, then Leonora down, giving them the painting appurtenances. "Off with you, then, and we'll say no more about it," he said with a smile.

They did not wait for him to get back into his carriage before stealthily entering the back way, Millie first to be sure the coast was clear, and then Leonora.

When they reached her bedchamber, Leonora dropped onto the bed, laughing heartily, but Millie was not quite so pleased, for only the chance of that nice gentleman turning up had saved them from a lot of trouble. In the future she would try to discourage her mistress from this kind of behavior.

Taking everything into consideration, the visit to Bath had been most worthwhile for all of them.

If a sampling of the waters had not improved her husband's health, Lady Clairmont was sure the regimen had done no harm either, and he seemed to have enjoyed, as she had, the young people who had gathered around her stepdaughter. And for her part, the visit had been quite necessary, for, city-bred, she had realized she could live happily only six months or so at a stretch in their remote area of Devon before spending time in a more civilized place.

For Lady Davenport it had been a wondrous holiday— perhaps the last she would have at her age—for she had visited with old friends she had not seen in years, including

Edward Torrington, the Earl of Edgeworth, with whom she had reminisced for a couple of hours or more before that delightful young grandson of his had brought her back to her family.

Lord Clairmont was feeling particularly pleased with himself, for he found he liked young Sinclair very much indeed. Though Sinclair was second in line for Lord Clairmont's own Bristol earldom, he gave this little thought, for Geoffrey would inherit that and, hopefully, produce a passel of sons. Sinclair was, however, in direct line for more than an earldom, for his grandfather was the Marquess of Croydon, and this title would pass to him after his father.

He would not think of forcing Leonora to marry against her will, but she had seemed to enjoy Sinclair's company, going out of her way to be more feminine and ladylike than usual, and the young man had paid her a great deal of attention. He had high hopes of a satisfactory outcome, for Sinclair now had a head start on the dandies Leonora would meet next Season in London.

Leonora felt ridiculously pleased with herself. In four weeks she knew she had acquired a considerable amount of poise, and despite the frequent visits of Lord Burlington, she had enjoyed herself very much. Though she acknowledged this was in some part due to the attentions of Gerard Sinclair, she would not yet admit to what extent, but she would admit to feeling like a completely different person than the one who had left Clairmont House a little less than a month ago.

She hoped to see Gerard before they went to London, for he had told her he would visit Clairmont House first, perhaps escorting them on their journey. He had also said how very much he looked forward to showing her all the sights, and she felt she just could not wait. Her heart beat faster at the thought of his staying at Clairmont. Her new-found poise disappeared and she became tongue-tied once more at the very idea of coming down on a morning and seeing him at breakfast, then taking him riding and sailing.

But it was still some weeks away, so she tried to put him

out of her mind. Today her immediate consideration was that of helping out the smugglers. She had received a note the day after her return, and unless she heard from them again, she would set the lights in place and then relax, for her additional services would not be required.

Having been away from Devon, she now saw this from a rather different perspective. She had begun to have doubts as to whether she should help them further than just putting out lights for markers once every month—an act that in itself was a crime.

Smugglers had been active for years, bringing in wine, brandy, tobacco, silks, and more for the wealthy who wished to avoid paying the government-imposed duty. When England went to war with France, legal import of such items ceased altogether, but not the demands of the wealthy. Unwilling to forgo their luxuries, the rich paid gladly for packages left for them in secret places, while patriotically denouncing smuggling and sending Revenue cutters to hunt the same men who supplied them. Smuggling was most definitely breaking the law, and if she was caught, her family would be shamed—and she dared not even think of the consequences to herself.

Ted had told her that almost every family in the village was involved in the distribution of the smuggled goods once they were brought in, but only the men she sailed with knew of her even more dangerous part in the operation.

6

It was in a still-thoughtful frame of mind that Leonora came down the stairs the second day after their return, to see a strange, solemn young man waiting in the hall. She was about to ask his business when the butler came out of the study and showed him in to see her father.

She and Smathers heard the crash at the same time, some minutes later, but Leonora was first to reach the study door, flinging it wide and bursting in, to stop only a few feet from where her father lay on the floor, the young man kneeling beside him.

"I believe his lordship has fainted," the stranger said quietly. "Could one of you get him a glass of brandy or something?"

As Smathers went over to a cabinet, Leonora bent down, glaring suspiciously at the man. "My father has never fainted in his life. What did you do to him?" she demanded fiercely.

"I'm afraid I brought bad news about his son," he said as he leaned forward and moistened Lord Clairmont's lips with the brandy Smathers had poured.

For a moment the man's face seemed to fade and the room swam around her, but she was determined not to lose control. To her ears her voice sounded faraway as she asked, "Has he been wounded? Where is he?"

"I'm sorry, miss, but it's worse than that. He has been reported killed in action," the young man replied, leaving Lord Clairmont in the hands of his butler and moving toward Leonora, but she held up a hand to stop him coming closer.

She shivered as an icy cold swept through her, but even

that could not dispel her need to know what had happened. "Tell me as much as you can, please," she requested in a hoarse voice.

"It was in the south of Spain, at a place called La Albuera. We repulsed Soult and forced him to retreat to Seville, but it was the worst battle of the war." She unconsciously noted how haunted his eyes seemed as he spoke.

"Will they be sending his b-body back to us?" she asked painfully.

"That I couldn't say, miss. It will be up to General Beresford, I suppose. It was on May 16. A fellow officer saw him struck down as the cavalry charged, and said there was no chance that he could have survived." He stood, not knowing quite what to do. "You're not going to faint, are you, miss?"

"No, I'm not," Leonora said determinedly, getting up and walking over to the bell pull. She gave it two sharp tugs, then picked up a piece of paper from the carpet that must have dropped out of her father's hand. "Is this the official notification?" she asked, and the young man nodded.

There was a knock on the door and a footman entered, looking first at the bent back of Smathers and then at Leonora.

"Ask Lady Clairmont to come at once, please, and have someone go as quickly as possible for the doctor," Leonora requested, feeling as though one part of her mind was functioning normally while the other had gone completely numb. "And take this gentleman to the kitchen for something to eat, for I imagine he's come a long way. I'll see you again before you leave," she said to the messenger.

"How is Papa?" she asked Smathers when they were alone.

"I think he's coming round, my lady." He looked at her with pained eyes and took her hand in both of his. "I'm so very sorry."

At his sincere sympathy, tears came to her eyes, but she

blinked them quickly back. "Thank you, Smathers, you loved Geoffrey too, I know."

Then the door was flung open and Lady Clairmont came hurriedly in. "What happened? I was told there was a messenger here. It's not Geoffrey, is it?"

Her stepdaughter's face confirmed her fears, and she dropped to the floor beside her husband, who had begun to stir. Smathers moved away. "I'll get some footmen to carry his lordship to his room, my lady," he said.

"Thank you, Smathers, that would be best, and send for the doctor," Lady Clairmont said as he left the room.

"I've already sent for the doctor, and the messenger is in the kitchen, Adele, if you should wish to speak with him. As soon as Smathers brings help, I'd like to go to my room until the doctor gets here," Leonora said quietly.

Lady Clairmont looked torn between the two people she loved. "Oh, darling, I'm so sorry. As soon as we know what has happened to your papa, I'll come to you, I promise," she said.

Leonora crossed toward her and took the hand she had proffered. "It's all right. You look after Papa, for I fear it was more than just a faint. I'll be all right," she assured her with a wan smile.

The next few hours were very busy ones, for it seemed her father had indeed had more than just a fainting spell. The doctor said it was a small seizure, brought on by the shocking news, and that he must be nursed carefully and kept as quiet as possible.

"This one appears to have done little damage, but there is considerable danger of others occurring, which frequently happens in such cases," he told Leonora and Lady Clairmont. "It would be best if the two of you could take turns nursing him for the next few days."

Putting a comforting arm around Leonora, Lady Clairmont said, "I'm not sure if my stepdaughter is up to such a task. She has had a terrible shock herself, for the two children were very close. I can arrange to stay with him and have my meals brought up to me."

Leonora shook her head firmly. "I'll not hear of it, Adele. He's my father and your husband and the two of us will care for him and help him get well again. I couldn't bear to lose him too."

The doctor smiled sadly. He had helped bring her into the world and seen her through her childhood illnesses, as he had Geoffrey also. She'd turned into a lovely young lady and she had a good head on her shoulders. He felt strangely proud of her now.

Despite their loving care, the earl showed little sign of improvement. He blamed himself for buying his only son a commission in the army and sending him to his death. It was a heavy load to bear. The fact that it was what the boy wanted more than anything else made little difference to his feelings. Over the next two weeks he had several more seizures, and when he recovered partially from one particularly severe one, he asked for pen and paper. He wished to see his heir, Gerard Sinclair.

Carefully he penned a brief message, requesting Sinclair's presence as soon as possible. It was Leonora who folded it and applied her father's seal, then placed it in the hands of a reliable groomsman who would take it to Gerard's home, just outside Bristol.

The man had scarcely passed through the gates when Lord Burlington arrived. He had paid his condolences previously and was now returning to try to ingratiate himself and see how the family was getting along. Smathers showed him into the drawing room and sent word to Leonora, as Lady Clairmont was resting.

"Good afternoon, my lord," Leonora said, stepping into the room and curtsying briefly. "You must excuse the absence of a chaperon, but my stepmama is taking a little well-earned sleep, for she was up most of the night with Papa."

She had been careful to leave the drawing-room door wide open and knew that the footman on duty would hear every word. Although her hair was so very dark, her skin was smooth and creamy and she looked pale but lovely in a simply styled black silk gown.

Burlington came forward and took her dainty hand in his large red one, but she withdrew it quickly, then adroitly sidestepped, seating herself on a straight-backed chair.

"Pray be seated, Lord Burlington," she said, pointing to the couch opposite her, but instead he grasped a chair and placed it close to her own.

Before seating himself, however, he started toward the door, saying, "What I have to say to you, my dear, cannot be said in front of servants. I'll just—"

"You'll just leave the door as it is, my lord, or I will have the footman stand inside the room instead of outside it. There is nothing you should say to me, a single young lady, that cannot be said within hearing of others." Her voice was loud enough to carry into the hall, and she was glad to see Smathers appear in the doorway and look questioningly at their neighbor.

Burlington returned to his chair, pulling it even nearer until his knees were almost touching hers, and as she edged away he reached out to grasp her arm.

"Stop being missish, Leonora," he ordered, trying to keep his harsh voice low. "What I have to say is not for the ears of servants. I understand that your father's health has not improved—in fact I know that it has worsened over these last two weeks."

Leonora said nothing, but looked pointedly at the hand that was still on her arm until, with a frown and a shake of his head, he removed it. Only then did she raise her head.

"Papa is ill, but not dangerously so at the moment, my lord," she said evenly, "but I cannot see why you should be so concerned. I assumed you had called to ask about him, not to tell me his condition."

"Of course I did," he said, blustering a little, "but you know how servants are—they keep me informed. What I really came here for was to offer you my help in any and every way. You possibly did not know that your brother and I were on the best of terms, and he often told me how worried he was because of your lack of suitable friends in the neighborhood. We spoke of you often, and I know he would have wished you to turn to me in your grief."

Leonora knew full well that Geoffrey had despised Burlington and avoided him whenever possible. He had considered him an odious, ill-mannered churl and warned Leonora to keep out of his way. However, she did not allow this knowledge to show on her face, but waited to hear what else he would say.

" 'She's had too much freedom,' he told me. 'With Papa in town so much of the time, she's had too much of her own way, Hector,' he said only a week before he left for Spain." Burlington stretched out his hand again, but this time Leonora was too fast for him and moved her arm out of reach. " 'What she needs is a strong man to guide her, someone like you.' That's what he told me, my dear. I'd swear to it on my mother's grave."

If he was going to make a fool of himself, he might just as well go all the way, Leonora decided coldly, and waited silently for him to continue.

"That's why I'm here today. I waited a few weeks for you to get over your grief, and now I'm here to ask for your hand in marriage. Of course, I'd have asked your father had he been well, but in that case it wouldn't have been necessary," he growled.

"It would have been more seemly if you had made your proposal to my stepmama, sir, but it really makes little difference, for I thank you for the honor but cannot accept," she told him icily, giving him a look of complete loathing.

"Now, don't be so hasty, missy," Burlington said angrily. "It would be an excellent arrangement, for the two properties could be joined and make one of the finest estates in the county. My first marriage was, unfortunately, childless, but I've plenty of proof that it was no fault of mine, and you're young enough to have a dozen or more youngsters to follow after."

"I hardly think that is a fitting subject to discuss with a maiden lady, sir," Leonora reproached him sternly, "and as far as my brother is concerned, I can assure you that we were very close. Close enough, in fact, for me to know that he despised you and would not have wished me to have anything to do with you."

His face went so red that she thought for a moment he might burst a blood vessel; then he took a deep breath, calmed down, and finally, still breathing quite heavily, said, "Now, you know you don't mean that, my girl. All the recent trouble you've had has unsettled you. You'll feel differently about it in a few weeks. There's no need to tell Lady Clairmont that I came for anything more than to ask after your father, but I'll be back in a week or two to talk about this again."

For the first time since she had entered the room, Leonora smiled. "By all means do so if you wish, sir, for by then my father's heir, Lord Gerard Sinclair, should be here, and you might wish to put your proposition to him. He will, of course, inherit the Clairmont estates eventually."

He jumped to his feet, and she thought that his eyebrows were going to rise right through his narrow forehead and meet his hairline. "Do you mean that fellow who was sniffing around you in Bath?" he asked. When Leonora nodded, trying hard to keep her triumphant feelings from showing, he walked to the door, then turned and faced her once more.

"He'll not have you, for I'll see he doesn't," he threatened, pointing a finger at her. "You're going to marry me eventually, so you'd best get used to the idea."

With that he flung out of the room. Leonora sat down, for she was shaking, but even she did not realize just how enraged Burlington was. She had insulted him and virtually called him a liar, and had thwarted his plan to own both estates. As he rode away, he made a vow to get even with her sometime, somewhere. Leonora had made a bitter enemy.

In telling him that Gerard would soon be here, she had, of course, put her own wishes into words. But she had little doubt about it, for hadn't he said he had accepted her papa's invitation to visit? And hadn't he said he would come and escort them to London?

A few days later, when she awoke from a heavy sleep, Leonora found that a note had arrived asking that she be at the jetty at the usual time. She wondered, at first, how she was going to arrange this and still sit up with her father, but then she realized that Adele would be sitting with him through that night, and unless there was any drastic change for the worse, Adele would not think of disturbing her stepdaughter's sleep.

Since the word had come of her brother's death, Leonora had once more reversed her feelings about working with the smugglers. It had now become the only thing she could still do for Geoffrey, to carry on the spirit of adventure he had reveled in. She forgot all her previous doubts and threw herself into it wholeheartedly, deliberately ignoring the dire consequences should she get caught.

She rang for Millie to help her dress, and when the girl started to arrange her hair, she was surprised to hear her say quietly, "Ted said to tell you 'e wouldn't 'ave asked so soon if they could've done without you, m'lady. 'E said you should tell me where to put the lights so as I can do that for you, and I'll wait at the top of the tunnel till you get back, if you like."

"How long have you known, Millie?" Leonora asked.

"Just since Ted and me started walking out together," the maid said, "and I was that surprised when 'e told me that you go out with them sometimes." She gave her mistress a worried look. "I wish you weren't doing it, m'lady. It's too dangerous for someone like you."

Leonora smiled at the girl in the mirror. "I'm sure he did not ask you to tell me that, Millie."

"That 'e didn't, but I worry enough when 'e's out without 'aving to worry about you as well."

"I'll be all right, and if you can take care of the lights, it will be a big help. Just keep your fingers crossed that we don't meet up with the Revenuers tonight, for I'd like it to be a quiet run if possible."

The run was a good one, with no sign of any boat but the Frenchy they were to meet; and on the way, the men came over to say how sorry they were about her brother.

Ted walked with her to the tunnel, and it was good to find Millie waiting to help her undress and slip into bed for several hours' sleep before she must relieve Adele at her father's bedside.

She had returned with a bolt of black lace, large enough to make a gown, but the best reward she had received tonight was the feeling that she was carrying on for Geoffrey.

7

Gerard Sinclair lost no time in reaching Clairmont House. He had intended to leave for Devon the following week, staying there until the Clairmonts were ready to journey to London, and then accompany them.

He was, of course, completely aware of the earl's wishes in regard to his only daughter. Unfortunately, he had grown accustomed to ambitious parents, usually mamas, using all kinds of wiles to bring their daughters to his attention. As a mere viscount, he would have been beneath the notice of many, but the inevitability of his becoming a marquess made him a high prize on the Marriage Mart.

To be held in such high esteem by so many matchmaking mamas had gone to the head of many a young man before him, but one factor had saved Gerard from growing too big for his breeches. He had a younger brother and two young sisters, and loving parents who had eloped when faced with the marquess's objections. They were bound and determined to treat all their children alike.

On returning home after his first couple of months in London many years ago, Gerard had been teased unmercifully when he showed a slight tendency to arrogance. After that, he had grown accustomed to recounting the more ludicrous attentions he received, and sharing their laughter.

Accustomed to meeting young ladies who had been taught how to please, if not actually seduce, such an eligible bachelor, he had found Leonora's lack of guile most refreshing, and when Lady Clairmont had gone so far as to insist her stepdaughter meet other young bachelors, she also had risen in his esteem.

He had enjoyed the earl's company and understood his concern for his only daughter, so when the note arrived, asking him to come as soon as possible, he had left at once, taking his valet and a minimum of baggage.

As he waited in the great hall, he saw a dark figure descending the huge stairs and was appalled to find, as it drew near, that it was Leonora. She was gowned in unrelieved black, and her pale, strained face made her blue eyes appear enormous, though their sparkle and life were sadly missing. He felt a deep urge to take her in his arms and soothe away the sadness, but their relationship had not progressed thus far as yet, so he had to be content with taking her hand and pressing his lips against it.

With eyebrows raised, he asked softly, "What has happened, my dear? How can I be of service?"

It was so good to see him, Leonora thought, despite the heaviness of her heart. Just his presence here eased the burden, but she knew it would do much more than that, or her father would not have sent for him.

Still holding her hand, he led her into the drawing room and sat beside her on a sofa while she told him all that had transpired since their return to Clairmont House.

"I would think Papa sent for you because you're now his heir," she concluded, realizing that her hands were still held comfortingly in his.

"How is Lady Clairmont taking this?" he asked.

"Very courageously. We've taken turns nursing Papa, and she tries to cheer him up as much as possible. Others may have thought theirs was a marriage of convenience, but she really loves him," she said, casting her eyes downward.

He reached out a finger and stroked her cheek. "Your father is fortunate to have two such devoted nurses. And how about Lady Davenport? She's too frail, I am sure, to be of much help."

"Of course. She's been so sweet that I miss her tart tongue, but can hardly tell her so." A trace of a smile lit her face, then quickly died away.

"I am glad I was at home when the summons arrived,"

Gerard said. "I came right away. My man, Jacobs, is taking care of my things, so whenever Lord Clairmont feels up to it, I will meet with him. I assume he knows I'm here."

"I'm sorry." She shook her head at her own forgetfullness. "I should have told you that I sent word to Adele before coming down. She was giving Papa some medicine, and as soon as she has him settled comfortably, we're to go to his room."

"Has there been a funeral service?" he asked, realizing that there might not have been anything done as yet.

"No," she replied softly. "We thought we might have a service when Papa feels better. The messenger didn't seem to know what would be done about the b-body, and I didn't know where to inquire."

He felt her hands tremble in his, and clasped them more tightly. "I'll instigate inquiries," he promised. "Do you know where and when it happened?"

"The messenger said it was at La Albuera on May 16," Leonora said painfully.

It was what Gerard had feared. There had been considerable speculation as to how General Beresford could have claimed La Albuera a victory when two-thirds of the British infantry, more than two thousand men, had been killed or wounded that day. It would not be easy to find her brother's body, but he would do his best.

A footman knocked and entered. "Lord Clairmont is ready to receive you, milord," he intoned.

"Thank you, Charles," Leonora said, getting up quickly. "I'll show Lord Sinclair the way."

When they reached the bedchamber, she was pleased to note a slight improvement in her father, for his color was a little better, and his eyes a little brighter.

"Good of you to come so quickly, my boy," he murmured, holding out his hand, which Gerard clasped firmly. "If you'll take that chair, we'll throw the ladies out and have a man-to-man talk. Off with you," he said to a surprised Adele. "If I need you, Gerard will come and get you, don't worry."

With some reluctance, Adele steered her stepdaughter out of the room as Gerard took the seat beside the bed.

"Now, the first thing I'd like you to do for me is to find out what happened to my son. I'd somehow feel better if I knew his body were buried here in our own cemetery, not rotting in some damned field in Spain. Have you any contacts with Wellington or any member of the Cabinet?"

Gerard nodded. "I've already spoken to Leonora about it. As it happens, Spencer Perceval owes me a favor and I shall ask him to look into the matter at the highest level. The battle was a fearful thing, though, with tremendous casualties on both sides, so it will probably take some time."

"If anyone can help us, Perceval can," the older man grunted. "So you're in the service of the Prime Minister, eh?"

"Yes, I am," Gerard admitted. "When this thing with Napoleon became serious, I tried desperately to buy myself into the army, despite my grandfather's objections, but I was politely informed that I was not eligible for military service. The marquess is a very wily old man, and he was one step ahead of me. Then Perceval asked for me. I performed one assignment to his satisfaction and am involved in a second one at this time."

The earl cleared his throat and took a sip of water before telling Gerard why he had sent for him.

"We discussed in Bath the fact that you were my heir, after my son, but had no notion then that a tragic event had already taken place. I knew that Geoffrey thought the world of his sister and that there would have always been room for her here if she should need a home."

Gerard began to speak, but the earl raised a hand. "From you I want more," he said bluntly. "You spent a great deal of time in my daughter's company in Bath, so I assume you have no commitments elsewhere. The two of you seemed to rub along together very well, so I would like you to carefully consider her for your wife.

"I'm not looking to see her a marchioness, so don't think I care about that. It's your character I like. I believe you're the right man to hold her in check without hurting her.'' He watched Gerard's face closely. "She has a good-size dowry from both her mama's and some of my mama's estates, aside from what you'll inherit from me.''

Gerard was surprised at the forthrightness of the request and, as the earl said, they had got along very well together. In fact, he could not remember when he had enjoyed a woman's company as much.

"Does your daughter not have a say in the matter?'' he asked. "I would not take an unwilling bride.''

"What do chits of her age know about such things?'' the earl asked querulously. "I wouldn't make her marry anyone she took in dislike, of course. For instance, that neighbor of ours, Burlington, has been asking for her ever since she turned sixteen, and I've told him she'll make up her own mind when the time comes. Of course, even if she said she wanted him, I'd not permit it.''

"I should think not, for I've met the man," Gerard said shortly. "But in that case, why do you allow him to call?''

"Because I'd rather not have bad blood between neighbors if I can help it. Once she's married to someone else, he'll not bother us anymore.'' He was growing tired and his pallor had returned, but he struggled to put forward his proposition. "With me away a month and ill ever since, this place must be going to rack and ruin, so I'd like you to stay with us and get things back in order. I've a good bailiff and he'll put you in the way of it.

"I won't deceive Leonora, but will tell her my wishes, and she'll have time to think on it over the next month or two. You know, nothing official for now, but just get to know each other and see how you both feel.'' He lay back against the pillows, breathing heavily.

"I know you're tired, sir, but I must say one thing more. Leonora is a very beautiful girl and she would not want for suitors in London. Should she not be given that opportunity?'' Gerard insisted.

"You know I had that in mind, of course, but now it won't do. She's in mourning and won't be able to go to London for another year. By that time I might well be dead and buried also, and then she'd be in mourning for another twelve months," the older man said emphatically.

"You've given it a lot of thought, sir, but I'd much rather see you get well and active enough to dance at our wedding if she will do me that very great honor." Gerard smiled understandingly at the older man, knowing perfectly how his mind had worked.

"Then you do like her?" The earl looked pleased with himself.

Gerard chuckled. "I never said I didn't, but I wouldn't want her forced into a marriage with me against her will or before she's ready."

Lord Clairmont nodded. "She'll be willing enough when the time comes, mark my words. So you'll stay and keep an eye on things for me?"

"Of course. You had only to ask, in any case. But I must leave for a few days from time to time to work on Perceval's assignment. Permit me to bring your lady back now, for I fear you have overtired yourself and need her gentle care to lull you to sleep." He squeezed the limp hand that lay on the bed, then went into the corridor, where an anxious Lady Clairmont waited.

"Is he all right?" she asked.

Gerard nodded. "He's tired now, for he did a lot of talking, but I believe his mind is much relieved."

She went into the bedchamber and Gerard was not at all surprised to see Leonora come from some room further along the corridor.

"Would you like me to show you the garden, my lord?" she asked, with the first hint of cheerfulness he had seen on her face since his arrival. He had meant to take a rest before dinner, but could not turn down her invitation, knowing how anxious she must be to find out what her father had wanted.

They left the house and crossed the smooth green lawn toward a wooded area a little beyond. Settling herself on an old tree stump, with her hands clasped together in her lap, she looked at him expectantly.

"Can you tell me what my papa wanted, or is it a secret?" she asked.

"It should not be a secret from you, and I think perhaps that I should be the first to explain it," he said seriously. "He would like me to stay here for some time, to get to know the running of the estate, see the bailiff, and bring the place back into shape after his absence now of nigh on two months."

She bit her lower lip and frowned. "He thinks he's going to die, and he doesn't care about that but does care about Clairmont House and lands. That's it, isn't it?" Her voice quavered a little, but she held back the tears that threatened.

He nodded. "To some extent," Gerard agreed, "but he also cares very much about you." He watched her face to see what her immediate reaction would be to his next words. "He would like us to marry, you and I, and wants us to get to know each other to see if we feel we might make a go of it."

Leonora jumped up, an expression of complete amazement on her face. "But that's preposterous! We've seen a little of each other in Bath and we dealt well together—or at least I thought we did—but that's not enough to base a marriage upon."

Standing also, Gerard put a hand on each of her shoulders and smiled deeply into her eyes, which showed the first signs of life since his arrival.

"I don't think he just got the idea, really. When I met him in Bath for the first time, he talked a great deal about you, how you had been brought up with just a number of governesses to care for you, and had become a bit of a hoyden. He was extremely anxious for me to meet you, and I got the idea he was playing matchmaker." His voice was soothing, with just a hint of humor in it as he tried to make her understand her father's foibles.

"I believe your stepmama saw through him also, for she had a strange gleam in her eye the day she insisted you help her entertain callers," he added.

"But Adele likes you, I know. She wouldn't have tried to stop us seeing each other, particularly against Papa's wishes," Leonora protested.

"I didn't say she would," he said, letting his hands slide from her shoulders to gently hold her upper arms. "What I believe she was doing was trying to slow down the process so that you might make comparisons. He'd probably hinted to her in the same way as he had to me." The corners of his mouth quirked in amusement as he waited for her to get used to the idea.

"Do you think he'll talk to me about it?" she asked, still not finding anything amusing about her father's maneuvering.

He nodded. "I'm sure he will. And I'd much prefer you to tell him what I told him. That we'll get to know each other better in the next few months. We'll do things together within the limitations of your mourning, and if we decide we could rub along well together, then we will become engaged to marry. If, however, either one of us has the slightest hesitation, we will not be forced into anything. Do you think you could tell him that?"

"Is there no one else you had thought of marrying?" she asked cautiously, for it was important she find out before agreeing to his suggestion.

"No one at all," he assured her, "until I met a delightfully refreshing young cousin, with black hair and sparkling blue eyes. Someone I looked forward to seeing much more of in London. But you're to be very honest with me now. You must not agree to something you don't want just for your father's sake, for marriage is for a very long time."

"I promise." This time her smile bore a distinct resemblance to its former beauty. "I'm so glad you're here, Gerard. This has been the worst month I've ever known in my life, and now it feels as though a huge weight has been removed."

"It will be easier from now on, I'm sure. But I believe we should return to the house to dress for dinner. I'll send my man back to get enough clothes for a stay of some length, and I'll discuss with you later the question of engaging a nurse to take care of your father. Even if he has taken a turn for the better, he's going to need a lot of attention, and you and Lady Clairmont are quite obviously close to exhaustion.''

"You'll talk to Adele about it first, won't you?" she asked hesitantly. "I'd hate her to take offense."

"I'll talk to both Lady Clairmont and your father before doing anything, of course. I'm only surprised the doctor has not suggested something of the sort before. And don't worry. I can be very persuasive when I set my mind to it," he added, looking at her so warmly that heat suffused her whole body, leaving her strangely tingling all over.

You can be most persuasive whether you set your mind to it or not, Leonora thought, for I've just agreed to everything my papa asked, when at first I was horrified.

They walked back to the house hand in hand. Then Leonora went to see her father, and Gerard retired to his bedchamber to get out of his traveling clothes and apprise his valet of the change in plans for a longer stay.

His opportunity to speak with Lady Clairmont came just before dinner, which she ate in the vast dining room a little earlier than the others while Leonora watched over her father. It needed little inducement for her to agree to Gerard's suggestion, for she was becoming extremely tired, and knew she must look as bad as, if not worse than, Leonora had until a few hours ago. Since Gerard's arrival, she had gained a little color in her cheeks and a brightness in her eyes.

With the earl's permission, Gerard consulted the doctor the following morning, and by evening a competent nurse had arrived and started into a routine.

8

The day had dawned bright and sunny, with just enough breeze to stop the heat from being oppressive.

Gerard had come into the room just as Leonora was finishing her breakfast, and he was glad to see her already looking more rested.

"What would you say, my dear, to packing a picnic and taking off in that sloop you sail so proficiently?" Gerard asked, and was delighted when her face lit with pleasure.

"Do you think we could, or might it be considered the wrong thing to do when in mourning?" she asked, hoping he'd say it was all right.

He reached a finger out and smoothed away the little frown that had formed between her eyebrows. "The thing you have to ask yourself is whether Geoffrey would think it wrong."

"Never in a million years would he think it wrong," she declared. "It will bring him closer to me, I believe, for we enjoyed so many happy hours together on the water. I'll have Cook prepare a picnic and tell Adele where we're going, and meet you here in half an hour. Do you think you could wear some of Geoffrey's things?"

"Would it bother you?" he asked, watching her face carefully.

She thought for a moment, then firmly shook her head. "No, not at all. He would have liked you to wear them, I'm sure," she said. "I'll pick something out and have it sent to your chamber."

She was one of the most punctual women he had ever known, and it was a minute short of the half-hour when she joined him and they left through the back of the house and took the path leading to the cliffs.

He could hardly take his eyes off her, for she was wearing a dark blue jersey that Geoffrey had grown out of years ago, and a pair of his old canvas trousers, bleached by the sun to a light beige and cut off at the ankles to accommodate her shorter legs. Her hair was fastened in a long braid down her back.

It was the very same way she had been garbed, except for the fishing hat, when he first saw her racing her sloop against that of one of the fishermen, and he felt a pang of unreasoning jealousy.

When they reached the edge of the cliff and he looked down into the sparkling cove, his eyes narrowed, searching for the footpath.

"I give up," he said finally. "Tell me how you get from here to the boat without breaking your neck."

"Oh, it's easy when you know where the path is," she said airily, heading for a clump of grass that looked no different from any of the others but behind which there was a steep, winding, rock-strewn trail that no self-respecting goat would have used, never mind human beings. "Just follow me and watch your step."

She was off—surefooted from many years of practice—before he could stop her. He followed at a more sedate pace, carrying the picnic basket and most certainly watching his step, for had he stumbled, he might easily have knocked her down the cliffs also.

The *Lady Leo* awaited them at the end of the small dock, and while Gerard stowed away the picnic hamper and prepared to cast off, Leonora unfurled and raised the sails and swung the sloop around to let the wind fill them.

Compared with bringing in the fishing lugger in the black of night, this was easy, and she felt at peace as she located the markers and cleared the cove, heading west-southwest to circle a small island where she and Geoffrey had often picnicked.

She was about to make for the island when she felt Gerard's hand lightly touch the tiller. "May I?" he asked, and she let him take over, hoping he knew what he was doing, but within a few minutes she saw that he was more than capable. She sat back and watched him circle the island once more, noticing how blond his hair was in the bright sun, and how straight and white his teeth were as he laughed with pure joy. She knew well the gladness he felt as the wind caressed his face and blew his hair into his eyes and his mouth.

She came to stand beside him and point out the best spot to land, where there was a small cut to run the sloop into, then jump overboard and haul it the rest of the way onto the sand.

They took off their shoes before jumping from the boat and pulling it ashore, then trod where the sea rarely reached and felt the gossamer heat of soft, silky sands loose enough to cover their ankles. She spread out towels for them to sit upon, then opened the picnic hamper and gasped.

"Cook has done us proud," she told him as she handed him cutlery and a napkin. "This is quite unlike the food she used to pack for Geoff and me when we came here."

He reached inside and brought out a cloth-wrapped bottle. "Can you find a corkscrew anywhere?" he asked. " 'Twould be a pity were we unable to open such an expensive French vintage wine."

"Here you are," she said, handing him the tool. "Would you like to start with the smoked salmon and then go on to turkey breast, Cornish pastries, and sliced tongue, or shall it be a little of each?"

"Why don't you make up one plate with some of everything on it, and we'll both eat from it," he suggested huskily, handing her a glass of wine. "But first, a toast to your father's recovery, my love, and then to us." He gazed longingly at her soft pink lips as they seemed to caress the rim of the glass, and he determined that before the day was out he would taste them.

They had raised their glasses for the first toast, but for the second one he insisted their arms be intertwined, forcing them to look at each other as they sipped the wine.

Leonora was breathing hard as he released her arm, and she concentrated on making up the plate, hoping he would not notice her flushed cheeks.

As soon as she was finished, he took up a fork, stabbing a piece of salmon, then rested it lightly on her bottom lip until she opened her mouth.

"My turn now," he murmured, and she forked a piece of tongue, then held it close to his lips, fearing to stab him if she went further. He reached for her wrist and drew it toward him, parting his lips to take the food inside, then slowly chewing it, watching her face the while.

By the time they had finished the plateful there was a decided current of excitement running between them, and Gerard swiftly pushed aside the remains of the picnic and pulled Leonora into his arms.

"I won't hurt you, my love," he whispered in her ear, though none but a few seagulls would have heard had he shouted it on the wind. "I just want to hold you for a few minutes, feel you close to me and kiss those tempting lips."

Her eyes opened wide, but she could not refuse for she was longing to know what it would feel like.

Gently he placed his lips against hers, touching them and sweetly probing while she listened to the thudding of her heart. Then he drew away and placed a tentative finger on her lower lip, pressing lightly until her mouth opened of its own volition. His own lips were back again, moving over hers like butterflies, teasing until her head started to swim and she gasped for air.

He released her mouth for a moment, smiling deeply into her eyes with such tenderness and understanding she wanted to stay like that forever. But his mouth came down on hers once more, now insistent and demanding, drawing a response from deep inside her and at the same time making her feel strangely languid and helpless. His tongue slipped between her lips, and her body quivered at the sensations it awoke in her.

When he finally, regretfully released her mouth, he continued to hold her lightly against him and she did not try to push away. Her head fell on his shoulder and her fingers crept up to her burning, swollen lips and then she clung to him, hiding her face against his chest. He had taken her into a new world of feelings she had never realized existed and she needed time to adjust before facing him under the bright, ruthless sun, which would surely reveal to him her wanton need.

"Are you all right now, my love?" he asked softly. "I had no idea one kiss could have such an effect on me. Did you feel the same?"

She lifted her head then and looked at him in wonder. "Isn't it always like that?" she asked.

"I hope it will always be so between you and me, but to answer your question, it is very rare indeed." He got up and gave her his hand to pull her onto her feet also.

"I think we'd best leave now, before I do something I will regret later. Your father has entrusted you to me, and I cannot betray that trust. I'll repack the hamper and then we'll start back."

Leonora was still in a dream, and she left the sailing to Gerard until they approached the cove; then she took over and brought the sloop through the channels and to their dock.

"Now I know what you meant when you said you climbed," Gerard said as he scrambled up the steep path. "I wonder how costly it might be to have a real path cut in the cliff, with steps and handrails. Or would that take away much of your fun, my love?"

"It never seemed worthwhile when only Geoff and I used it, but as we grow older it might be a problem," she admitted with a grin. "Can you imagine me climbing down here with my walking stick, like Aunt Charlotte?"

Gerard had been gone for a week, and Leonora was surprised how very much she missed him. She was quite cross that he had not told her where he would be, except to say, in answer to her question, that he would not be visiting his family.

Even more exasperating, in her present mood, was the

fact that her papa quite obviously knew where he had gone but simply refused to tell her, saying, "You're not in his pocket yet, girl, and if he'd wanted you to know what he was doing, he would have told you himself."

One thing Gerard had suggested before leaving was that she order a riding habit in black so that she might accompany him around the estate and also go with him for rides in the country.

She had just tried on the new habit, and found that the style suited her very well and the fit was perfect. She twirled around, watching the way the skirts fell into place, and imagined how attractive it would look later with a brightly colored hat and scarf, though she knew she looked extremely well in the black shako and white cravat she had donned.

Suddenly impatient with Gerard for not being here to see how well she looked, she glared at her reflection and stamped her booted foot. She would go for a ride by herself, she decided, and sent her maid, Millie, to the stables to order Lady Luck saddled. A moment later there was a light tap on the door and Adele came in.

"How becoming that habit is!" she exclaimed, walking completely around her stepdaughter to view it from all sides. "Were you just trying it on for fit?"

"I was," Leonora said, pouting a little, "but I've now decided to go for a ride. It's a lovely day and Lady Luck needs exercise."

"I'm sure the grooms are more than happy to exercise all the horses, for it must be quite the pleasantest of their tasks," Adele said dryly, "but I trust you do not intend to go further afield than our own lands?"

"I don't know where I'm going yet," Leonora replied rebelliously, "but I'll take a groom along if that's what you're worried about."

Adele smiled rather sadly, for she was very fond of her stepdaughter but could exert little influence over her when she was in one of these moods. "What's the point in taking a groom when you know you're going to outride him as soon as you leave the grounds?"

"Then if that's how you feel, I won't," Leonora said with a toss of her head. "And Papa is hardly in a position to carry out his threats of some months back, is he?"

Lady Clairmont shrugged. "If he decides to delegate his authority to Gerard, you may be sorry."

"Gerard wouldn't dare touch me, with or without my father's permission, Adele. If he did, then I wouldn't marry him, that's all."

"I don't think for a moment that he would spank you as your father threatened to do, but I know I would not like to receive a dressing-down from that young man," Adele warned.

"He shouldn't go away and leave me like this without even telling me where he's going or when he'll be back," Leonora retorted, smarting from what she felt was a complete disregard of her burgeoning feelings.

"There's probably a very good reason why he couldn't tell you, my dear. Don't do anything foolish that might spoil your budding relationship, or you might regret it for a very long time." Adele gave her a sympathetic hug, then left her alone to think about it.

Leonora took one more look in the mirror and decided it was a waste not to go riding now that she was dressed for it, then hurried down to the stables, where one of the grooms was holding a decidedly frisky Lady Luck.

"Shall I accompany you, m'lady, or are you just going around the estate?" he asked.

"It's all right, Jim, I'll not go too far, so you needn't come with me," she said when she was mounted; then she turned sharply and let the mare have her head, racing across the field and jumping the fence at the far side.

Because of her lack of suitable attire, she had not ridden since before they went to Bath, and the wind felt good on her face as she took the cliff path, avoiding the village. She headed toward the seldom-used moorland road, letting her horse set the pace until she realized she had come much further than she intended, and swung around.

But she had gone no more than a hundred yards when she realized Lady Luck was limping badly, and she immediately dismounted and examined her carefully, angry with herself for not noticing sooner. To her relief, it was nothing more than a large stone that had become wedged under her shoe, but Leonora had nothing with which to remove it. She broke a nail poking at it with her finger, but could not dislodge it. She could not remount and add to her horse's discomfort, so she grasped the reins and walked the six or more miles back to Clairmont House.

Leaving Lady Luck in the hands of Fred, the head groom, she went in through the back of the house, hoping her long absence had not been noted, but aware she had been gone close to four hours and had missed luncheon.

Refusing to sneak up the back stairs like a thief in the night, she walked through the corridor and into the main hall, and had just passed the drawing-room door when a voice called, "Is that you, Leonora?"

She stopped, her heart turning a somersault at the sound of Gerard's voice, then turned back and entered the room, regretting her unkempt appearance, for her hair had come loose and her habit was dusty from the long walk home.

Gerard was with Adele in the drawing room, and he rose and came toward her, holding out his hands.

"We were about to send out a search party but had no idea which way you had gone," he said as she placed her hands in his and felt their reassuring warmth. "What happened?"

"Nothing terrible," she told him, explaining about the stone. "We were halfway across the moors before I noticed her limp, so we had a long walk back." She shrugged slightly, as though it was something she could not have helped, then looked into his eyes and knew she was not home-free.

Adele rose. "I'll leave you two together and see if Cook has something left over from luncheon for Leonora," she said.

"Please don't bother, Adele, for I don't think I could eat anything." Leonora felt her insides start to quake. "I'll wait until dinner now."

As soon as Adele had left the room and closed the door

behind her, Gerard pointed to a seat, and when she took it, he sat down across from her.

"We have all been worried sick for this past hour or more, in case something dreadful had occurred. You know that it would finish your father at once should anything happen to you, Leonora, and you also know that fretting about you is the worst treatment he can give his heart," he said sternly.

"I couldn't help Lady Luck picking up a big stone, could I?" she asked defensively.

"You could help being out there alone, for if a groom had been with you he would have walked and you would have ridden his horse directly home," he retorted. "Will you tell me why you insist on going off on your own?"

"Because the groom can never keep up with me," she said, remembering using the same words earlier in the day to Adele.

"That's utter nonsense, and you know it." His lips curled scornfully. "There are at least three other horses in the stable with as much speed as Lady Luck, and if you picked a young groom who loves to ride, I guarantee he could easily outdistance you if he dared to do so."

She looked thoughtful, for it had never occurred to her to use anyone except the older man that Fred probably gave her because he was also a slow worker.

"Your father has told me, and Lady Clairmont would not deny it, that you have always been strong-willed and stubborn, yet apart from the first time I ever saw you, you have shown little of such tendencies in front of me. Are they right, and have you just been hiding them from me?"

"I suppose . . ." she began, studying the carpet as she spoke.

"Look at me, please, when you're speaking to me, Leonora," he said harshly.

Suddenly she was very angry. "How would he know?" she asked, her blue eyes flashing. "Until nine months ago he hardly ever saw either me or Geoffrey. He spent as much time away from here as he could, and when he was here he was too busy with his neglected estates to bother with us. We did grow up wild, but it wasn't our fault, for we only had each other." She was almost sobbing but could stop now.

"He wanted Geoffrey to learn about the estates, but Geoff knew Papa would never come home if he did, for he'd have no need to. He only came home last year and married Adele so that she could bring me out and find me a husband—and take care of him in his old age. Geoff and I both loved him but he didn't care about us, and he only let Geoffrey go into the army because he didn't know what to do with him. And now he's dead and he was all I had—the only one who cared."

Gerard was across the room and gathering her into his arms before the words turned into heartbreaking sobs. Holding her close and murmuring soothingly, he let her cry it out of her system. Her sorrow for both her brother and her father had been bottled up inside of her for a long time, he thought, and needed to come out.

As the sobs turned to sniffs, Gerard reached into a pocket and gave her his handkerchief. She wiped her face and blew her nose loudly, and then noticed the mark she had left on the shoulder of his coat.

Following her gaze, he gave a soft chuckle. "Jacobs will take care of that, I'm sure. Do you feel better now?" he asked gently.

She nodded and smiled a little tremulously, then told him, "I suppose the answer to your previous question is, yes, I am strong-willed and stubborn, but, no, I wasn't deliberately hiding it from you. I just never felt that way when I was with you."

Her hair fell over her face and he stroked it back out of her eyes. "I was harsh with you, I know, love, but I was scared witless that something terrible had happened—and I didn't even know in which direction to look for you.

"Will you give me your promise that you'll never take a horse out again, off the estates, unless a groom is with you who can keep up?" He looked intently at her as he spoke, and saw her sheepish smile at his last few words.

"I promise," she said contritely. "I'm sorry I had you so worried."

He bent to wipe away a forgotten tear, and she tilted her head, inadvertently brushing her lips against his, then drew back sharply, startled by the heat that rose inside her at the slight contact.

"Please do that again," he begged, and she raised her face shyly toward him, pressing her lips against his in an unconsciously full, open kiss. When she finally drew away, she was shaking and her face was red with embarrassment.

Gerard grinned, delighted at her confusion. "I think after that you should make an honest man of me," he said. "Will you marry me, Leonora? I know how I feel about you, and I hope you feel the same way."

She nodded, unable to speak for a moment, then said simply, "I know, too, and I want to marry you very much."

There was a knock on the door and they sprang guiltily apart as Adele entered. A maid followed, with a tray she placed on the tea table, then left the room.

"I thought Leonora might be hungry despite what she said, but now I wonder if I should have left you alone." She looked at them reproachfully.

Gerard raised an eyebrow to Leonora and she nodded, smiling a little shyly. "You may wish us happy, Adele. Leonora has just consented to become my wife—when, of course, she is out of mourning."

"My darling," Adele said as she threw her arms around her stepdaughter. "I am so very pleased for you both, for I don't know when I saw a better matched couple. Come sit down and have a cup of tea while I go upstairs and give your father the good news."

Leonora nibbled at the food while Gerard joined her in a cup of tea. But as she ate, she became very serious and finally asked him, "After we are married, you won't still go away for days on end and not tell me where you are going, will you?"

He saw that she was quite concerned, and turned her toward him, smoothing away the frown that creased her brow.

"From time to time the Prime Minister has asked me to do certain things for him which have entailed spending a few days away from home. I believe it was my grandfather's consolation prize for stopping me going into the army, for it gives me a way of being of service to my country." He paused, for he was only human and could not help enjoying the surprise on her face.

"These assignments are highly confidential, and that is why I didn't tell you where I spent my week away from here. I shall continue to do whatever I am asked after we are married. If I can tell you about it, I will, but you will have to be understanding when I cannot."

"I feel better, now that you've explained it to me. But you could hardly expect me to like it when you left without explanation, could you?" Leonora asked calmly, but inwardly she was quaking as she recalled that he had been asking questions at the inn. Could he be working with the Revenuers, looking for smugglers?

"You have a point, my love, but after all, we were not promised to each other then, were we? And speaking of that, I'll send a messenger to my home right away, for I must have the family betrothal ring to put upon your finger," he said. "I have a feeling you will like it, for it is a very pretty ring of sapphires and diamonds."

She looked up in delight, for she had never worn any ring before. He caught her chin in his hand, stroking his lips over hers. She closed her eyes to better enjoy this new, wonderful sensation, and he slipped his arms around her, cradling her in a tender embrace while he kissed her mouth, her eyelids, her forehead, and finally he just held her close to his chest, where she could feel his heart beating rapidly in tune with her own.

For once, Leonora was incapable of speech. She felt a joy more intense than she'd ever believed possible. It shone from her eyes when she looked up at him, and was reflected in his as he slowly released her, placing a last lingering kiss in the palm of her hand.

"How warm and natural you are, my love," he murmured. "Stay that way and I can promise you will have a most happy and contented husband."

9

Lord Clairmont was delighted when Adele told him the good news, and despite her misgivings, he insisted that a bottle of champagne be opened and a small celebration held in his bedchamber before dinner.

But as Adele had feared, the excitement was too much for him, and during the early hours of the morning his condition had worsened. After examining him, the doctor was grave. "These seizures are taking their toll on him," he said brusquely, "and the life he's led is mostly the cause. It's a pity he was not in your care sooner, Lady Clairmont."

By the end of a week there was little improvement; then one afternoon Lord Clairmont told his wife that he wished to speak to Leonora and Gerard.

When they entered the room, he appeared to be sleeping, but then he opened his eyes and beckoned them closer. "Get her out of here," he said faintly, pointing to the nurse. "I must talk to you."

The woman, who had risen at their entrance, slipped out of the room and Leonora took her seat by the side of the bed and reached for her father's hand. He smiled faintly and brought her hand closer to his face to look at the betrothal ring, which had arrived that morning.

He gave a satisfied grunt, then said, "I left you alone too much after your mother died. Shouldn't have done it, but I was no good at bringing up babes." He looked up at Gerard. "I want to see her wed before I go."

Gerard raised his eyebrows in question to Leonora, and when she nodded her agreement, he smiled at her tenderly.

"Nothing havey-cavey, mind you." Lord Clairmont had

gathered his strength a little and he knew what he wanted. "Known the bishop for years—used to play cards with him. I'll send him a note and tell him to bring a special license."

"I'll take your message myself, sir," Gerard said quietly, "and bring him back with me. In the meantime, the ladies can make whatever plans they think necessary for a ceremony at home."

"Knew you'd a head on your shoulders when I saw you." Lord Clairmont's growl was getting fainter and Leonora rose to bend over and kiss his cheek.

"Get some rest now, Papa. We'll take care of everything," she whispered before slipping her hand into Gerard's and leaving the room.

They descended the steps in silence, and it was not until they returned to the drawing room, where Adele was waiting, and had firmly closed the door behind them that they spoke a word.

"Are you sure you want to do this, my love?" Gerard asked, turning Leonora toward him and watching her expressive face.

"Yes. I always wanted to be married in a church, but I suppose it will be just as binding if the bishop performs the nuptials," she said seriously.

He smiled a little grimly. "It will be binding, I can assure you, but we can always have a second ceremony in a church later, should you wish to make the bonds even more secure."

Adele was looking at them with concern. "He wants you to marry right away?" she asked.

They explained her husband's wishes, and she agreed with Gerard. "Under the circumstances, should you desire to have a second, more elaborate ceremony a year later, no one would think anything about it, Leonora. That is, if you were not . . ." She hesitated and her cheeks turned a deep pink as she murmured, "Oh, dear."

"Precisely," Gerard said with a grin. "And now I think I'd best prepare to leave, for I believe 'twere well it were done quickly."

"Will you return soon?" Leonora asked.

He stroked her cheek gently with one finger and let it stray across her soft lips, as though implanting the memory of his kisses. He felt their tremor and wished he could be alone with her for a few hours to offer her comfort, but the matter was urgent and he must be on his way.

"It's not very far, my love," he said tenderly, "but I do appreciate your concern, and if all goes well, I'll be back by tomorrow night or early the next morning."

When he had gone, she turned to Adele and was surprised to find that she looked very much better than she had when they first revealed Lord Clairmont's plans. Her stepmama's next words confirmed this.

"It is such a relief to have a man of his stature around, for he seems to be able to take command of any situation, yet does not ride roughshod over the feelings of others. The more I see of him, the more pleased I am that he is to be your husband. You are fortunate indeed," she told Leonora, "and for this at least you can thank your papa, for had he not sent for him, it is possible you would never have met."

Leonora smiled faintly. He was indeed a man of many facets. She could still feel his touch on her lips, and she, too, wished there had been time for a few moments alone together before he left.

"While I have you to myself, I suppose we had better talk a little about what happens between a husband and wife once they are married," Adele said thoughtfully. "I do hope that Geoffrey did not put any strange ideas into your head, for I've no doubt you discussed all manner of most unsuitable things."

"We were certainly close, but most of the time he didn't act as if I was a girl at all, though he did make it clear there was a great difference between me and the women he met drinking and gambling," Leonora told her. "And he was furious and pulled me away quickly when some of them came over to talk to him one day."

"I should think so," her stepmama said, slightly shocked, then turned back to the matter at hand. "Did one of your governesses perhaps say anything to you when you started . . . ?'' She hesitated as Leonora chuckled.

"Geoffrey told me about that,'' she said offhandedly, "for I thought surely I was going into a sickly decline. And you should have seen how shocked Miss Worthington was when he told her about it.''

"I've no doubt she was, but it was natural, I suppose, under the circumstances, that you would turn to your brother before you would turn to a governess. Did he tell you anything else?''

Leonora shook her head. "Geoffrey said it was something to do with babies, and I'd know all about it when I grew up,'' Leonora offered. "What else should I know?'' she asked gently, her eyes twinkling with secret amusement at Adele's obvious embarrassment.

"Nothing you need worry about with a man of Gerard's sensitivity, I'm sure. Once you are married, he will come to your chamber and make love to you, and though it may hurt a little, I am sure he'll be as gentle as he can. If you're lucky, you may have a baby.'' Adele looked a little envious, for she had always wanted children of her own.

Leonora did not really understand much of what Adele had told her, but her stepmama quite obviously felt he'd made it all quite clear.

Dinner was a comparatively quiet meal without Gerard. Aunt Charlotte was more subdued than usual, for she was fond of her nephew, and the news of his worsening served to depress her. To Leonora's relief, she excused herself once they were finished, saying her maid would bring tea to her room a little later.

Adele was anxious to get back to her husband's bedside, so instead of retiring to the drawing room, Leonora asked for tea to be brought to her bedchamber also, giving weariness from the excitement as an excuse.

The fact of the matter was, however, that she had received a note from Ted. As it contained only the word "Wednesday,'' she was much relieved, for she had to admit that in all the confusion of her papa's illness, she hadn't time to think about the smugglers. She needed to sit down and decide what she would do about her part in their activities once she was married. What if Gerard found out? What if he were actually pursuing smugglers, and the very ring she was helping? She tossed about as these questions repeated themselves endlessly in her mind. But eventually fatigue caught up with her, and she fell into a sound sleep.

The next day Leonora busied herself deciding which chambers would be suitable for her and Gerard, selecting furniture to be moved into them, and supervising the placement of it, so that it was not until she had retired for the last time to her old bedchamber that she thought about the smugglers again. She must stay awake tonight to put the lights in place.

"If you like, milady," Millie said rather hesitantly when she came in to help her into bed, "I could set out the lights from tonight on. I told Ted that you were to be wed and that I thought I should do that for you in future. He seemed pleased. He said he'll only trouble you if Bob Bowers can't go out."

Leonora was relieved, for she had been concerned about this. "Very well, but be sure they're burning brightly, for the men's lives may be at stake," she warned. "And I would still like his note to come to me, so that I know what night I might be needed."

When she was alone she started to ponder how she might be able to get away, when necessary, after her marriage. Millie had solved the problem of the lights, but there still remained the times when she must go out with the men. She could not let Gerard find out about her involvement, for, even if his assignment had nothing to do with smugglers, she knew he would never permit her either to run such risks or to associate with such men.

It was worrisome indeed, but she was determined to continue, for when she was with Ted and the others, she felt closer to Geoffrey. Since Gerard had entered her life, memories of Geoffrey had faded somewhat, and helping the smugglers was a way of remembering her childhood and holding on to it—a way of keeping her brother's memory sacred.

* * *

Adele was unhappy that Leonora could not be married in anything lighter than her best black dress, with neither flowers nor veil to relieve her somber attire. Though it was a wedding without a party and guests, there was one thing Adele could do for the couple. She spent considerable time making arrangements with Cook so that there would be a proper wedding feast.

Gerard and the bishop arrived at midmorning. The latter spent more than an hour with Lord Clairmont, who seemed much stronger, before coming down to luncheon with Gerard and the three ladies.

"It is my hope that it is not just the occasion that is making my old friend a little better," the bishop said in a resounding voice as he took his seat at table. "He was always a rascal, and I hate to see him so low. I have spoken to him at length about his son's death, for which he blames himself, and I believe I have been able to ease his conscience in the matter."

"What time did you wish to have the ceremony, sir?" Adele asked him. "You will, of course, spend at least the night with us, so perhaps the late afternoon would be suitable?"

"That was just what I was going to suggest," he boomed. "Give old Roland a chance to sleep for an hour or so after his luncheon, for excitement does not sit well on a full stomach."

Adele turned next to Leonora. "Is that all right with you, my dear?" she asked, hoping she would not disagree, for it would interfere with her plans for later. "You have already changed, I see."

"Of course, and if Papa is still sleeping this afternoon, then we'll just wait until he awakes," Leonora said, sounding far more relaxed and amenable than she felt, for as the time drew near, she was becoming a little nervous. It was a big step to take and she hoped she was doing the best thing, for she had started to realize that she really did not know Gerard very well. "It's not as though we have to worry about keeping guests waiting," she said.

She looked over to where Gerard sat, and he gave her a reassuring smile. He looked rested, so she assumed he had found the bishop at home and had not lost sleep seeking him. After he arrived he had gone directly to his chamber to change out of riding clothes, so she had not had a chance to see him alone.

"If you've finished luncheon, would you like to take a stroll in the garden, my love?" Gerard asked. Leonora accepted with alacrity, for she had been dreading the idea of just sitting around and becoming more and more nervous.

"That's the way," Aunt Charlotte said with a chortle. She had taken a sip of sherry before luncheon and was feeling much livelier than she had for days. "You young lovebirds make the most of it while you can, for it'll not be long before little ones come along, and there'll be no time then for walks in the garden."

Leonora blushed a deep pink, and was grateful when Gerard grasped her arm firmly and steered her out of the room.

"I know you would have preferred to be married in the church, but under the circumstances, it couldn't be. Did you have any further thoughts about having a second service later?" he asked when they had found their favorite spot amid the roses.

Leonora had given it a great deal of thought while he had been away, and she was hoping he would not think her wishes foolish. "Not a service, exactly, and you may laugh at what I have in mind," she said with some hesitation, "but do you think we could go together to St. Petrox Church within the next few days? It's a place I dearly love, and I think I would be contented if we could just sit for a while in the ancient chapel.

"You might find Dartmouth Castle, which is built into the same piece of rock, of more interest. When it was finished, it was said to be the most advanced fortification in the whole of England, and it guards the entrance to the River Dart. There is supposed to be chain running under the estuary and fastened on the other side to Kingswear

Castle, which could be pulled tight when necessary to keep enemy ships out.''

He grinned. ''It sounds to me as though one of your governesses used to be fond of historical ruins and took you there on outings.''

''How did you guess?'' Leonora laughed. ''She was interested in little else. Taking me to visit ancient buildings and old ruins was as much for her own as my benefit, I'm sure.''

''We'll most certainly go there, if that's what you would like. I'll plan a short trip around the area, and let Adele know where we will be staying each night so that she can reach us if necessary. Would you like that?'' he asked, wishing to have her to himself for a while, and also to give her a taste, if only a small one, of a honeymoon trip.

''Thank you. I'd like it very much, and you, too, should know a little of the area where you are residing,'' she said.

He nodded, fortunately deciding not to tell her he had been in almost every town and village along the South Coast in the last six months, working with the Revenue officers, and had helped them catch quite a number of smugglers and several French spies they had brought into the country. Leonora's nervous state would have considerably worsened had she known for sure that this was the assignment on which he was working for the Prime Minister.

His hand, linked in hers, was warm and comforting, and they strolled slowly back to the house to find that Lord Clairmont was now awake and anxious to get started with the ceremony.

What it lacked in surroundings was certainly made up for by the presence of the bishop, who donned his robes and performed the service with his resonant voice as solemnly as if he had been in a cathedral. When the vows were exchanged, Gerard turned to face Leonora and looked into her eyes as he made his promise and she, in turn, could do no less.

Toasts with champagne followed, until Gerard, glancing at his new father-in-law, noticed that the older man was showing signs of tiring, and suggested they adjourn to the drawing room.

After sipping the heady champagne, Leonora took Gerard's arm and seemed to float down the stairs and into the drawing room, where, to her complete amazement, the household staff was assembled to toast the happy couple and wish them well. Plates of sweet and savory pastries covered the sideboard, and in the center was a magnificent wedding cake. Cook stood proudly beside it, holding a knife with which the pair were to cut the first slice.

Most of the staff had known Leonora all her life and were delighted to see her wed. Their wishes for her happiness were heartfelt if a little blunt. Cook's departure seemed to be the signal for a general exodus, and soon Leonora and Gerard found themsleves alone, for Adele, the bishop, and even Aunt Charlotte, who had been trying to persuade that gentleman to give her a game of whist, were suddenly nowhere to be seen.

Taking advantage of the moment, Gerard drew his bride into his arms, tilted her head toward him, and first circled her mouth with the tip of his finger, then with the tip of his tongue, after which he gently brushed his lips against hers. Her whole body came instantly alive, and when his lips abandoned hers and trailed down her cheek, they left a path of fire in their wake.

It was some time before either of them realized that Smathers was in the doorway, loudly clearing his throat.

When he had their complete attention at last, he looked not a little embarrassed, but his voice was steady as he said, "If you will follow me, milord, milady, dinner is served," and led them, not toward the dining room, but up the stairs and into the sitting room between their two bed-chambers.

A fire had been lit to take the chill off the evening air, and in front of it a table was set for two, decorated with trailing red roses and forget-me-nots. On a sideboard were a number of covered dishes, and once Gerard had seated Leonora, Smathers proceeded to serve them, first presenting a bottle of the finest claret for Gerard's inspection.

Leonora could not have told anyone later what she ate for dinner, but she knew it was delectable. Either the wine or the warmth in Gerard's eyes set her aglow, and she suspected it was a little of both.

They ended the meal with small cups of coffee and the best French cognac, and as they sipped the fragrant beverages, Smathers cleared away all signs of their feast and then disappeared.

Pleasantly drowsy, Leonora was curious but not at all apprehensive about what was to happen next as she allowed Gerard to lead her into her chamber. She shivered with pleasure as he started to unfasten the tiny buttons down the back of her gown, dropping kisses on the bare skin as each inch was revealed. Then he turned her around and cupped her face in her hands.

"I think you can manage the rest yourself, my love, while I get into something more comfortable. Let me know if you need any further help, for I am your maid this evening."

Dropping a kiss on the tip of her nose, he left her to finish undressing, and when she was down to her drawers, she went to get her nightrail from the bed and found that a most beautiful white gossamer gown had replaced her old flannel one.

She was sitting up in bed by the time Gerard returned, looking strange but extremely handsome in his dark blue dressing gown as he proceeded to snuff the candles.

"Don't put them all out yet, Gerard," Leonora said softly. "I think I'd like to see what happens next."

He couldn't help chuckling as he realized, to his delight, that she was not going to be a frightened, quaking bride. "There'll be a glow from the fire for a while, but I'll leave the candles lit nearest the bed if you wish," he agreed. Their eyes met and held as he walked toward her, untying the sash of his gown as he drew near.

"You look beautiful. Like one of the statues I saw in Bath," she said in a surprised voice.

"Not anywhere near as beautiful as you, my love," he murmured, flinging his gown onto a chair and bending to place a soft kiss on the tip of her nose. "Perhaps it is as well we did not have a traditional wedding, for you are not at all the traditional quaking bride, for which I am truly thankful.''

Stretching out on the bed, he slipped an arm around her shoulders and she tentatively reached across to touch the bright golden hairs on his chest. They felt silky and she knew that before the night was out she would satisfy her urge to rub her cheek against their softness. His smile was tender, but his eyes burned with passion as his mouth captured hers and his tongue teased relentlessly. Slowly, almost casually, his hand began to stroke the velvety skin at her throat, then moved down, untying the ribbons of her gown when they hampered his slow, sensuous progress.

When his hand reached her waist and slid below, she gasped with joy at the waves of inner passion he aroused. Then he moved closer, and their bodies touched, his hard and muscular, hers soft and yielding. His desire heightened as he felt her instinctive response, but he knew he must go slowly, for her wonderful natural feelings could be shattered if he should frighten her. He slid her gown over her head and tossed it onto the floor. His mouth found the soft mound of a breast and she gasped as his lips sent unbelievable sensations like messages through her body to where his fingers were gently stroking the velvety skin and easing her legs apart.

The fires he had lit threatened to consume her, and she clung to him desperately, feeling the hard planes of his muscled back and shoulders beneath her hands. Then his mouth was on hers again, more demanding this time, sending her into a swirling, cascading world of passion, through which she only faintly heard him say, ''This will hurt a little, love, but only this once, I promise.''

There was a sharp pain deep down, and she was unaware that she cried out, as it was quickly forgotten and she was swept away on a sea of sensations, one cresting wave after another, until, when she thought she could bear it no longer, there was a breaker more magnificent than the last, followed by a glorious feeling of peace and well-being.

After what seemed an age, but was really little more than a few minutes, she opened her eyes and looked at her husband lying beside her on the bed. He was gazing at her through half-closed eyes, a secret smile on his face, and he reached out and cupped her breast in his palm.

"For once I hardly know what to say," she murmured. "Is it always like that?"

He laughed softly, shaking his head at the innocence of her response. "No, my love, it couldn't be, or we'd be dead before the week was out. I don't think you knew much of what was happening, and I was little better. Let's lie still for a while and rest."

"Can we do it again later, or is it just once a night?" she asked innocently.

He cradled her in his arms, and she snuggled against him, loving his faint masculine smell. Her cheek rested, as she had known it would, in those soft golden hairs.

"There are really no rules to this, my love, or at least not for us. If we both feel like it, then we may do it again, or we may just become too exhausted and go to sleep instead," he murmured, his warm breath caressing her ear.

To her delight, they were not too tired, and it was just as wonderful, but in a different way, for she approached the second time with more awareness and just as much joy. She was crazily, unbelievably in love with him, and, it seemed, he felt the same way about her. She knew she would feel like this always, and she prayed that he would also.

10

"Here you are, Adele," Gerard said, handing her a list of inns. "We'll try to stay with this plan, but if by any chance there is no room for the night at one of them, we will still ask there for any messages."

He and Leonora were setting out on a small trip around the countryside, not journeying any distance that would prevent them from returning to Clairmont House the same day if the need should arise.

"Enjoy yourselves," Adele said, "and I'll try to see that the improvement in Lord Clairmont's health continues. Just knowing that Leonora is secure has set his mind at rest, and he is in complete agreement that you both deserve some time alone."

She looked at the piece of paper. "I see you will be spending tonight at Dartmouth, and I can highly recommend the inn, for I stayed there once several years ago and found the beds clean and the food excellent. Now, do drive carefully, for the roads are narrow and young men these days race along them as though they own the earth."

Leonora laughed. "You sound like a mother hen, Adele, and you forget that Gerard is a young man also."

"Oh, no, I didn't forget," her stepmama said with an amused glance in Gerard's direction. "I was trying to give him a subtle hint, that's all."

"I will take very good care of my wife, dear stepmama," he said, putting one arm around Leonora and reaching the other out to take Adele's hand. "My days of racing recklessly along narrow country lanes have been sadly curtailed, I fear." He raised her hand to his lips and smiled warmly. "Don't forget to take care of yourself, as well as Lord Clairmont, and if all is well, we'll see you in a week's time."

Adele went to the door with them, and stood on the step watching as he helped Leonora into the curricle and took the reins; then they both waved until they were out of sight.

"Did I tell you how beautiful you look today?" Gerard asked when they were proceeding at a moderate pace. "Your skin is as soft as rose petals, and the sparkle in your eyes is brighter by far than the sapphire you wear for me."

Leonora's cheeks turned a rosy pink, and her whole face glowed with happiness. She had been married two wonderful days!

Cook had packed a picnic lunch, and they ate it beneath the shade of a large oak while the young tiger watered the horses.

"We'll be in Dartmouth in about an hour," Gerard said. "Do you want to go directly to St. Petrox Church, or should we first see if the inn has a room for the night?"

"Why don't we go to the inn, and you can secure a room for the night and send in our baggage while I wait in the carriage?" Leonora suggested. "Then we can continue to the church, which is a little way from the town, if I recall."

"Brains as well as beauty. Now, why did I not think of that?" he said with a rueful grin.

There was not a hint of sarcasm in his voice, but Leonora still felt somewhat discomfited, for she had not meant to tell him what to do. Her cheeks reddened and, seeing them, Gerard put an arm around her shoulders and drew her close, resting his face against hers, then turning his head to place a tender kiss on her mouth.

"We're partners now, love," he said softly. "I'd never let you become a shrew, but neither do I want you to hold back your undoubtedly intelligent suggestions."

They started out once more and it was not long before they reached the outskirts of the port town and then the inn itself. As she had suggested, Gerard went inside, leaving her in the carriage with the tiger holding the horses.

He had been gone hardly a moment, however, when she heard an all-too-familiar voice behind her. "Well, well. What are you doing so far from Clairmont House, Leonora?"

It was hard to repress a shudder when the owner of the voice, Baron Hector Burlington, rode up astride a coal-black stallion, leaned forward, and grasped the side of the carriage.

"Good afternoon, Lord Burlington," Leonora said, inclining her head slightly.

His glance encompassed the stylish curricle, finely matched chestnuts, and the uniformed tiger at the horses' heads. "Whose equipage might this be, young lady, for it certainly is not in Lord Clairmont's style," he demanded harshly.

Leonora flushed, but held her head high. "It belongs to my husband, my lord, and he will be back in just a moment . . ."

As she spoke, Gerard came out of the inn closely followed by the innkeeper and a couple of servants, who picked up the baggage and hurried back inside.

"Good afternoon, Burlington," he said curtly, looking pointedly at the hand that grasped the carriage. He turned to Leonora. "Are you all right, my dear?"

She gave him a bright smile and nodded as Burlington took his hand off the carriage with obvious reluctance, then said coldly, "I understand I am to congratulate you, Lord Sinclair. May I ask when the happy occasion took place?"

"The bishop married us two days ago, at Lord Clairmont's bedside," Gerard said coldly, "and, under the circumstances, there were no announcements made, and no guests except the immediate family."

"I see. I have been away for several days or I would have known about it, I'm sure. I trust Lord Clairmont has not taken a turn for the worse?" Burlington offered, turning back to Leonora, but there was no sympathy in either his expression or his voice.

"He had, but has since recovered a little, thank you,"

Leonora told him. "Are we ready, darling?" she asked Gerard.

"Yes, my dear. Thank you for your congratulations, Burlington, and now we must be off." He jumped up into the carriage, took the reins in hand, and with a wave of his whip they departed, leaving a disgruntled Lord Burlington glaring after them.

"Has his behavior always been so familiar?" Gerard asked, frowning slightly. "I know he's a neighbor and all that, but there seems to be something presumptuous in the way he addresses you. I remember thinking so when I saw him with you in Bath."

"He wasn't with me in Bath, just paying an afternoon call," she reminded him, then decided it might be prudent to tell him of her last extremely distasteful meeting with their obnoxious neighbor. "He came supposedly to offer his condolences when we first returned to Clairmont House, and he was most unpleasant."

"In what way?" Gerard asked offhandedly, trying to hide his concern at her remarks.

"He tried to tell me that he had been close to Geoffrey and said my brother would have wanted me to turn to him for comfort," Leonora said irritably, then added, "I practically told him he was a liar and asked him to leave."

"Was Adele with you when you met with him?" he asked, for it was not at all the thing, of course, for a young lady to entertain a man alone.

"Adele had just gone to sleep after nursing Papa all night, and Aunt Charlotte was also resting, so I reluctantly saw him alone. But I stationed a footman outside the open door," she told him, "and though I didn't ask him to, Smathers also stayed within hearing."

"If you implied he was a liar within the hearing of servants, he must have been quite beside himself," Gerard said, now distinctly alarmed on her behalf.

"He went very red in the face, but he also proposed marriage to me. I declined, of course. I also told him he should have waited and asked you when you arrived, which did not please him at all." She shrugged. "But at least it put him off, for he hasn't called since."

Gerard said nothing more, but vowed to keep a close eye on the man in the future. They strongly disliked each other, which was understandable, but it was possible that Leonora's words had turned a would-be suitor into an enemy.

They were driving along the road that topped the cliff now, and soon the castle and St. Petrox Church came into sight a little below them.

Leaving the carriage in the charge of the tiger, with instructions to him to walk the horses to a spot higher up, where the road widened enough to turn, Gerard helped his bride down the steep footpath and into the ancient church.

It was delightfully cool inside, and they walked slowly down the aisle, stepping on stone slabs on which were recorded the burials of worthy parishioners, and toward the altar with a magnificent arched stained-glass window behind.

Before reaching it, Leonora stepped into one of the pews to her right and sat in silence for several minutes, then dropped to her knees in prayer, and Gerard followed suit. After ten or more minutes she rose, and when they were in the aisle once more, he took her hand and led her to the altar, where they knelt again, still holding hands.

When Leonora rose this time, she looked peaceful and serene. He drew her into his arms and pressed a soft kiss on her lips; then they turned and walked slowly back the way they had come, pausing while Gerard dropped some coins in the offertory box, and then moving out into the bright sunlight.

Only then did Leonora realize they had been in such attunement that neither of them had spoken a single word from entering the church to leaving it.

After that, Dartmouth Castle seemed an anticlimax, but they dutifully climbed down into the dungeons and up onto the battlements to see the view across the water and the town in the distance.

The next day they went to Plymouth, where Sir Francis Drake had played on the bowling green until the Spanish Armada came close enough for him to attack and defeat, and from where he, as well as Hawkins and Raleigh, had

set sail to explore the New World. It was still an exciting,
bustling seaport, and Leonora enjoyed the harbor filled
with vessels of all shapes and sizes, the sounds of hammers
and the shouts of men as boats were repaired, and the
strong, not unpleasing smell of seaweed, tar, hemp, rum,
and a myriad other things all blended into one.

They went to Tavistock, seat of the Duke of Bedford,
and Newton Abbot, but were careful to avoid Dartmoor
Prison, which had been completed just two years before to
house French captives from the war with Napoleon.

The days passed swiftly as Leonora saw places she had
heard of but never seen before, and the nights passed even
more swiftly as Gerard made passionate love to her and she
learned how to please and even torment him.

"I've never known a week go so quickly," Leonora said
with a heavy sigh, for they would be back at Clairmont
House in an hour, their short honeymoon over, "but I
suppose all good things have to come to an end
sometime."

Gerard took his eyes off the road for a moment and was
surprised to see sadness in her face. "Now, come along,
Leonora, you know better than that," he scolded lightly.
"Nothing is coming to an end for us. We've had a
delightful week alone, and now we are returning to begin
our life together as husband and wife. I am sure that Adele
will gratefully relinquish some of her duties to you, so that
she may have more time to be with your father."

"But you will be out all day supervising the estates, and
I will see little of you," she said fretfully, then suddenly
laughed at herself as she realized how petty she had
sounded. "My goodness, have I become so spoiled in just a
week? I'm sorry, darling. You're quite right, of course, for
there will be much for both of us to do and it will be good
to see Papa and Adele again."

"Actually, you will need to come with me at first as I
inspect the lands and farms, for the tenants would be hurt
if they could not see their favorite 'little lady' turned
miraculously into an elegant young matron," he warned.
"And I will thoroughly enjoy showing you off. It's a little

difficult, for the local gentry cannot entertain you as they would like while you are in mourning, but I am sure they will invite you to have tea with them.''

Soon the Clairmonts' huge house came into view, sitting elegantly amid the well-tended lawns and gardens, its creamy stone gleaming in the late-afternoon sunshine.

"It's strange, but suddenly it feels so good to be home, when just a few moments ago I was complaining,'' Leonora admitted. ''You know, when I was little I used to love to count all the windows. There are thirty-seven in the front alone, and I would pretend there were people in all the rooms, glad to see me returning, and waving to me.'' She shrugged. ''Of course, I used to wave also, and sometimes Smathers would lower his dignity and wave to me from the door.''

As Gerard envisioned the formal butler waving to his little mistress, he felt sorry for all the childhood joys she had missed. ''What lonely children you must have been, left for servants to look after in this great house,'' he remarked, taking her hand and placing it upon his knee. ''Our children won't be lonely, I promise, for there'll always be one of us to welcome them home.''

As they drove up to the door, Adele hurried out to meet them, and for a moment Leonora was frightened, until she saw the wide smile on her stepmother's face.

"How nice to see you looking so well-rested, Adele,'' she said when Gerard had lifted her down from the curricle. ''Papa must be feeling better, I'm sure.''

"Oh, my dears, he really is,'' Adele assured them. ''It would seem that your marriage set his mind at rest and he's been sitting up in bed and soundly beating me at piquet almost every night since you left. He observed your carriage approaching long before I did, and is most anxious to see you.''

"Then we won't keep him waiting,'' Gerard told her. ''He'll not mind our dusty appearance, I'm sure.''

They hurried up the stairs, and before Gerard could knock on Lord Clairmont's door, the nurse opened it and they went in.

"Papa," a beaming Leonora said as she hurried to the bed and kissed his cheek, "it's good to see you looking so much better, but poor Adele—fancy you trouncing her at cards. We'll have to see if my husband is a more worthy opponent."

Gerard echoed her remarks and added, "We had a delightful week, but are both glad to be back here with you, sir."

The older man's smile was a little tired, for the excitement was taking its toll. "You can tell me all about it tonight," he said, "but I just wanted to have a look at you both before I take my nap. It's good to have you back."

As they left the chamber, promising to return later, they met Adele coming to attend to her husband. "This came for you shortly after you left," she said to Gerard, and gave him an official-looking letter. "I hope it's not urgent."

He thanked her and glanced at the seal, then slipped it into his pocket.

"Is it from the Prime Minister?" Leonora asked, curious as to what it might be. She grew pale. "Is it word about Geoffrey?"

Gerard shook his head but did not look happy. "No, it's not from Perceval, but unfortunately it might mean I have to go away for a few days, and I had hoped to have more time with you. Will you mind very much, my love?"

"Not if it's only for a few days, but couldn't I go with you?" she asked.

"I'm afraid not, my dear, but let's not speculate unnecessarily. I'll go directly to the study and join you in a half-hour. I'm sure you are anxious to take off that heavy carriage dress and rest before changing for dinner." He made sure no servants were around, then kissed her softly on the lips, turned her in the direction of her chamber, and gave her a love pat on her bottom. Then he ran lightly down the stairs to open and read his letter in the privacy of the study.

Although she had said she would understand, Leonora nonetheless felt hurt that Gerard still kept secrets from her.

He had said firmly that it was not from the Prime Minister. Who else would write to him in such secrecy? she wondered as she walked slowly toward her bedchamber.

On entering her room, where Millie waited to help her undress, she forgot about Gerard's letter for the time being. She really was tired, and once she stretched out upon the bed, she fell asleep immediately.

She dreamed she was sailing her sloop out of the cove, standing at the helm with Gerard, and the wind was blowing gently on her face. Then she heard a familiar silky voice murmur, "You look so happy, love, I really should allow you to sleep."

In an instant she was awake, her eyes opening wide to see Gerard sitting on the other side of her bed, grinning and waving one of her large bamboo fans to and fro in front of her face.

"Where were you, and whom were you with, you little wretch?" he teased. "There was such a happy, satisfied smile on your face that you had better have been dreaming of me or you'll be in deep trouble."

She laughed. "You should have said deep water, for I was sailing my sloop, and beside me was a tall, good-looking, black-haired—" She leapt off the bed as he lunged toward her, and she darted behind a screen, tipping it in his direction as he followed her, then raced for her dressing room, but his outstretched hand grasped her robe and they fell together onto the softly sprung chaise longue.

"Now, who was that you were describing?" he asked, holding a feather pillow threateningly above her.

"It was a woman, a black-haired woman, I promise," she cried between gurgles of laughter. "Kind sir, have pity on an innocent maiden—unless, of course, you mean to ravish her?"

"What a good idea," Gerard said, his silvery eyes sparkling with fun as he threw the pillow aside and pinned her hands above her head. "Now what are you going to do?"

"Confess, of course, and throw myself on your mercy," she cried, wriggling her body from side to side. She started to say something more, but his lips pressing firmly against her effectively stopped her.

His free hand found the sensitive parts of her body that he now knew so well, provoking even more squirming, until she could stand it no longer and they came together with a force that left them both completely exhausted and temporarily speechless.

For a while they lay side by side, Leonora's head on Gerard's shoulder and his arm around her; then she turned to look at his face and nudge his chin with the top of her head. "If that is ravishing, I think I like it," she said softly.

"Me too," he mumbled as he sought to remove her hair from his mouth. "You didn't get much sleep, though, did you?"

"That was much better than sleep," she whispered. "I feel wonderful now. But I have an awful feeling you're going to tell me you have to go away tonight."

"Not tonight, love." His voice was soft in her ear. "We have a few days before I need go, and then I'll not be gone long. A couple of days, or perhaps three, is all it will take."

Leonora sighed. She realized he was not about to say more, and she would just have to be patient until such time as he felt he could trust her, but for some reason she had an awful sense of foreboding.

11

"What's Ted doing, Millie, sending me a note one day that he needs my services, and the next day changing his plans?" Leonora asked irritably. "With Lord Sinclair away, tonight would have been the best possible time for me. Did Bob make a miraculous recovery?"

Without thinking, she screwed the slip of paper into a ball and threw it carelessly at the litter basket, not realizing that it hit the edge and bounced out.

" 'E said as 'ow they're not going out at all. Something about the Revenuers watching round 'ere tonight," Millie said with a frown.

"How could he know in advance, I wonder," Leonora said slowly, "unless he has one of them for an informer. If I was Ted I would worry that he might be a turncoat and snitch on us."

"I really shouldn't tell it, milady, but I know it's safe with you. My sister, Dottie, lives in Dartmouth and 'as been walking out with one o' them Revenuers. 'E's a nice-enough feller, she says, an' comes from Brighton way. She was the one 'as sent word," Millie explained.

Leonora smiled at her maid. "That's a relief to know, anyway. I was concerned because I heard somewhere that they're never assigned close to their home towns in case they have smuggler friends or relatives there."

"Dottie's a good girl, milady. She was sweet on one of the gentlemen 'ere before 'er mistress, old Mrs. Thompson, died an' she 'ad to go away to find work."

"Oh, yes," Leonora mused, "one of the 'gentlemen.' I'd almost forgotten that was what they were called."

After a last look to make sure that her mistress looked

her best, the maid gathered the soiled linens and left the chamber. Leonora glanced at her reflection with little interest. To her, one black dress was much like another, and having to change for dinner was pointless when she and Adele would be dining alone again. Perhaps by tomorrow Gerard would be home.

But when her husband had not returned by late the next morning, she grew impatient and decided to go for a ride, being careful to have the young groomsman Gerard had suggested accompany her.

As she raced along the cliffs, she smiled with satisfaction as she saw what was obviously a black Revenue cutter a little way out to sea, going in the direction of Dartmouth. They'd probably been out all night, searching the coastline, she thought, and sincerely hoped they were going back empty-handed. The normally fast vessel was moving slowly, and she could see crewmen looking at the water, some with telescopes to their eyes, probably trying to spot the bobbing corks that marked where kegs of wine and brandy had been dropped overboard for later collection.

For once she did not stay out long, for she wanted to be there when Gerard returned, but as she dismounted and left her horse with the groomsman, she saw that Gerard's matched chestnuts were being rubbed down.

It took all of her newly learned restraint to proceed at a normal pace to the house, allow the footman to open doors for her instead of racing through them as she would have a few months ago, and walk, not run, up the stairs and into her chamber.

Had she entered that room ten minutes earlier, she would have found an anxious husband looking for her, for on his return Gerard had quickly thrown down his whip and gloves and hastened to her chamber.

When he reached the center of the room, he had paused, looking to see if her maid was in the dressing room and might know where he could find his wife. But his eye lit on something white sticking out from under the dressing table and he stooped to pick it up. Finding it to be a discarded piece of paper, he automatically smoothed it out with his fingers and glanced at it to see if it might be of importance. Three words were printed on the small scrap of paper: "Can't meet tonight." Beneath them was the single letter T.

Turning quickly, he went through the sitting room that separated their chambers, and entered his own room, closing and locking the door behind him. He wanted to confront Leonora, ask her whom she was having an assignation with, and shake her until the bones rattled in her body.

He recalled how familiarly she had behaved toward the village men when she had raced her sloop against one of them, but could scarcely believe that a lady of rank would associate with one of their sort.

He sat for a moment with his head in his hands, trying to decide how to handle the matter. He heard the knob rattle as his wife tried to open the door, and her voice calling his name, but he ignored it. He was not ready to see her just yet.

Slowly he changed from his traveling clothes, declining the help of his valet, who had been told of his return, for he needed to be alone to think. By the time he was ready for luncheon, his cravat tied to perfection in the waterfall and his hair carefully brushed into the Brutus style, he had decided how to handle Leonora.

He would behave exactly as before, enjoy her body at night and her company during the day, but nothing would be the same for him, of course, for his heart would not be in it. And he would watch her carefully, checking where she went, whom she spoke with and, particularly, any messages she received.

He had passed her door and started down the stairs when he heard her come out of her chamber.

"Gerard, where have you been, darling?" she called, hurrying to catch up with him, then slowed a little as she noticed a maid dusting a nearby table.

"It's good to have you home," she said as she slipped an arm through his, then whispered softly, "I missed you so very much and couldn't wait until you got back."

"Did you really, Leonora?"

He tried to sound normal, but she noticed something in his voice, and though he smiled, it did not reach his eyes. For a moment she looked bewildered.

"Of course I did. Every single minute of each day," she told him, and he marveled at how sincere she could make her lies sound.

They went in to luncheon, where Adele was waiting, and when the teasing and joking that usually went on among the three of them did not seem any different, Leonora wondered if she had been mistaken. Perhaps Gerard had just been tired after his journey and she had misread weariness for coldness.

Over the next few days, however, though they did exactly the same things as before, and he came to her bed each evening, Leonora knew something had to have happened while he was away.

Could he have met someone, another woman more experienced than she was, willing to fill his lonely nights? It was possible, she knew, for she had heard that some married men openly kept mistresses in London.

Whilst away, Gerard had been given some rather disconcerting information. the lieutenant commander of the Preventive Water-Guard—the official name for the Revenue Service—stationed at Dartmouth, had informed him that on more than one occasion a fishing lugger they believed to be on a smuggling run had escaped into the cove beneath Clairmont House.

"It's actually been going on for years, my lord," the lieutenant said. "And we've set up watches on the house, but no one from there has been seen anywhere near a fishing lugger."

"This, of course, is not actually of concern to me unless you have reason to believe they are bringing in spies. Have you spoken to Lord Clairmont about it?" Gerard asked.

The officer shook his head. "We've no evidence that spies have ever been brought in by this ring, or anything else for that matter. But when a lugger runs when it sights a cutter, we become suspicious. As for Lord Clairmont, we've been to the house, but it seemed he was hardly ever there, and we've asked for him a couple of times this last six months, but were told he's gravely ill. We would not, of course, trouble Lady Clairmont under such circumstances."

"I would think not," Gerard said sternly. "She has enough to do nursing her husband without involving herself in such matters. Why does the Revenue cutter lose its quarry? With its running bowsprit, surely it's much faster than a fishing lugger?"

"Because we'd rather lose the smugglers than the cutter, for they're costly to build and carry expensive equipment. Ours is one of the finest, built by Gely of Cowes some years ago, and cost two thousand, five hundred pounds. If I lost it, it would be the end of my career," the lieutenant explained. "There're rocks under those waters that have caused many a vessel to founder. Only someone who knows the channels could get into that cove by day, and at night they would have to know them like the back of their hand to negotiate them."

"What does your quarry do? Surely you could sit outside and wait it out, for they've got to come out sometime," Gerard suggested.

"There are too many other smugglers around, much bigger rings than we believe this one to be, for us to sit waiting for long. At one time it was thought that Lord Clairmont's son might be behind this ring, for we had a tip from one of their neighbors."

"Don't tell me," Gerard said, "let me guess. Lord Burlington?"

"That's right, sir. How did you know, for we keep the names of informers under tight security."

"It's just the kind of thing he would dream up to try to make mischief," Gerard said in disgust. "But as the young man was killed in action in Spain, he could hardly be operating a smuggling ring, could he?"

"I was sorry to hear that, my lord, but, in any case, we found no evidence to link him to the ring," the lieutenant

said, shaking his head. "You know, we've even chased the
lugger into the cove and then come back at dawn to wait
for it to come out, but found no sign of it there."

"You saw the small sloop, tied up at the jetty, though,
didn't you?"

"Yes, my lord, we did, and we see her many a time
during daylight hours, with the young lady of the house at
the helm. As a matter of fact, that's what I was wondering
about." The officer paused, knowing he might be asking
the impossible. "Do you think she might be persuaded to
show our helmsman how to get in and out of the cove
safely?"

Gerard frowned. "Definitely not," he said curtly.
"That young lady happens to be my wife, and I would not
think of allowing her on a Revenue Cutter. However,
I have another thought. In the next few months I will
have her show me, and after that I will teach your
man."

"Splendid, sir." The young officer looked vastly
relieved. "And I do apologize for mentioning the other
idea, for I did not know she was now Lady Sinclair."

Gerard had thought about this conversation several
times since his return home, but since finding what he
thought to be proof of her unfaithfulness, he had not felt
inclined to ask any favors of Leonora.

She, on the other hand, was trying everything she could
think of to tease or cajole him into a better humor. The
more she tried, however, the gloomier he became, for he
was sure it was an attempt to prevent him becoming
suspicious.

"I don't know what happened when you went away,
Gerard, and I know you can't tell me. All I know is that
something very bad has brought your spirits low," she
finally said, having decided to stop pretending she didn't
notice. "You enjoyed the day we sailed out to the island
and shared a picnic. Do you think you might enjoy doing it
again tomorrow?"

Part of the old Gerard seemed to come back as he smiled
broadly, then told her, "I was going to suggest something
of the sort, as a matter of fact. And while you're about it,

you can show me how to get in and out of the cove, tell me what you use for markers, and how you time it.''

Perhaps it was something in his eyes, or an inflection in his voice, but Leonora suddenly had an awful suspicion.

"Why do you want to learn?" she asked quietly. "I know you sail, but you've never shown any inclination to take her out alone. In any case, the waters are treacherous and it would be quite a while before you were competent."

Gerard shrugged. "You may as well know the reason, and I'm sure you'll be just as surprised as I was. Apparently a group of smugglers frequently use the cove to shelter from the Revenue cutter. I don't know how they learned the way in, but perhaps your brother took one of them fishing a few times and showed him."

Inwardly horrified, Leonora carefully controlled her expression so as not to give anything away.

"Anyway, the commander at Dartmouth approached me and asked that we teach them how to get in and out of the cove, and take the advantage away from the particular gang that is using it." He looked at her set face and remembered how reluctant local people were to aid the law. "Smugglers are not the romantic figures young girls dream about, you know. They're hardened criminals, and some of the gangs have been known to capture and viciously kill and maim Revenue officers."

Leonora had heard of some large gangs who operated from vessels every bit as large and well-equipped as the Revenue cutters. They even turned on, attacked, and sank cutters and preventive boats instead of running from them.

They were armed with the same cannon as the Revenue cutters, and on land they openly unloaded their duty-free goods and marched with them through small towns, some fifty strong, while the townsfolk turned away from their windows so that they did not see them.

To compare Ted and his fisherman friends, who smuggled to make up the living they lost in having to fish close to shore, with vicious men like these was ludicrous indeed!

Then there was something else that no one wanted to think about, but she had to say it.

"If people like you, my father, the Prince Regent, and probably the Prime Minister and his Cabinet also, refused to buy French brandies, wine, and tobacco, and to dress your wives in French silks and laces, there would be no problem, for there would be no market for the smuggled goods," Leonora said scornfully. "Is your secret work for the Prime Minister the chasing and capture of these men?" she asked, silently adding the words "and women."

Gerard did not at all like her attitude, but he needed her help if he was to keep his promise to the Revenue officer. He forced a smile. "No, it is not, and I cannot disagree with the point you have made. When would you like to take the sloop out? Perhaps we could take a picnic lunch tomorrow, as you suggested?"

Leonora rose. "I don't want to fight you, Gerard, but I will not teach you or anyone else how to get in and out of Clairmont Cove."

He crossed the room and grasped her shoulders, his fingers hard, forcing her to look at him. "I can be every bit as obstinate as you, my dear. I will not permit you to go sailing unless you cooperate."

He expected anger and tantrums, but instead there was a look of unbelievable sadness on her face as she said, "Then I will not sail my sloop, that's all." She looked pointedly at his hands, and when he removed them she walked slowly from the room.

12

With the improvement in her husband's condition, Lady Clairmont spent more, rather than less time with him, for he became quickly bored with lying abed and needed entertainment rather than nursing at this stage.

She had left the newlyweds to their own devices, taking her meals with her husband in his chamber, so it was some time before she realized that all was not well between them. She knew that, with their short honeymoon and Gerard's need to be away soon afterward, and again a week later, there was much work to oversee around the estates, so she was not at all surprised to learn that he rode off early most days and did not return until nightfall.

She was surprised, however, when she found that Leonora never accompanied him. When Adele finally emerged from her husband's bedchamber for a more-civilized meal in the dining room, she was shocked to find that they were barely polite to each other.

Lady Davenport had, it seemed, taken to dining in her chamber also, to let them have time to themselves, so no hint had come from that direction.

When the two ladies were having their tea afterward, Adele asked Leonora about it. "For an arranged marriage, my dear, I felt at first that I'd never seen two people so obviously in love. Please tell me how long this estrangement has been going on, and what has caused it, for I want to help if I can."

"I don't want to talk about it," Leonora muttered.

Adele took her tea and sat on the couch next to her stepdaughter, placing her arm around her shoulders and observing as she did that she seemed to have lost weight.

"You must, my dear, for you'll be ill if this goes on much longer. I noticed that at supper you ate barely enough to keep a bird alive, as Aunt Charlotte would say."

Leonora bit her lip to hold back the tears that threatened, and she swallowed hard before saying very quietly, "I think he's installed a mistress somewhere and sees her when he goes on these so-called missions for the Prime Minister."

"Have you a sound reason for thinking so?" Adele asked.

"No, I haven't, but ever since he came back from that short trip just after we were married, he's been completely different."

"Does he come to your chamber at night?" Adele hated to ask the question, but knew it was of the utmost importance.

"He did after he went away the first time, but it wasn't the same . . . he seemed to be pretending. He stopped altogether, however, after I refused to do something he asked of me, and now he rarely even speaks to me." She looked unhappily at her stepmama.

"What do you do with yourself all day while I'm with your father?" Adele asked. "I had thought you frequently accompanied Gerard around the estates. Do you go sailing a lot like you used to?"

"No, he's forbidden me to take out my sloop, so I ride with a groom occasionally and I've been painting a great deal." Her smile was a little like her old self as she added, "And I'd better tell you what I refused to do, for I know you'll find out eventually."

She explained what Gerard had asked of her, then added, "I know who the smugglers are, Adele. They're men I've known all my life. I know their wives and their children, and I can't betray them, I can't cause them to be captured and hanged. Gerard's not from these parts so he doesn't understand, nor will you, I suppose."

"But of course I understand, my dear, and Gerard's not seeing straight if he can't see your point of view. With your permission I would like to talk to him, for I cannot sit back and watch you become more and more unhappy. And if your father should realize what has happened, it could cause him to have a relapse. Will you let me try?''

"If you wish, Adele," Leonora agreed. "You can't make matters much worse, and it might possibly help a little.''

"Good. Now, there's no time like the present, so why don't you go off to bed," Adele suggested, "and I'll find out where that husband of yours is hiding himself and see what I can do.''

Leonora left at once, though she did not for a moment think that her stepmama would have success. In fact, Gerard might be furious with her for discussing their relationship with someone else. Adele had not seen this side of Gerard, and Leonora herself had found it hard to believe that the man who had made love to her with such joyous abandon could now become so distant and cold.

It had become her habit to retire around this hour, so Millie was waiting for her and helped her into bed, placed the novel she was reading by the bedside, then left.

Leonora had read almost two chapters and was getting a little sleepy when she heard the sound of the handle being turned and smelled the familiar scent of Gerard's shaving soap. Suddenly she was frightened and did not want to turn around, but knew she must.

He was wearing his blue satin robe. He looked serious, but not angry, as he pulled a chair close to the bed and sat down.

"Why didn't you tell me that you knew who the smugglers were?" he asked quietly.

"Because I thought you would try to make me give you their names." Her voice was almost a whisper. "They're not what you said they are—murderers and traitors.''

He shook his head and his face had softened. "You silly girl. If you had told me, I would have understood. Do you realize that we've both been miserable for the last few weeks for no reason at all?''

"Not for no reason at all," Leonora said. "If everything

had been all right between us I would have been able to
explain to you. But it wasn't, was it?''

He frowned, looking puzzled. ''What on earth made
you think that I had taken a mistress? I can assure you,
Leonora, that I have not made love to anyone but you
since we first met in Bath. Do you believe me, and can you
say the same?''

She looked up into his face and could not deny the
honesty she saw there. ''I believe you, for I don't think
you've ever lied to me. Of course you're the only person
who has ever touched me, Gerard. You should know
that.'' She paused before asking, ''Why did you seem so
different when you returned from that first trip?''

''It must have been your imagination, my dear, for I was
not aware that I treated you in any way differently from
before.''

Leonora knew without a doubt that he had done so, but
realized he might not have been aware of it. It was a small
point, and she felt this was not the time to press it. She
knew also that the next move was up to her, so she pulled
back the bedclothes in an invitation he willingly accepted.

''Oh, my love, I've missed you so very much,'' he
whispered, and though Leonora recognized the very same
words she had said to him when he returned from the
three-day absence, she said nothing, for it was enough just
to be together once more.

It seemed he could not get enough of her. His hands
were everywhere at once, stroking her back, her hair, and
that tender spot at the base of her throat where his caresses
always drove her out of her mind.

A shower of kisses followed his hands, and only when
she could stand no more and ached with desire did he give
her fulfillment, loving her with a newer, wilder abandon
than ever before.

Just before dawn she awoke to feel his arms pull her
close as he dried her face with part of the sheet. She must
have been crying in her sleep, as she had been doing
frequently since he had stopped coming to her bed.

His hands stroked her tenderly while he murmured

soothingly in her ear until she fell asleep once more and did not awaken until much later than her usual hour.

Millie, wondering why her mistress had not rung for her hot chocolate, knocked lightly on the door, then peeped inside, and when she saw the entwined forms, both still fast asleep, she smiled with relief and closed the door quietly behind her.

Now she could tell Ted that he need not worry any more about his little Leo. When word had come that her brother had been killed, Ted had sort of taken over for Geoffrey, keeping a careful eye on little Leo, as he called her.

And after her marriage, Ted had tried not to call upon her except in real emergency, which was what Leonora had wanted at first. Then, when she had said, some weeks ago, that it didn't matter anymore and she'd be happy to go as often as he wanted her to, he had put two and two together and realized she and her new husband were having serious problems. He wasn't treating her right.

"I'd like to wring 'is bloody neck," he had confided to Millie. " 'E mustn't be warming 'er bed at night, or she'd not be able to get away so easy-like."

The night of the bad storm, Millie had waited in the passage, scared silly for their safety. The second helmsman was making hard work of it, and was seasick into the bargain, according to what Ted had told her later.

That's when little Leo took over. She really needn't have gone out, for they'd nothing to fear from the Revenue men that night. The Revenuers wouldn't put out in such high seas, so normally she wouldn't have been needed.

It wasn't until they were back at the jetty, he had said, that little Leo admitted she'd been terrified, not for herself, but for the crew. It had bothered Ted something awful that she'd not cared about herself, for it showed how very unhappy she really was.

That night he swore to Millie that he'd get even, on little Leo's behalf, with the high-and-mighty Lord Sinclair if he ever got the chance. Millie just hoped that the chance never came, for she didn't want Ted to get hurt, and she'd seen his lordship's muscles.

13

Gerard was away once more. This time Leonora missed him but was not unhappy, for everything was right between them again.

The only thing that would make her happier than she was at the moment would be confirmation that she was increasing. She had a strong suspicion that this time it was not a false alarm, as had happened before. She also knew that once she was sure, she would somehow have to train one of the men to get in and out of the cove, for she could not risk losing her baby.

Leonora's portrait of Gerard, which she had secretly been working on since they had reconciled, was almost completed. She felt very pleased with it, for she had drawn the cleft in his chin perfectly and depicted the exact shape of his beautiful mouth. Considering he had not sat for it even once and, in fact, had no idea that she was painting it at all, she knew it to be an excellent likeness, one that he would be proud to hang anywhere.

She had received word this morning from Ted that Bob was out of sorts again, and she would be needed tonight, but with Gerard away she had no cause for concern. As this would probably be the last time she would go out with them, she felt even more excited than usual.

When she went down to dinner, Adele remarked upon the fact that she looked better than she had for some time. "You have an attractive flush to your cheeks, my dear, and a sparkle in your eyes that is most becoming."

"Perhaps it's because I'm so happy, Adele, and that is thanks to you, of course. I shall be forever in your debt for interfering at the right moment," she said.

"Just stay happy now, and learn to talk out any differences as they arise," Adele advised, "for mole hills do eventually become mountains if they're allowed to grow. And speaking of growing, is there any chance that you might make your papa a grandpapa? He continues to do well and I do know that it would make him so happy. You have a certain look about you that I've noticed before when my sisters were in that condition."

Leonora's cheeks reddened. "I'm hoping it's not a false alarm, but it's a little too early to be sure. Please don't say anything, Adele, but I do so hope you are right."

"I'll say nothing at all until you choose to make your announcement, but then I shall expect you to behave sensibly and curtail the kind of activities you enjoy so much, such as sailing and horseback riding, which are far too dangerous when one is enceinte," Adele said with a twinkle. "However, I imagine Gerard will take you in hand and make sure you behave."

Leonora grinned sheepishly. "He does have a way of making his point with emphasis, I'm afraid. I remember so well the last day I went riding beyond the estates without a groom. You had told me times without number, but he had to say so only once and I never dared do it again."

What a good thing it is that both Adele and Gerard are unaware of my one activity that has the strongest element of danger, she thought, then realized her stepmama was speaking.

"He does listen to reason, though," Adele remarked. "I had no difficulty whatsoever when I attempted to resolve your misunderstanding, for he sat and quietly listened to everything I had to say, and he wanted that reconcilation every bit as much as you did."

Leonora had a sudden idea. "When you're finished with dinner, could you spare a moment to come and see the painting I've just completed, Adele? I'd like your opinion on it."

"I'm finished now, and we can have tea brought up to your chamber if you'd like," her stepmama said eagerly. "What is the subject?"

"I won't tell you," Leonora said mischievously. "Wait and see." They gave the necessary instructions to Smathers, then made their way up the stairs and into the young couple's sitting room.

"Now, close your eyes and don't open them until I have it in place. I want to get your very first impression," Leonora said earnestly.

Adele had no idea what to expect. She knew how talented her stepdaughter was, but when she opened her eyes it was as though Gerard was looking directly at her from the painting.

She caught her breath. "It's magnificent, my dear. The best thing you've ever done. Where are you going to put it?"

"I'd like to hang it in here, over the fireplace, and take away that old thing that's there now. It's the same size, though, so I could put it in the same frame for the time being. The hook is in just the right place," Leonora said thoughtfully. "But I will cover it and have Gerard do the unveiling. I do so hope he likes it."

"There's no question but that he will, and I'm sure he'll want to have it framed properly, but he can attend to that later. Let me help you put it there now in case he comes home tomorrow earlier than you expected. Ring for Millie, and she can bring a duster and a stool to stand on," Adele said, enjoying the project enormously.

An hour later when the painting was in place, Millie produced a piece of cloth and a cord and positioned them so that a small tug would uncover the portrait.

Leonora could hardly wait for Gerard's comments, but she had not forgotten that she had a mission tonight, so she let Millie help her into bed for a few hours' sleep before setting out for the jetty.

"Boat on the horizon," came the call, and Leonora was alert and making for the helm before confirmation came that it looked like a Revenue cutter, probably the one out of Darmouth.

No matter how often she did it, Leonora found the race

to reach the cove ahead of the cutter was tremendously exciting, but tonight it seemed more so, for it was likely tō be her last time. She was making good speed with the wind just right, but a glance back told her that it was just right for the cutter also, for it was gaining on them fast.

Now she was at the entrance to the cove with only minutes to spare and had begun the swing through the deep but narrow channel, when shots rang out.

At first she thought it was the cutter firing its cannons just out of range, but then she realized there were the faint outlines of men on her own strip of beach near her sloop. She would have to pass close by, and they must have rifles, for she could actually see the flashes as they fired. Just a little closer and an expert marksman could easily pick her off, she realized with a gasp of almost despair.

It couldn't happen, mustn't happen now, not on her very last run, she prayed. Then Ted was beside her, protecting her with his own body from any bullets that came her way. "If there's any chance you can come about, Leo, we're in luck," he said urgently. "The cutter got a little bit too clever and is stuck on the rocks."

She blinked back tears of relief as she nodded. He called to his men, "Coming about," as she put the lugger hard over.

"They'll not be expecting us back," he said with satisfaction as he felt the boat swing around, and moved to remain between her and the sharpshooters.

Later, Leonora could not have told anyone how she felt at that moment. It was as if her prayer had been answered, for had they been only a little further along, the channel would have been too narrow to bring the boat about and they'd have headed straight into the gunfire.

She had never sailed the lugger out of the cove before, but the darkness worked to their advantage. She kept looking back at the lights as she steered, and she breathed a sigh of relief as they passed the Revenue boat.

Had the commander of the cutter suspected they were coming back out, he could have brought the swivel guns at its stem and stern into action faster. But he and the crew were busy trying to get the two rowing boats launched, and by the time he realized the lugger was approaching fast, it had turned once more toward the open sea and the shots fired were out of range.

The lugger rounded the next headland and they let the sheets run free as they dropped the roped-together casks of brandy overboard some distance from shore, with small corks as markers. As they hauled in the sheets and got under way again, making straight for the village jetty, Leonora felt the tension slowly draining from her body.

It was fortunate that tonight they had no silks, laces, or the precious Brittany salt the fish packers in the next village needed so badly. They were able to drop anchor and leave the boat with no evidence that it had ever been out.

With a letdown feeling after all the excitement of the chase, Leonora left her oilskins in the boat with the others and started the long walk up the main street and onto the cliff road. Ted, as usual, had insisted on accompanying her, and their feet made no sound as they deliberately walked on the grass at the roadside.

They were both exhausted after their efforts, and maintained a comfortable silence that was broken suddenly by the sound of horses' hooves. They saw the outlines of about a dozen men on horseback, coming directly toward them.

Thinking quickly, Ted pushed Leonora into the dark of the bushes and bracken, then ran out into the open to draw the men after him in the other diection. Leonora was sure that Ted could easily evade them, for he knew every inch of the countryside, so she set off at a trot along a path that led to the hidden passage.

"Halt or I'll fire!"

Something about the voice sounded familiar, and for a moment Leonora paused in panic; then she took to her heels and raced for the thick, prickly shrubs she knew her pursuer's horse could not get through.

She heard the sound of the first bullet as it whistled close to her ear; then, just as she reached for the ring to open the hatch, she felt an agonizing pain in her left side and she fell to the ground. The door was open, for she had pulled it with her as she fell, but she did not have the strength to get herself inside.

Gerard believed he was chasing a young boy, and when the lad went into the bushes, he swiftly dismounted and followed on foot. As he roughly pushed the bushes aside, he saw the open door and the passage beyond, but a crouching figure blocked the entrance.

He grabbed the lad's arm to pull him to his feet; then, clearly visible in the light of a lantern that had been left in readiness, he recognized the frightened blue eyes and deathly white face of his wife.

The sound of the Revenue men returning compelled him to act swiftly. Pushing Leonora inside the passage with a muttered, "I'll be back. Don't you dare move from there," he returned to his waiting horse, mounted, and rode to meet them.

"Did you catch the varmint?" he asked, knowing full well they probably had not. "I thought I saw a second man, but I must have been mistaken."

The sergeant in charge grunted. "There was only one, and you'd think we could 'ave caught 'im, but 'e knew where 'e was going and we didn't."

"I'm not far from my home, so I'll spend the night there. It has been an eventful but disappointing evening and I'll be interested to see the reports that are filed." With that Gerard turned his horse and rode off in the opposite direction from the men, doubling back when they were out of earshot and heading once more for the hidden passage where he had left Leonora.

Now that he knew where it was, it was easy enough to find again even in the darkness. He tied the horse to a tree, walked over to the bush that hid the door, and stepped inside.

Leonora seemed to have fallen asleep where he had left her, and he grabbed her arm, shaking it and saying, "Get up, you little fool. I'm taking you home, and when we get there, you'll have a lot of explaining to do."

But Leonora made no effort to get up; in fact, the arm

he grabbed dropped lifelessly to the floor when he released it, and her eyes remained closed. Then he saw, to his horror, that her other hand was pressed to her side and there was a considerable amount of blood on the floor.

Her eyelids flickered as though she was trying to lift them, and he bent down and spoke in her ear. "Nod if you can hear me, love," he ordered softly, and it was with relief he saw her head move slowly but definitely.

"Now, does the passage to the right lead to the house?" he asked, and her head went from side to side.

He tried again. "Does the passage to the left lead to the house?" he asked, and was grateful when she nodded slowly.

"Good," he said. "I'll go send my horse back home, then return right away to take you inside. Do you understand?"

When the slow nod came again, he went to where he had left the horse, untied it and pointed it in the direction of the house, then gave it a hard slap on the rump. It trotted off into the darkness as he returned to the passage, arranging the bush and closing the door behind him.

He picked up Leonora and the lantern, and was surprised at how little she weighed, but knew he'd be glad of it by the time he got to the end of the passage, for they were quite obviously a considerable distance from the house.

Walking slowly in order to keep from jolting Leonora, he finally reached the end, and was surprised but glad enough to see Millie waiting there with a lighted candle.

She looked shocked when she saw them. Without a word, she took the lantern from him, put out the light, and placed it on a shelf in the passage. Then, when he had passed through into the wine cellar, she closed the door and slid the cask back into place.

"Go ahead of me and put a large kettle of water to heat," he ordered. "Then get cloths and laudanum and take them to your mistress's bedchamber. I don't want anyone in this house to know she's injured. Is that clear?"

The maid nodded and went to poke up the kitchen fire that had been banked for the night, setting a kettle of water on it. Then she scurried ahead of him, lighting the way with her candle until she reached the chamber. She ran in and pulled back the covers from Leonora's bed, then lit every candle she could find.

As he placed Leonora on the bed, Millie tried to start undressing her, but Gerard stopped her. "Go get the water and the things I asked you for. I'll take care of her clothes."

He would not admit, even to himself, how worried he was that the bullet he had fired might have penetrated deeply, and he was anxious to check the wound as quickly as possible.

As the motion ceased, Leonora opened her eyes. "What happened?" she asked, but when he swung around, her eyes were slowly closing once more and they remained so while he took a knife and cut her clothes away from her wounded side.

To his relief, he saw that the bullet did not appear to have entered her body but had ripped through the flesh between two ribs for several inches, scraping the bones but leaving no lasting damage.

While he waited for Millie to return with the supplies he had asked for, he got the rest of Leonora's clothes off, cutting them away and throwing them in a heap on the floor.

He examined her very carefully to be sure there was no further injury, then turned her on her side again, tying her hands loosely together with a kerchief so that she could not move her left arm and hamper his work. He then tucked a blanket around her, for she felt icy cold to his touch.

As he worked, he felt sick at heart, for she had given him her word that no one but him had ever touched her, and he had believed her. He had only a brief recall of the man who had been with her, but there was no doubt that her lover was a fisherman, who would not, of course, have ever been accepted by her father.

He wondered how long the affair had been going on, and cursed softly to himself as he thought of what they probably did in that dark, secret passage.

Millie returned then, and without asking, she poked the dying fire into a blaze and added wood, while Gerard lifted Leonora and held her gently, making her sip a mixture of laudanum and hot water.

"If you don't need me, milord," Millie whispered, "I'd best get back to the kitchen and tidy it up before anyone gets up. I'll come back as soon as I'm done."

"No, I'll finish up here and watch her for the rest of the night. You'd best get some sleep, for you'll be needed tomorrow," he told her.

She nodded and left, and the thought crossed his mind that she had a remarkable head on her shoulders for a maidservant.

He bathed and disinfected the wound, and as he stitched it, Leonora moaned softly, but she quieted as he padded it and bound it tightly to stop the bleeding.

When he had done all he could, he unfastened her hands and covered her with woolen blankets, tucking them in firmly in case she should become restless. Then he bent and touched her lips with his own before stretching out on the chaise longue and falling asleep.

He was a light sleeper, and twice he heard Leonora call out, but the words were indistinct except for the name Ted, which she said several times. Easing her up, he gave her a little more laudanum, and checked to be sure there was no sign of a fever before tucking her in once more.

After the second time, Gerard changed into a dressing robe before returning to the chaise longue, and despite his weariness, it was some time before he fell asleep again. He kept trying to recall what the man had looked like who ran off into the dark, but all he could remember was a tall figure and a broad-sounding voice calling the riders so that they would follow him and not see his lady friend.

14

Leonora awoke with a gasp. She had the most agonizing pain in her side when she tried to move her left arm, and she was finding it hard to breathe. Then she felt with her right hand and found that cloths were wrapped around her middle in Egyptian-mummy fashion.

She opened her eyes and first saw Gerard's dressing robe on the chaise longue, and her gladness that he was back was somehow overshadowed by something she could not quite remember.

When the dressing robe moved and Gerard rose and came toward her, she tried to hold her arms out to him, but the pain was too much and she fell back against the pillow with a little cry.

"It's so good to have you back," she tried to say, but he must not have heard her, for he said nothing, but bent and looked at her side.

"Good, it's not seeping through," he said. "I think I'd better give you a little more laudanum and let you sleep most of the day. I'll tell Adele you're just a little under the weather."

She did not understand what he was talking about, but she was thirsty and gulped down the water he gave her, then the diluted laudanum, but before it took hold she looked pleadingly at him, touched her mouth, and whispered, "Kiss me again."

As he pressed his lips to hers and felt her response, he was confused, but then there was a knock on the door and Millie entered.

"How is she, milord?" she asked, after dropping a curtsy to him.

"Better than she deserves, I've no doubt," he said grimly, "for there's no fever as yet, and she recognized me, I'm sure, when she woke just now.

"It's best that she sleep as much as possible today, I think, and you'd better stay with her. I'll get dressed and make my presence known. If Lady Clairmont comes in, try to keep her away from the bed. I'll hint to her that Lady Sinclair has a heavy cold, and she'll be careful then not to catch it."

Millie had taken a nightgown from a drawer. "Would you want to 'old 'er up while I put this on, sir?" she suggested.

He nodded. "Of course," he said, and eased Leonora up from her pillow. "You seem to have your wits about you, Millie, and a fondness for your mistress."

"That I 'ave, sir," she said, and added, "I've known 'er since we were little girls."

"Well, I'll have some questions to put to you later in the day, and I'll want some truthful answers, so you can be thinking about it and what will happen to you if you don't tell me what I want to know."

He saw the fear in her eyes, but turned his back and went through to his own chamber.

In the absence of his valet, who was still at the inn where they had planned to spend the night, Gerard took more time to dress than usual. He wanted to look as well as possible to allay any suspicions the family or servants might have.

When he entered the dining room, Lady Davenport looked up in surprise, but Adele just smiled. "Good morning, Gerard," she said. "I heard that you had returned very early, and thought you might have spent today resting from your journey."

"I am a little tired," he admitted, glad of the excuse, "and I'll not be doing too much today, for Leonora seems to be a little under the weather."

Adele looked surprised, for her stepdaughter had seemed particularly well yesterday evening.

"It's nothing much, I'm sure. Probably a chill she's taken or a cold she's picked up. I wouldn't go too close to her if I were you, in case you should catch it, and she'll probably sleep most of the day anyway."

"Is Millie with her?" Adele asked, and when he nodded she said, "Then she's in good hands, for that girl is a jewel and worships her. I'll look in on her a little later in the day."

"Let the gal be," Lady Davenport said loudly. "She's got a husband to look after her now, and you've enough to take care of with your own husband. She'll be up and about again in a couple of days, I'll warrant."

When Adele left the breakfast room, Gerard rose and followed her, making his excuses to Lady Davenport.

"Could I see you for a moment in the study?" he asked her. "There is a matter of some importance I would like to speak with you about."

She looked startled but followed him and allowed him to seat her before asking, "Leonora's indisposition is not worse than you indicated, is it?"

Gerard shook his head. "No, of course not, but I have some news that I wish to impart to you alone, and I trust you will not betray my confidence in you."

"You know I can be trusted, Gerard, but I dislike keeping anything from my husband, as I am sure you will understand," she warned.

"I think you will agree to keep this from him for the time being," Gerard said. "You see, while I was away I received a communication from the Prime Minister. He had agreed to look further into the matter of Geoffrey's death and have a search made for the body."

"I'm not sure I understand," Adele whispered.

Gerard stopped pacing in front of her and faced her. "At Lord Clairmont's request, I asked Perceval to do what he could to have someone locate Geoffrey's body and send it back here. He gave the necessary orders, but it seems that no one can find any proof that he was actually killed."

"But the man who came here said that a fellow officer had seen him struck down," she protested.

Gerard nodded. "I know, and it has been a more difficult task because it was such a horrendous battle and so many men were lost. However, he is the only officer unaccounted for and, at Perceval's request, they are now listing him as missing instead of killed in action."

"Then he feels there is some hope that Geoffrey is still alive?"

"I believe so. There is a possibility, of course, that he deserted, but I hope for his father's sake that is not the case," he said. "And there is a chance that he was killed and his body stripped, so after some time it would be impossible to identify him."

"I agree that no one else should be told of this for now," Adele said sadly. "The alternatives you offer would surely make his father suffer a relapse."

"There is one other possibility," Gerard said, "and that is that he could have sustained an injury, for the officer did say he was struck down, and perhaps he either wandered or was taken away suffering from a loss of memory."

Adele rose. "I'm glad you told me, for I will be prepared should we hear anything further. I am in complete agreement that, until more is known, his immediate family should be left in ignorance," she told him. "Tell Leonora that I will come and see her this afternoon."

"I'll look forward to seeing you then," Gerard said with a small bow, and held the door open for her.

As Gerard had predicted, Leonora slept most of the day, and he stayed around the house and stables, looking in on her occasionally, then retired to his chamber in the afternoon, giving the quite truthful excuse that he needed to catch up on the sleep he had missed the night before.

What he really wanted was to be there when Leonora finally awoke, and to talk with her before she was able to find out from Millie what had happened.

He opened the doors between the rooms and sent the maid off with instructions to go to bed and not get up until evening; then he stretched out upon his own bed and fell asleep.

When a crash sounded, he awoke instantly, and he was in Leonora's room in a flash, expecting to find her on the floor, but all she had done was knock over a chair.

She stood, leaning heavily against the dressing table, and her cheeks reddened with embarrassment as she said weakly, "I need to use the chamber pot."

He sighed with relief, then went over and took out the receptable. "I thought you'd fallen and opened up that wound. Come along, don't poker up. Just close your eyes and pretend that I'm Millie, for you cannot contrive without my assistance."

By the time she slipped back into bed, Leonora felt as though her whole body was one big blush of embarrassment, but Gerard seemed not at all concerned as he tucked a second pillow behind her so that she could sit up for a while.

"Would you like a drink of water?" he asked solicitously.

"Yes, please, but don't put any more laudanum in it, for I need to think clearly," she told him.

"You certainly do, young lady," he said, trying to sound stern but reluctant to add to her suffering. "And I want some answers before you are well enough to foist me off with a Banbury story."

"You shot me, didn't you?" she said accusingly.

"To my chagrin, I'm afraid I did, love," he admitted. "I did not shoot at you, but rather in the direction of a ragamuffin lad who I thought was running away from the Revenue men.

"You'll be all right so long as no infection sets in. The bullet did not enter, but tore the flesh and bruised the ribs," he said, gently cupping her chin in his hand, "and though I'm more than a little cross with you right now, I'm very sorry to have caused you this pain."

"Where is Millie?" she asked, for she must find out if Ted had escaped.

As if reading her mind, Gerard said coldly, "If you're wondering if your lover was captured, you can set your mind at rest, for he was not. He got away from the men, but I promise you he won't get away from me."

She sighed heavily, for it was all too complicated for her drugged mind to straighten out. She really had made a botch of it, and wanted to tell him that he was her only lover, but then how could she explain what she was doing alone with Ted at that hour?

"What are you going to do?" she asked.

"First, get you well again. Adele may stop in to see you, but she'll probably keep her distance, for I have told her you may have picked up a cold."

Leonora suddenly remembered the painting. "I know this isn't the right time," she told him with a wan smile, "but she and I were planning a surprise for you, and she'll suspect I have more than a cold if you haven't seen it by now. Will you please go into the sitting room and take the cover off the picture above the fireplace?" she asked more appealingly than she realized.

Gerard looked at her a little oddly, then got up to do as she asked.

He was gone for a number of minutes, and when he returned he sat on the bed, facing her. "It's quite remarkable. You must know my face very well to have achieved such a likeness without a single sitting," he told her, looking into her eyes and trying to understand how she could have a lover, yet behave as though she still loved him.

"I do know your face very well," she said softly. "The planes of your cheeks, the straight lines of your eyebrows, the hollow in your chin that is neither a cleft nor a dimple, and the tightening of your lips when you're cross with me, as you are now. And the wonderful softness that comes over every feature when we make love." She paused, then added, "I know every inch of your magnificent body, also."

There was anguish in his voice as he asked harshly, "And do you know every part of your lover so well?"

Leonora shook her head. She wanted to tell him, but how could she explain who Ted really was? She also wanted to know if the cutter had managed to free itself from the rocks with no injuries to the men, for she knew they were only doing their job.

She closed her eyes and winced as a spasm of pain shot through her side. "No, you don't understand . . ."

There was a light knock on the door, and Adele put her head inside. Seeing her stepdaughter sitting up, she entered the room. Gerard rose courteously.

"I won't come too close in case what you have is catching, but I just wanted to make sure you were all right, my dear," she said. "You are a little pale, though. Do you have a fever?"

"I really don't think so," Leonora assured her. "I'll stay in bed for the rest of the day, and then perhaps tomorrow I'll be up and about again. Don't worry about me, and don't tell Papa I'm in bed or he'll be concerned."

Adele hovered at a distance, wanting to come closer, yet afraid of carrying a cold to her husband. "How did Gerard like your gift?"

Leonora smiled up at him, glad she had thought to have him unveil it.

"She is quite an artist," he said emphatically. "I don't think I could name anyone who could have done a better portrait of me. But it's not my birthday for a long time yet."

Leonora's smile remained. "I'll find something equally suitable for that occasion," she assured him. "And now I think I'm going to sleep for a while, for I cannot keep my eyes open any longer."

Adele left then, and Gerard removed the extra pillow and helped his wife slide into a comfortable position. He could tell from her face that she was in pain and, without asking, put several drops of laudanum into some water.

"Drink this, my love. I know you don't want it, but it will help ease the hurt." He supported her with one arm while he held the glass to her lips, then lowered her once more.

Before he replaced the blankets, he lifted her nightgown and checked to be sure the wound was not bleeding, then kissed her tenderly on the lips before going over to a wing chair and sitting down.

He realized he must have dozed off when he opened his eyes and saw Millie moving about the room, straightening the blankets, and putting things away. Leonora was still sleeping, so he stood up and signaled the maid to come into the sitting room.

He did not close the door, but left it open just a crack in case his wife should waken; then he turned to question the maid.

"Did you manage to get some sleep, Millie?" he asked.

"Oh, yes, milord," she assured him. "I did just what you said, and then when I woke I went to the kitchen to get a bite of food. 'Ow 'as she been?"

"She's all right, don't worry. She was awake for a while, and we talked, but when she tired I gave her some more laudanum, for she is still in considerable pain," he told her.

"I'm sure she is, milord, poor thing. Did you want me to stay with 'er all night?"

"No, Millie, just during the evening while I am dining. Was it, by any chance, your evening off?"

"Oh, no, sir." She shook her head.

"Are you from the village, Millie, courting one of the young men there, perhaps?" He was hoping that she would let slip the name of his wife's lover.

The maid looked shy. "Yes, milord, my mam and dad live 'ere, and I'm walking out with one of the fishermen, Ted Peterson. We 'ope to get married next year."

"Is Ted a common name locally, for I heard the land-lord of the inn speaking to a man called Ted. He was a short black-haired fellow."

"It couldn't 'ave been my Ted," she said, "for 'e's tall—almost as tall as you, sir, and 'is 'air is more ginger than anything. It must 'ave been a stranger, for there's only one Ted round 'ere."

Gerard nodded, trying to appear casual, but finding it impossible to believe his wife would be going out with her maid's young man. The height fit the man who had run off last night, though.

"I'll get changed now, Millie. Keep an eye on my lady, and don't hesitate to fetch me if she seems any worse, or starts to bleed through the bandages."

He went into his own chamber and was pleased to find that his valet, Jacobs, had arrived, for he had to dress for dinner and join the ladies within the hour.

"Have you heard any talk belowstairs about a fellow by the name of Peterson, first name Ted, I believe?" he asked his man as he was adding the finishing touches to his appearance.

"As a matter of fact, I met him, milord. He had come to inquire after her ladyship, I understand, though I thought it strange that news of her cold would have spread to the village."

"What kind of a man is he?" Gerard asked, trying hard to sound casual.

"About your height, milord, and probably about the same weight, but there the resemblance ends, for he is a rough-and-ready fisherman, as my nose was quick to inform me. He hadn't even taken the time to shave before coming to the house," he said in disgust.

Gerard nodded, then went down to join Lady Clairmont and Lady Davenport for a predinner glass of sherry in the drawing room.

15

"How is Leonora feeling this evening?" Lady Davenport asked. "I've not known her to stay in bed more than a day since I came to Clairmont House.

"She broke her leg when she was about eleven or twelve, but there was no tying her down. She came down the stairs on her bottom until one of the grooms put four wheels on the lid of a barrel, and then she scooted faster than you could walk." She gave a cackle. "She didn't want to give it up when the leg was healed, but she had to after she ran into a footman carrying a tray of dirty dishes, and down he went. What a mess that was!"

Gerard smiled. "I don't blame her wanting to keep using it, for it sounds as though it would be fun in a house this size, where the downstairs rooms lead one into another. And I should think there was a distinct shortage of fun for a young girl left to be brought up by servants. Was she difficult to control?"

Lady Davenport shook her head, enjoying reminiscing. "She was always up to a lot of mischief and wanted to do everything Geoffrey did, but if you explained why she shouldn't do something, she understood, and you didn't have to tell her twice."

"And one thing about Leonora I have always liked," Adele said, "is that she does not tell lies. She may prevaricate at times, but when it comes down to it she will not tell a direct lie."

She turned to Lady Davenport. "When she is feeling better, you must ask to see the lovely portrait she has painted of Lord Sinclair. It is a wonderful likeness, do you not agree, Gerard?"

"I certainly do, and am amazed at her talent. When

things have settled down a little and Lord Clairmont is back on his feet, God willing, I think I will encourage her to take lessons, preferably with someone in London. How did she learn to paint?''

"It was before I came here," Lady Davenport said. "It seems that one of her governesses tired of trying to teach her to sew, and started her painting instead.''

"Lord Clairmont told me his father painted very well in his younger days," Adele broke in, "but he had to stop when the estates took up too much of his time.''

There was the sound of a discreet cough, repeated twice, and they looked over to see Smathers standing at the door. "Dinner is served, my lord, my ladies," he pronounced, and they followed him into the dining room.

The three made general conversation between courses, and when the ladies retired to the drawing room for tea, Gerard made his excuses and returned to his bedchamber. After dismissing Millie, he stood for some time looking at Leonora as she slept peacefully. Then, having come to a decision, he returned to his own chamber, leaving the doors between their rooms open in case she should wake in the night.

Leonora had a good night's rest, and was still sleeping the next morning when Gerard left the house. After taking care of a few matters on the estate that were urgent, he rode down into the village and made his first stop at the village inn.

Now that he was part of the Clairmont family, the inn-keeper was a deal more friendly than he had been when Gerard and Sir Timothy had stopped by. When he asked where he might find Ted Peterson at this hour, the man grinned widely, deciding that the young viscount must be wanting to acquire a little duty-free brandy for himself.

"Down on the jetty's where you'll find Ted, my lord. He'll be cleaning out his fishing boat ready for his next run," he told him.

Leaving his horse at the inn, Gerard walked slowly down the main street and onto the dock. Though there were a number of men there, most of whom turned to stare as he approached, it was not difficult to find Peterson, for his height and red hair made him stand out.

As Gerard walked toward him, the fisherman stopped what he was doing and met him on the wide jetty. Thinking the two had business together, the other men started to go about theirs.

"You looking for me?" the fisherman asked, standing facing him with arms akimbo.

"If you're Peterson, then I am looking for you," Gerard said grimly. "I believe you have been carrying on with my wife, and I'm here to put a stop to it once and for all."

Peterson let out a loud guffaw. "You are, are you? And 'ow do you mean to do that, your 'igh-an'mighty lordship?"

"By pounding you to pulp, that's how," Gerard said with a cold smile.

"If you want to try, don't say I didn't warn you. Take your jacket off and we'll see about it. Broughton's prize-ring rules, or rough-and-ready?"

"Whichever you wish," Gerard said as he stripped off his coat and put it on the wall.

"I can take you fighting clean. Broughton's it is."

Word that there was to be a mill went round faster than if it had been shouted from the hilltops, and the fishermen all stopped working and left their boats to watch one of their own fighting a gentry cove.

Gerard had frequently sparred at 'Gentleman' John Jackson's and knew how to use his fists, and though Peterson might have fought dirty under other circumstances, he recognized the other man's expertise and determined that, win or lose, it would be a good clean fight.

When another fisherman tried to join in, it was Peterson who turned on him and sent him flying with a right hook to the jaw, and the fight continued to an end that left Peterson on his back, but with neither man really claiming a victory. They had been equally matched.

The fisherman got up and offered a work-hardened hand, and Gerard grasped it firmly, though his much softer hands were bruised and the knuckles bleeding.

"I think you'd better come with me to the pub and get yourself cleaned up a bit," Peterson said as Gerard picked up his jacket but did not put it on. "We've got a bit of talking to do, you and me."

Most of the village had been watching the fight, including the innkeeper, and he hurried back to see that the snug, the small room at the back, was emptied for them and left that way. He also set a bowl of water and a towel on the table for his lordship's use.

Almost before they were settled he came back with foaming tankards of ale, then went out, closing the door behind him.

"Now, Sinclair, let's get one thing straight," Peterson began, smiling despite his battered face. "It's an insult to 'er ladyship to say she's 'aving anything to do with me that way. And I 'ave too much respect for 'er to let you or anyone else insult 'er."

The way he said it, Gerard believed him, but that was not enough. "Then what were the pair of you doing walking together from the village in the early hours of the morning?"

"She didn't tell you?" Peterson grinned, and looked at him over the top of his tankard as he took a long thirst-quenching drink, then wiped his mouth on the back of his hand and said, "I'm sure she didn't say we were carrying on together, as you put it."

"No," Gerard admitted, "but when I accused her, she didn't completely deny it either."

Peterson leaned forward, resting an elbow on the polished wood table and his chin on his hand. "Were you down on the sands of Clairmont Cove the other night?"

"Yes," Gerard growled, "which means that you were on the lugger." He paused. "You're a smuggler, aren't you?"

"That's right. You get a medal for that deduction," Peterson said. "I'm a smuggler, all right, and so is little Leo, as we call your wife. Matter of fact, it was Leo the Revenuers were firing at till I got in front of 'er. She was bringing us in."

As realization of what the fisherman was saying finally came to Gerard, he put his head into his bruised hands. "Oh, no," he groaned. "They might have killed her."

"They tried," Peterson said grimly, "and so did you. That's what this was about." He made a fist and touched Gerard lightly on the chin with it.

"No, never," Gerard said vehemently, shaking his head in protest. "I was shooting wide, trying to make what I thought was a young boy stop, but she lunged to the left, attempting to reach the hatch to the passage. The bullet is still in the wood. How did she start doing something like this?"

"She didn't exactly volunteer, if that's what you think. Young Geoff was doin' it for a bit of excitement. There's nothing much around these parts for a young gent to do.

" 'E wouldn't take anything from us except a keg o' brandy once in a while, cos 'e knew we did it to make up what we've lost in fish, with the catch not being 'alf what it used to be."

"How's that?" Gerard asked curiously.

"When the fish are running, we daren't follow them too far now in case there's a Frenchy warship waiting to take us prisoner. Two boats from the other side of Dartmouth disappeared out there last month, and they even got a Revenue cutter a while back," Ted said with a pleased grin.

"Then you're not operating the kind of large ring I've been hearing about?" Gerard asked.

Ted shook his head. "No, and I wouldn't want to be, from what I've 'eard of them. The lads and me bring the stuff in, and 'alf the village make deliveries, so it' elps feed a lot of mouths. You're not Revenue, so what interest do you 'ave in the smuggling?"

"None at all, Ted, unless you're bringing in spies," Gerard told him, watching his face carefully and seeing an expression of disgust come over it.

"We wouldn't 'ave anything to do with spies, and Frenchy knows it," he said firmly. "We've lads from the village fighting out there in Spain, and we may not be much, but we're not traitors."

"I was pretty sure of that, or I would not have been talking to you so freely," Gerard said. "You were telling me about Geoff, but I still don't know how my wife got involved."

"When 'e went into the army Geoff told us she would 'elp if we needed 'er," Ted said, smiling to himself as he remembered her surprise. "She'll tell you all about it now if you ask 'er. She's only been out with us about 'alf a dozen times.

" 'E shouldn't 'ave done it. 'E should 'ave shown somebody 'ow to get into the cove besides Bob, but 'e didn't, and we were stuck." There was a look of understanding in his eyes. "Now I think you want to get back to 'er, don't you, and make it right?"

"How did you guess?" Gerard asked dryly, getting to his feet and offering his hand once more. "You also know you can trust me, don't you?"

"Yes, but it's not because we'd tell on little Leo if you turned us in, for we'd never 'arm 'er no matter what." He grinned again. "It's funny, Millie told me just this morning that you were a good sort, and she was right, but I still wanted a go at you for what you'd done to little Leo. And I'd 'ave come looking for you if you 'adn't come 'ere first."

With a wave of his hand, Peterson set off back down the main street and Gerard collected his horse from the stable. When he reached Clairmont House, the head groom took one look at Gerard and respectfully suggested he go in the back way.

"I'll look in the kitchen for your valet and send him along to you, if you like, my lord," he said with a grin.

Gerard reached his room without meeting anyone, but when Jacobs came in, he stared at Gerard in horror.

"It looks much worse than it is," Gerard told him. "Just get whatever you need to clean up my face and hands, and take out fresh clothes."

But it was almost an hour before he was reasonably presentable. He looked a little the worse for wear, but no damage had been done that would not be gone in a few days.

16

When Gerard entered the room, Leonora's face was toward him as she slept peacefully on her right side, but as he approached the bed she stirred and her eyes opened slowly, then widened suddenly. She let out a tiny scream at the sight of his bruised face and partially closed eye.

Instinctively she tried to get out of bed to go to him, alarm in her own wide eyes, but she fell back as a stabbing pain shot through her. Gerard was by her side in a moment, easing her against the soft pillow and gently smoothing her hair away from her face.

"Don't be scared, my love. It's not half as bad as it looks—that is, as long as I don't try to laugh," he told her.

She stared at his bruised jaw and numerous small cuts, then reached her right hand upward to touch his swollen lips. "What happened, darling?" she asked. "Were you attacked by ruffians, or did you have an accident?"

He smiled a little crookedly, wincing at the effort. "Not exactly, love. It's a long story, and you'd best get into a comfortable position while I tell it, and while you provide me with some more answers. Can I get you a cool drink or something before I begin?"

Though she was a little thirsty, she shook her head, for she had always hated the waiting more than the scolding itself, and a certain glint in his good eye told her he knew much, if not all that she had been doing these past months. He pulled a chair close to the bed and sat down.

"First of all, young lady, why did you let me think you were having an affair with Ted Peterson?"

"I didn't, but I couldn't tell you the truth," she answered, looking at the bedcovers as though she'd never seen them before. She hoped he was not going to ask her too many questions, for she had no wish to reveal something of which he might be unaware.

"Look at me, love," he said quietly, though his voice held a warning.

When she raised her head, he told her, "You'll not betray any of Ted's secrets, for he and I have just had a long talk."

Her eyes filled with a sudden fear and her lips trembled. "But Millie said he wasn't captured. Have they arrested him? Is that how you got hurt?"

He sighed and shook his head slowly. "No, it is not. Trust me, will you? We talked alone in the snug at the inn after we'd had as dandy a mill on the jetty as any fighting man could wish." He saw her eyebrows lift. "Officially I beat him, for he was the one on the ground at the end, but it was as close a match as any I've had."

Leonora could not believe it. "You mean you, Viscount Gerard Sinclair, had a fistfight with a fisherman? Who started it?" she asked, looking quite appalled.

"I thought I did, as a matter of fact, but I found out at the end that he would have come looking for me sooner or later had I not gone down there. He thinks a lot of you and he knew that I had hurt you and he wanted to even the score." He watched the uncertain emotions that flickered over her face. "He's very protective where you're concerned, but now I know I have no cause to be jealous.

"I went looking for him because I thought he was your lover and I wanted to beat the living daylights out of him for daring to take what is mine," he said grimly.

"I never said he was," she said softly. "I couldn't lie to you, but if I'd told you he wasn't, you wouldn't have believed me."

"I know I wouldn't, for, you see, some time ago I had found something in your chamber, a scrap of paper screwed up and carelessly dropped, canceling an assignation and signed with the letter T."

Leonora looked puzzled, remembering a run had been planned and then canceled and trying to recall when it had

been. Surely it had been a long time ago, just after they
returned from their honeymoon trip. Suddenly she knew,
and she sighed with relief as everything began to fall into
place.

"So that was why you were so different and cool toward
me." She reached out a hand and he took it in his. "It was
just after we returned from our honeymoon, when you
came back from that first short trip. Ted had found out
that the Revenuers would be looking for them that night,
so he called it off."

Nothing had been said, as yet, about her part in the
smuggling activities, but she realized he was aware of what
she had been doing and was coming to it eventually in his
own good time.

"They guessed as much when they saw no sign of the
lugger," Gerard said, "but to my knowledge they never
found out who had given them away. Thank God he did
find out and canceled the run."

"Were you aboard the cutter, then?" Leonora asked,
trying to conceal her amusement.

He nodded, and added, "Yes, and I know now, of
course, that you would have been at the helm of the lugger
had it gone out. I also know now how you got started with
the smuggling ring, but I don't understand at all how your
brother could have involved you the way he did. He had no
right to do so, and you must realize that, love. Weren't you
frightened every time you went out?"

Leonora tried not to laugh, holding her side as she did
so. "I was horrified when I first found out I was on a
smuggling vessel," she admitted, "and scared, for my eyes
were glued to the horizon all the way back, in case a
Revenue boat came in sight." She shook her head slightly.
"I'd have been shaking in my boots, though, had I known
they expected me to take the helm if we were spotted."

"What did Ted say when you told him that?"

With a wide grin, Leonora said, "I've never heard him
swear in front of me since, but he did that night. He
couldn't get over it, and that was part of the reason why I
started helping them. The other reason was, of course, that

I found I enjoyed the excitement and adventure of it. It was exceedingly dull here, you know, once Geoffrey left."

"And was being married to me so unexciting that you were forced to continue, to add a little spice to your life?" he asked quite sternly.

"Oh, no, darling, please don't think that for even a moment. But, you see, Bob is not a healthy man and he's the only one Geoffrey showed how to get into the cove. After we got married I told them to call me only if it was absolutely vital I be there, for I knew you would not like it."

"That must be the biggest understatement I've ever heard," Gerard remarked. "Smuggling is just about the very last thing I would have suspected you of being involved in. And had you not already been injured when I found out, I would have been sorely tempted to put you over my knee and soundly thrash you."

"I was not aware when we wed that you were a wife beater, sir," Leonora said cautiously.

"Believe me, my love, I am not, and I have no time for men who treat their wives thus. However, in this case I think the extreme provocation would have justified such action. And let this be a warning should you ever defy me and go out with them again."

She looked at the poor swollen hand that held her own so comfortingly, and saw the cut and bruised knuckles. It had often caressed her lovingly from head to toe, had held her gently as he had carried her through the tunnel and to her chamber, and, though mistakenly, it had fought a punishing battle today for her love. She knew in absolute certainty that it would never be used violently against her, no matter the provocation, and she lifted it to her lips and pressed soft kisses against it.

"If you want for excitement, then I must try to provide it for you, my dear," Gerard said sagely. "You have proved to my cost that you can keep a still tongue in your head, so when next I have to leave, be it for one or seven nights, then I shall take you along. Do you think you will like that?"

He saw the pleasure on her face before she murmured, "Oh, yes, I know I will."

"And as soon as your mourning period is up, I will take you to London for the Season that you missed. I will dance with you until your feet are sore, take you to see all the sights, and generally become the most unfashionable husband in London by not leaving your side for a moment," he warned, his eyes sparkling with devilment.

There was a silence while he sat and watched her expression of pure delight; then another thought occurred to him.

"I've been told that your brother took no part of the profits, except for the odd keg of brandy on occasion, but what about you? You didn't, by any chance, add to your father's cellar, did you?" he asked, a stern expression on his face.

Leonora went red and bit her upper lip. "Ted sometimes gave me a package when we reached the tunnel," she muttered.

"Oh, no, that puts it in an entirely different light. You'd better tell me what was in the package," he said grimly.

"Ted said it was 'laces for a lady,' " she said, "yards and yards of the most beautiful French laces I have ever seen. You saw some of it on the gowns I wore in Bath, and I have more hidden away. Please don't say I can't keep it," she begged.

"I'll not say that," he said seriously, "for it's not up to me, of course, but I would feel happier if you had never received any recompense for your services. However, what's done is done. I do remember a particularly beautiful gown trimmed in white lace," he said with a shake of his head, but his face had softened.

"Is the scold over now?" she asked appealingly, and when he nodded, she said, "That's good, for I have a favor to ask of you. Could you bring my painting of you in here so that I could look at it and you side by side?"

"I shall demand a reward if I do," he threatened.

"Anything you want," Leonora rashly promised, smiling happily.

He went into the sitting room and came out with his portrait, placing it where Leonora could see it clearly.

"I'm afraid you cannot make a fair comparison right now, and will not be able to do so for a day or two, but I know it to be an excellent likeness," he assured her.

"I had an excellent subject, sir," she said sincerely. "I wanted to capture you now, and then I think perhaps I will do one every ten years to reflect the changes."

He nodded. "In London, we must have you sit for one of the members of the Royal Academy. We will need a good portrait to hang one day in the gallery of Croydon House and perhaps also we'll arrange for you to study under a master," he suggested, his voice deliberately casual.

"Gerard, do you really mean it?" Leonora was immediately excited and eager for the opportunity. "It would be wonderful just to study the techniques and try new media."

"Of course I mean it, love," he murmured. "But now you have to give me my reward." He lifted her gently over to one side of the bed, then settled himself on the other side and took her into his arms, careful not to rest any weight on the wound.

Pushing back her hair, he traced a delicate pattern around her shell-like ear, first with one finger, then with his warm, wet tongue and heated breath, sending her into an incredible rapture and making her feel deprived when he stopped for a moment. She sighed with pleasure, however, when he started to give the other ear the same delicate attention.

Next, her eyelids received butterfly kisses, and then her throat as his lips slowly moved down her soft, velvety skin.

Lifting her nightgown, he let his fingers lightly caress first one breast and then the other in ever-diminishing circles, until he reached the bud at the center. Then he lowered his head and flicked them with his tongue until she whimpered with pleasure.

"I don't know if this was a good idea," she gasped, "but don't stop, please."

"I'll have to soon, love, for you're in no condition to finish this the way I would like," he whispered. "When I think of how near I came to losing you—if that bullet had been just a couple of inches to the right—I want to hold you like this and never let you go."

"I've thought about that also," she murmured, her breath caressing his cheek, "and how you would never have been able to live with yourself—and all because of my foolishness."

Slowly, tenderly, his lips descended on hers, and what the kiss lacked in pressure was more than made up by the feathery delicacy and the depth of feeling that flowed between them. It was a kiss of forgiveness on both sides, and a promise of a new beginning with more trusting and a better understanding.

And it might have gone on for much longer had a light knock not sounded on the door. They separated like a guilty engaged couple about to anticipate their marriage, Gerard jumping off the bed and hastily straightening the blankets.

He called, "Come in," and Adele put her head around the door, then stepped inside.

"I must say, you really don't look very sick, Leonora," she said, somewhat puzzled by her stepdaughter's behavior. "Is there something you're both hiding from me?"

Leonora flushed, but was saved from replying when Adele took a good look at Gerard, blinked her eyes in disbelief, then looked again.

"Then the rumor I heard is true, isn't it?" she said in surprise.

"That depends on what you heard, Adele," Gerard said with a slow smile. "What rumor is being spread along the Clairmont House grapevine? I'd be most interested in the latest version."

"Now, stop roasting me, Gerard, for, by the look of your face, this is not a laughing matter. My abigail tells me that you had an argument and knocked one of the fishermen down on the docks, but Lord Clairmont's valet has a

different story. He says you had a fistfight with the fisherman, and he's very upset that he wasn't there or he would
have put his money on you and won a great deal. Whom
should I believe?'' Adele waited expectantly.

Gerard shrugged. "Both and neither, I suppose," he
started to say, when Leonora interrupted.

"Young men today are not much different from what
they were in your day, Adele," she said placatingly. "They
still enjoy boxing and fencing with instructors and each
other, for I heard 'Gentleman' John's mentioned when I
was in Bath. But I suppose that occasionally they have to
show off their prowess a little, invent some provocation,
and settle it by engaging in fisticuffs. Incredible though it
sounds to you and me, Adele, Gerard seems to have
thoroughly enjoyed himself, and he and his opponent are
now the best of friends."

"You are asking for trouble, young lady," Gerard
threatened, grinning and shaking a bruised fist at her.

"Can't you see how I tremble with fear?" Leonora
asked her stepmama with a soft chuckle.

"Not at all," Adele told her with a smile, "but what I
can see is someone who never stays in bed unless she's
almost dying, happily lying there in the middle of the afternoon." With raised eyebrows she waited for an answer.

"Oh, it was a false alarm and there's nothing wrong
with me at all," Leonora said airily. "If I can ever get my
bedchamber to myself again, I intend to send for Millie to
help me dress for dinner."

"I believe she's hinting for us to go," Gerard said,
tugging on the bell pull, then taking Adele by the arm.
"Let's leave her to Millie's tender care."

When they were outside the door and walking toward
the stairs, Adele said, "Come into my sitting room for a
moment, for we cannot talk here."

Gerard knew her to be a very sensible and sensitive
woman, and willingly followed her, closing the door firmly
behind them.

She allowed him to seat her, then came directly to the
point. "Something has obviously been going on that I

know nothing about, and of which you would rather I remain in ignorance. Am I correct, Gerard?" she asked.

He nodded. "In this case, Adele, the less you know, the better, and her father must never find out or it could be the end of him," he told her quietly.

"Has she been injured? Is that why she looked so pale yesterday?"

Gerard nodded. "She's all right now. There's nothing to worry about, and as far as my actions on the dock are concerned, I was under a misapprehension, but no harm was done."

Adele sighed heavily. "Then you're probably right. If it's something so serious, it is best that I don't know. If I should hear of any strange rumors going around, however, I will come to you right away for the truth." She rose and stood on tiptoe to kiss his cheek. "I'm glad she has you, for you're good for her."

He opened the door and waited for her to pass through, but she turned back. "Are you sure she's well enough to come down to dinner?"

"No, I'm not at all sure, Adele, but I don't know how I can stop her now," he said with a frown.

"I do. Tell her that Aunt Charlotte is having supper in her room, as she often does, and I've decided to dine with Lord Clairmont in his chamber this evening. Then I will arrange for you to have dinner served in your sitting room as you did on your wedding night," she suggested.

Gerard nodded. "An excellent idea, but this time we'll have the dishes left on the sideboard and I will serve us both, and then if she feels tired she can have a tray at the side of the bed. Thank you, indeed, my dear. An excellent idea!"

When he left Adele, Gerard hurried back to Leonora's chamber, and found Millie giving her mistress a bed bath so as not to overtire her. A dinner gown hung ready for her to wear.

He watched until the task was finished and Leonora lay back, exhausted for the moment; then he followed Millie into the dressing room.

"She's determined to get into that gown and join you downstairs, milord, but she's not fit for it yet," Millie told him, a worried look on her face.

"It's all right, Millie," he told her. "There's been a change of plan. Lord and Lady Clairmont are dining in their chamber, and we will be dining here. She need only wear her prettiest dressing gown, and if she tires, I will have her quickly back into bed."

Leonora had sharp ears and had caught most of what Gerard said. "I cannot dine with you in a dressing gown, my lord," she protested.

"Of course you can, for won't you look silly in that dinner gown with me in my robe?" he teased.

"But if Smathers serves us as he did last time—" she began, but he effectively stopped her protest with a gentle kiss.

When he raised his head, he told her, "Smathers will not be serving us, for the dishes will be placed on the sideboard and we will serve ourselves. It was Adele's idea, for I think she feared my ugly face might put her off her meal."

She laughed, then said seriously, "She suspected something, didn't she?"

"Of course she did," Gerard said, "for your stepmama is no one's fool, but I told her she would be happier not knowing."

"And she did not press you further?" Leonora asked, then, when he shook his head, added, "You must have a way with her, for I would never have been so indulged. She'll probably keep pressing me until I get annoyed."

"No, she won't in this instance, love. I guarantee she will never mention it again, and that she will keep your Aunt Charlotte quiet on the subject also."

"I hope you are right," Leonora said, "and you seem so sure that I know you must be. What time will dinner be brought up?"

"No earlier than usual, for we could hardly expect Cook to change the dinner hour at such short notice," Gerard said. "It will give you plenty of time to rest before having your first meal out of bed."

Millie had put away the dinner gown and set out a pale

blue velvet dressing gown before leaving them, and Gerard took advantage of the fact that they were alone to ask a question that had puzzled him for some time.

"Tell me, love. What made you think I had taken a mistress just a few weeks after our marriage?" he asked. "It has worried me ever since Adele mentioned it, for though I thought you had a lover, I made sure to behave exactly as before."

Leonora shook her head. "You probably thought you were doing so, but there was something missing. Laughter was no longer spontaneous, the special tenderness when we made love was not there, and I'd see you looking at me strangely when you thought I didn't know you had entered a room. And the next time you went away, you seemed glad to be going instead of hating to leave me as you did the first time."

He nodded. "I can see what you mean. A misunderstanding is like a wound that festers from lack of attention. We'll never let that happen again, love, for we'll talk about any problems as they arise, won't we?"

"Of course we will. We both know the signs of misunderstanding now, and we'll stop it before it even gets started," she agreed happily.

17

"I was riding along the cliff just now and saw a lugger in our cove, Leonora, though there was no sign of the fishing fleet further out. Have you any idea who it could be?"

Gerard bent to kiss his wife before going over to the sideboard and helping himself to a large breakfast. Taking a seat facing her, he waited for an answer to his question, observing with considerable amusement the guilty expression on her face.

"All right, you'd better tell me what you've been up to," he said, "for you know I'll find out for myself if you don't."

When she met his eyes she saw how they sparkled with suppressed laughter and knew that, though she should have checked with him first, he was most unlikely to put a stop to what she had arranged.

"It was probably Bob showing one of the other men how to get in and out of the cove," she told him. "I said it would be all right as long as they practiced early in the morning when few people were around to notice."

"And you thought I would not notice either, I suppose. Don't you know by now that I'd not have opposed it as long as you didn't teach him yourself? Of course, you're not yet in a condition to do any sailing, for the stretching might open up the wound. How do you feel this morning?" He was looking at her tenderly as he recalled how she had responded to his very gentle loving last night.

Her cheeks turned a delicate pink. "Wonderful," she murmured. "I'm much stronger than you think, but it's nice to be treated like a piece of delicate china for a change."

"I'm not rough with you as a rule, am I, darling?" he asked softly. "That's the last thing I would ever want to be."

"No, not at all, but last night I felt as though I was a fragile flower and you were a butterfly trying hard not to bruise my petals. I wouldn't want it that way every time, but it was a lovely new experience." She grinned wickedly. "I don't suppose you enjoy being likened to a butterfly, however."

"Not in the normal way, but the metaphor is apt for the particular circumstances," he began, but stopped as the door opened and Adele came in.

"You mustn't get up, Gerard," she admonished as he started to rise. "I'll just serve myself and join you two, if I may. I must say, it's nice to see you down to breakfast again, Leonora. You must be feeling better."

"I'm fine now, thank you. How is Papa today?" Leonora asked.

"Doing very well, my dear. I'm glad you stopped in to see him yesterday, for he was getting a little worried about you, but you looked so well and happy, I think it brightened his spirits," she said cheerfully. "Are you not going riding this morning?"

Leonora glanced at her husband. "I'm taking her out in the curricle after breakfast," he said quickly, making a mental note to be sure Adele was not there when he lifted Leonora into the vehicle, for it would be a little more awkward than usual.

He was glad of the interruption when Smathers knocked and entered. "There's a messenger here, milord, with a letter from London for you."

Gerard rose at once and followed the butler out.

"Oh, dear," Leonora said a little petulantly. "I do hope he does not have to go away again just now. He said he would take me with him in the future, but he may not think me well enough as yet."

"Gerard must have been spoiling you these last few days, my pet, for it is unlike you to take that tone," Adele said a little sharply. "It's possible he won't have to go right away, and can wait until you feel like traveling, though you look remarkably fit to me.'' She gazed speculatively at her stepdaughter.

Gerard's return precluded the need for Leonora to make a response to her stepmama, for there was an unmistakable air of excitement about him. He carefully closed the door behind him, and made no attempt to resume his seat, but pulled a chair close to hers, sat down, and put an arm around her. In his hand he held a piece of white paper.

He waited patiently until she had swallowed the sip of tea she had just taken, then said, ''The Prime Minister had good news for us. He says that Geoffrey is alive . . .'' he began, and waited for his words to have their effect upon his wife.

''Alive?'' she gasped. ''Are you sure?''

He nodded and pulled her toward him, holding her close as tears of relief streamed down her face.

Adele's eyes had filled also, and she moved closer to Leonora. ''That's wonderful, Gerard, simply wonderful,'' she breathed. ''I can hardly believe it myself.''

Leonora drew away from him, sniffing and wiping her face with the back of her hand until he handed her a kerchief.

''Where is he?'' she asked. ''Is he coming home?''

Adele reached over to clasp her hand, and the two women waited to hear what else the Prime Minister had written.

''He says that Geoffrey had head injuries and a subsequent loss of memory, and that some kind Spanish peasants looked after him until the wound was healed. Then he lived and worked with them until his memory returned.

''He is apparently now fit and well, and back with Wellington. He has written a letter to his father, which should arrive any day, but naturally, Perceval's correspondence moves more swiftly.'' Gerard looked with compassion into his wife's tearstained face. ''You can't quite believe it, love, can you?''

She shook her head. ''It seems too good to be true, but I

know it must be," she said shakily, then frowned as a thought occurred to her. "Do you really think he's well enough to go on fighting? Shouldn't he be sent home to recuperate?"

"He's probably in better health now than most of his regiment, love, for he got a chance to get over the injury before being thrust right back into the fighting. Don't forget, it's been a long time since the Battle of La Albuera." He put a finger under her chin and looked into her face. "Are you all right now?"

"Yes," she said, nodding, "but how are we going to tell Papa?"

"Very gently," Adele said, "for I'd hate the shock of good news to set him back."

"Then you had best tell him, Adele," Leonora said firmly, "for I would have to blurt it out, I know. I couldn't help myself."

"I think I'll wait an hour or so until he wakes from his morning nap, when he's well-rested, and tell him then." Adele looked at Gerard. "Don't you think that would be best?"

"I think this is completely up to you, my dear," he told her gently. "When he's over the first shock, Leonora and I can come in and explain in more detail what happened. In the meantime, I think we should go for that drive. Do you want to run upstairs now and meet me at the stables, Leonora? And, by the way, I wouldn't tell any of the servants until Lord Clairmont has been informed, for I'd hate one of them to let it slip."

Both women nodded their agreement, and Leonora hurried out to get ready.

"She's more shaken than she appears," Gerard said to Adele. "I think a quiet drive may calm her down and enable her to help with her father. You look very serious. Are you worried about telling him?"

"Oh, no, for I know how to go about that," she said calmly. "I was just wondering what kind of an injury she could have sustained that horseback riding could damage but bouncing about in a curricle won't harm."

"You're too perceptive by far, Adele," he said bluntly. "But you're wasting your time, for I don't think you could ever guess what happened if you tried from now until doomsday." He walked toward the door. "I had better change, too, and get the smell of horseflesh off me."

He held the door for Adele, then took the stairs two at a time, for he had no wish to keep his wife waiting. As it happened, though, they arrived at the stables at almost the same moment, and while a stableboy held the horses, Gerard lifted Leonora carefully into the carriage, then got in himself.

"How long do you suppose it will be before Geoffrey's letter arrives?" she asked as they set out at a steady trot down the lane.

"I would say a minimum of a week—maybe two weeks," Gerard said, not wanting her to be disappointed each day until it arrived. "Normally it would take much longer than that, but I'm counting on the fact that he may know one of Wellington's senior officers who will push it through quickly. And the fact that the Prime Minister was inquiring might help."

They drove in silence as Leonora thought of her brother and how good it would be to see him again when he got leave.

"Do you mind no longer being heir to all this?" she asked suddenly, indicating the lands that stretched before them.

He shook his head. "Not at all, for we never needed it, as you know. Unless Geoffrey is coming home on leave at once, we'll go to London, I think, as we intended to do once you were out of mourning. Then we'll come back here until he returns and is settled in, and after that we'll go to Bristol. Do you agree?"

"We will?" she asked doubtfully. "I never thought I would have to live away from Clairmont House."

He looked at her intently. "I don't believe you married me in order to go on living here. I know that we married in part because your father wished it, but things have changed between us since then, and I am sure what we now have could not be called anything but a love match.''

She moved close and slipped her hand under his arm. ''I didn't mean to imply it was not. I don't really care where I live as long as it's with you,'' she said quietly.

He turned and smiled down at her upturned face. ''I know, love,'' he said. ''Let's not make any mistakes about that. The next few days are going to be a little trying, I think, but I believe you can start ordering gowns for London right away. How much French lace did you say you have?'' he asked with a chuckle.

She smiled and shook her head. ''Not sufficient for a Season in London, but I have some beautiful silks also, so I will not look a dowd. It will be delightful to wear bright colors and pastels again, and though I have a lovely piece of black lace, I doubt that I will have it made up for a long time, for I'm so tired of wearing black.''

''You mustn't forget to pack your easel and paints, for I meant what I said about arranging lessons with a master,'' Gerard reminded her.

Suddenly it was very exciting. She had been adamant that she did not want a Season in London before she met and married Gerard, but now she could hardly wait.

''We'll turn back now, I think, for I would like to be in the house when Adele tells your father, just in case there should be any problem.'' As he spoke, he swung into a farmyard and out again, then set off for home.

''You must not be disappointed if Geoffrey has changed a great deal from the lighthearted youth he must have been. War has a way of making young men grow up quickly, and I'm sure he'll be a deal more responsible than when he left and dropped the problem of the smugglers into your lap.''

She let her hand come naturally to rest on his thigh, feeling the strength in the muscles, and he turned his head and smiled fondly at her.

''I'm sure he will, and though you may not think so, I have grown up a lot also since he went away,'' she told him. ''If, before I met you, I'd been forced to stay home and not go riding or sailing because of an injury, I would have been completely impossible to live with. Now it doesn't matter as much, for I know I'll be able to resume these activities in a while."

"You've become a very lovely, delightful companion, my dear, and though we cannot breathe a word about it now, I can just see us telling our grandchildren of their grandmama's smuggling days, and they'll never believe it of such a dignified old lady."

"You surely don't think they'll not hear about you as well, for I won't be the only one with an interesting past. When they hear how you fought and knocked down the head smuggler because of me, they'll be fascinated, I'm sure," she countered, grinning widely.

"Now, there's no need to tell them things like that, Leonora. We don't want them to grow into little ruffians," Gerard said with mock severity.

They were quiet for a moment, for the road was narrow and a large coach was coming toward them. There was something Leonora wanted to talk to him about, and once he had steered them carefully past the larger vehicle, she plucked up the necessary courage.

"We've never talked about it, so perhaps we should now. Do you want a lot of children, darling?" she asked him a little shyly.

Gerard had seen her grow quiet. It was a serious question and he considered carefully before replying. "I will be happy with however many we have, love, but I've always thought four was a nice number. It gives the older ones a sense of responsibility, and the younger ones have someone to look up to. What do you think?"

"Certainly more than two, for when one goes away, as Geoffrey did, it's very lonely for the one left at home," she said knowingly.

"Yes, but it was even worse for you, because you had neither mother nor father at home for all those years. I still can't understand how your father could have left you so much to your own devices," he said with some impatience. "However, he made up for it, in my opinion, by arranging for us to meet."

They were passing through the home woods, and Leonora moved closer and snuggled against him. He immediately pulled to a stop and drew her even closer.

"I hope this is a sign of affection and not just a way of keeping warm on this chilly day," he said, then swooped down to steal what he had meant to be a brief kiss, but her warm lips felt so good he lingered, tasting the sweetness and enjoying her swift, eager response.

"Was there any special reason why you brought up the question of children, my love?" he asked.

For a moment she almost told him that she might be increasing, then decided it was too soon yet. It could still be a false alarm, but just in case, she would make sure that the gowns she ordered were not too tight, and that some could be enlarged by loosening a drawstring.

If she mentioned it now, Gerard might not want her to travel, which was, of course, nonsense. She wanted those painting lessons with a master more than she wanted to dance at Almack's and drive in Hyde Park, and she could always return home if she had to.

"No, darling, none at all, but I just realized we'd never talked about children," she said, lifting her face for another kiss.

It was not until one of his chestnuts gave its opinion of their activities with a loud snort that they realized where they were, and they drew apart slowly, a longing in their eyes which could only be fulfilled at some other time and place.

"Your father should be awake by now," Gerard said gruffly as they neared the house, "so I'll leave my coat with Smathers and seek out Adele, if she's not waiting for us downstairs."

He jumped down at the front door and helped her out very carefully, giving the reins to his tiger, who had been watching for their return.

Leonora hastened up the stairs and into her chamber, where Millie was waiting to help her off with her coat and bonnet and give her hair as much attention as her mistress would permit, for she was anxious to see her father.

As she opened her chamber door, Gerard was just coming toward her.

"He woke a few minutes ago, and Adele is with him now. We'll knock and wait a moment before going in, I think," he said, putting a comforting arm around her and leading her along the corridor.

In response to their knock, Adele called for them to come in, and they found Lord Clairmont sitting up in bed with Adele holding his hand, tears running down his face. He beckoned for them to come to the other side of the bed, and Leonora went ahead and into his outstretched arm, placing her cheek against his while their tears intermingled.

Over his daughter's head, his eyes met Gerard's. He's going to be all right, Gerard thought, and reached into his pocket for the letter he knew the older man wanted to see.

Leonora moved back a little, and Gerard placed a kerchief in her hand and the letter in her father's.

Lord Clairmont read the letter quickly, then read it again, more slowly this time to absorb its contents. "I may keep this?" he asked out of politeness only, for he had no intention of releasing the precious document.

"Of course, sir," Gerard said, "and may I say how happy I am to have brought you such good news."

"It's a miracle, my boy. I need this scrap of paper to look at and know it's true and not just something I dreamed," he said in a voice that was stronger already. "I can't thank you enough for all you've done for us, particularly for turning my little hoyden here into a beautiful lady."

"My pleasure entirely, sir," Gerard said, smiling warmly at Leonora. "As soon as you are feeling stronger, we are planning to make that long-postponed trip to London and let her have a taste of the Season."

"That's a splendid idea, and I know I would have thought of it myself before long. Adele will enjoy helping her order gowns and such, and you'll stay in our town house on Hill Street, for it's been empty except for servants for too long.

"We'll stay here, of course, and await Geoffrey's

return. And I may as well tell you, I intend to persuade him, using any means at my disposal, to let me buy him out," Lord Clairmont said firmly.

"You may find that he needs little persuasion, sir. He's been through a bad time and may just be ready to settle down," Gerard suggested.

"I hope you're right, my boy, for I know I can't go through that a second time," the older man said, shaking his head.

"Don't worry about it now, my dear," Adele advised, "for if worse comes to worst and he cannot be persuaded, I'll see that he trips and breaks a leg or something and has to stay home."

"And I'll help you, Adele," Leonora added.

The two men shared an understanding laugh at the ferocity of their womenfolk; then Gerard took his wife's arm.

"Come along, love, for I fear we will tire your father out. We'll come back and talk more this afternoon if you like," he suggested.

She pulled away to kiss her papa's cheek, then tucked her hand through Gerard's arm and they left the room.

The next week was a busy one as Leonora selected fabrics or stood impatiently while pelisses, cloaks, riding habits, and gowns for every occasion were fitted time after time.

Adele helped, of course, but she was spending more and more of her leisure hours keeping her husband entertained, as Lord Clairmont was so much improved that he was inclined to overdo and needed careful watching.

Gerard was out most days around the estates, as he wished to be sure everything was running smoothly and would continue to do so in his absence, for Lord Clairmont would not be well enough to personally oversee these matters for many months. But by then, of course, Geoffrey might be home.

Two days before they were to leave, Adele took Gerard on one side.

"How badly would you feel if Aunt Charlotte came with you to London?" she asked, knowing the answer, of course.

"Oh, no, Adele," he groaned. "That's a little too much. We've not had a real honeymoon and were looking forward to making a leisurely journey there and then having the house to ourselves in London."

Adele was very understanding. "I know you were. Do you want me to tell her your decision or do you wish to speak to Leonora first?"

"I haven't made a decision yet, but I'll discuss it with Leonora and let you know what we both decide. I hate to disappoint the old lady if she thinks she's up to the journey," he admitted. He knew, however, that unless Leonora strongly objected, which was most unlikely, then they would take her with them, for he did not think he could tell the old lady that she could not come.

It was not until they were dressing for dinner that night that he was able to see Leonora alone and bring up the matter.

The ladies had abandoned their blacks the day Perceval's letter had come, and Leonora was changing tonight into a blue satin gown, almost the color of her eyes, with cream ribbons floating down the front. The neckline was lower than she was accustomed to, and she came into Gerard's chamber to seek his opinion on it.

With a nod he dismissed his valet, then stretched out his hands in welcome. She placed her hands in his and just gazed lovingly at this handsome man who was her husband.

He was wearing dark blue pantaloons and a white waistcoat, and his snowy white neckcloth cascaded in his own variation of the waterfall. His sandy hair was dressed in the slightly windswept style he preferred, and his coat, in a lighter blue, hung waiting for him to don just before leaving.

"Mm," he murmured in approval. "You look quite ravishing, my dear. Is that one of your new gowns?"

"Yes, and I'm very much afraid the neckline is cut too

low for modesty. Do you not agree?'' she asked, frowning up at him.

"Not at all, love. When you get to London, you will think this not daring in the slightest, for I'm afraid that many ladies who have far less attractive figures than yours try to make up for their deficiencies by showing as much flesh as they dare. I have often thought that some of them, if they breathed heavily, would come right out of the tops.''

"Oh, Gerard, stop teasing and tell me if I should fill it in a little with a fichu,'' she said, moving closer and tilting her head to look eagerly up into his face.

"Your modiste would probably leave on the spot if you ruined her design with such an abhorrence,'' he told her as he glanced at the moderate expanse of flesh the gown revealed. Then he looked at the longing in her bright blue eyes and the temptation of her moist red lips and grinned appreciatively. "You look as though you would like to ravish me, and I must warn you that if you do, I will insist that you marry me and save my good name,'' he twitted her.

As Leonora had been hoping he would want to have an early night, preferably in her bed, she was disconcerted that he read her so well, and she blushed prettily.

He touched her pink cheek with his fingers. "I hope you never get over this kind of embarrassment, as it is one of the delightful things about you, my love. If you eat up all your supper, I will allow you to do your worst tonight,'' he teasingly promised, then became serious as he remembered his talk with Adele. "Your Aunt Charlotte wants to come to London with us.''

Leonora's face fell, then brightened. "You are still joking, aren't you?'' she asked hopefully.

"I'm afraid not, love. She didn't even dare to ask us herself, but mentioned the matter to Adele,'' he told her.

"But I wanted to be alone with you. I've been looking forward to that part of our journey most of all,'' she bemoaned, gazing at him with an almost beseeching expression on her face.

"I know, my dear, but have we the heart to say she can't come?" he asked, holding her close and gently pressing kisses onto her forehead.

"You know we haven't, but just the same, I wish she hadn't asked," she muttered crossly. "You'll be all right, for you'll ride much of the way and leave me in the carriage listening to her snoring."

He cupped her chin in his hand and raised her face, then looked at her intently, smiling when he saw her shame-faced expression. "Will you tell her she can come, or shall I, my love?"

"I'll tell her tonight when we go into the drawing room for tea," Leonora said softly. "I'll tell her that we'd love to have her with us."

"That's my girl," Gerard said, placing a soft kiss on her slightly parted lips, but Leonora needed more. She put her hand behind his head and held him there, deepening the kiss and making him forget all about Aunt Charlotte and London, and almost about dinner.

When they drew apart, she asked a little shakily, "Do you want me to help you with your coat instead of Jacobs?"

He nodded, his eyes still dark with passion. "Dinner will seem endless tonight, but I'll join you ladies with one glass of port. Then I will slowly and deliberately kidnap you and carry you off to my lair."

"What will you do when you have me at your mercy, sir?" Leonora asked gleefully.

"Guess."

"You'll bring out all of your stockings that have holes in them and make me mend every one?" she ventured.

He shook his head solemnly from side to side. "I believe Jacobs sells them, holes and all, for a tidy sum," he said. "Guess again."

"You'll make me learn to tie your cravat in a waterfall to rival Beau Brummell's," she suggested.

"No, but I might make you wash and iron the dozen or so that are discarded every day," he threatened.

"I do know what you'll do, you know." Leonora's

voice became soft and sultry, and her eyes revealed some of the passion she felt deep inside.

"Tell me," he said huskily.

"You'll undress and lie down on the bed, then you'll make me run the tips of my fingers slowly over your beautiful body," she breathed, "starting with the lightest touches in your ears, and down to your throat, stroking the little pulses that will start beating rapidly halfway down your neck."

"There must be more than that," he challenged, tugging at the collar of his shirt, as it seemed to have suddenly tightened.

"Of course, for then you'll force me to run my fingers through that silky gold hair on your chest, circling the two little bumps that harden so quickly at my touch. You'll make me stroke that flat stomach you're so proud of, and watch the muscles tighten as my fingers go gradually lower and lower," she murmured. "Then . . ."

"That's enough," he groaned, grabbing her arm and pulling her toward the door. "If we don't go down to dinner immediately, I swear I'll not be able to."

Her laughter tinkled delightfully as they stepped into the hall, and she asked, "Are you sure you won't want to dawdle over that glass of port?"

He gave her posterior a light love tap, placed her hand on his arm, and escorted her sedately down the stairs. Just before they reached the last step, he whispered in her ear, "Eat well and build up your strength, my love, for I shall expect all of that and more from you before the night is out."

"It's a promise," Leonora mouthed, and her dancing eyes confirmed it.

18

The journey had been long and tedious, as they expected, with Gerard riding when they first set out each morning, then joining the ladies in the carriage after luncheon. True to Leonora's prediction, Aunt Charlotte had slept most of each afternoon.

As they neared the capital, Leonora had been most disappointed at the dirt and poverty to be seen everywhere, and it was not until they turned into Knightsbridge and passed the Hyde Park turnpike that she became excited once again.

It was only a matter of ten minutes later, that they came to Berkeley Square and turned into Hill Street, stopping at what seemed to be the largest house on the street, number thirty-one.

It was a handsome town house, small in comparison to Clairmont House, of course, but quite large for London.

Their first visitor was, as they expected, Sir Timothy Torrington, Gerard's friend, and he brought with him his young sister, Margaret, a pretty golden-haired young lady of nineteen years.

"This is what is known as the Little Season," Margaret explained to a surprised Leonora. "There are not nearly so many people in town, but it is a good time to accustom oneself to London society and the rigid code of the *ton*."

"Can it be so very different from Bath?" Leonora asked, not having realized she would still have to learn how to get along in society here.

"Oh, yes, very different," her newfound friend told her. "For instance, you have to wait until someone puts your name forward to one of the seven patronesses at Almack's

Assembly Rooms on King Street. Then, if they find you acceptable, they send you a voucher to attend their Wednesday-night balls.''

"And what if they don't find you acceptable? You just have to go to balls elsewhere, I suppose," Leonora rejoined, but Margaret shook her head.

"If Almack's refuses vouchers, you might just as well return to the country, for just about everyone who is anybody is seen there. Not that you need to worry," Margaret added, "For I am sure your family has already taken care of it and you will be receiving vouchers right away.''

Leonora was slightly taken aback, for it had never occurred to her that anyone of rank was refused entrance anywhere. "I suppose it is a very grand place," she suggested.

Margaret laughed. "Not really, though it does have enormous crystal chandeliers and a musicians' balcony, but the supper is most unappetizing and I never have cared for orgeat or lemonade. The waltz is considered rather wicked, and a lady has to have approval from a patroness before she is allowed to dance it for the first time there.''

"What a lot of nonsense it all sounds," Leonora declared, "but I suppose I will do whatever Gerard thinks best, for even if they send vouchers, we don't have to go, do we?''

"But you must, my dear," Margaret said persuasively, "if only to watch the others and say you have been. I felt just the same as you do when I first came to town, but it is surprising how one becomes accustomed after a while.''

The two gentlemen returned, having been to Tattersall's looking for a matched pair of horses for the curricle Sir Timothy had just acquired. Gerard's would be arriving any day, as his groom and valet were bringing it from Devon.

"Margaret has been telling me the most extraordinary story about seven ladies of rank who decide who will and will not be accepted by London society," Leonora told her husband. "And she thinks we may be receiving vouchers from them to the famous Almack's.''

Gerard came over and bent to kiss her cheek. "We

already got them, my love," he said. "And the four of us will go together next Wednesday night."

"And what about me, young man?"

They all turned to face the door as Aunt Charlotte came in, leaning on her cane. "I believe I'm a tad too old for dancing, but there'll be some there who still remember me."

As Sir Timothy helped her into a chair, Gerard said, "Then of course you will come with us, Lady Davenport. Anytime you wish to go somewhere we're going, you only have to say so, for there's always room for a little one in the carriage."

She looked at him fiercely. "I'm not as little as I used to be, young man. Comes of all this rich living in the country and no exercise. There was a day when I liked to walk, and I could keep up with the best of them, but those days are long gone now," she said.

Sir Timothy and Lady Margaret rose to take their leave, promising to be back the next day, and Leonora rang for some fresh tea for her aunt.

"According to Lady Margaret, there is a quite specific code of behavior at this Almack's place," Leonora told them as she offered a piece of cake to her aunt. "Something about not being able to waltz without their approval."

"The men can," Gerard said with a grin, "but we'll have to get their permission before you waltz there the first time. It's quite ridiculous, but it makes them feel important. And if you're not inside the doors by eleven o'clock sharp, they close them and not even Prinny is allowed in."

Leonora made a face. "Who are these female tyrants who have such an influence on half of London?" she asked.

Gerard was amused at his wife's intolerance. "Not half of London, my love, just the aristocracy or *beau monde*. And the tyrants, or patronesses, are Ladies Castlereagh, Jersey, Cowper, and Sefton, Mrs. Drummond-Burrell, the Princess Esterhazy, and the Countess Lieven. Mrs. Drummond-Burrell is the haughty one, Lady Sefton is the most charming, if Sally Jersey likes you she is also excellent company, and you will probably meet Lady Castereagh a little less formally when we dine with the Percevals.''

Leonora knew she would never remember all the names the first time, but viewed a dinner with the Prime Minister with even more alarm.

"Oh, no," she wailed. "When will that be, and who else will be there?"

"There's nothing to get yourself in a fret about in dining with a bunch of politicians, my gal," Lady Davenport said with a snort. "The men will jaw at each other all through the meal, and their womenfolk will chatter like magpies over tea, for it's the only chance they have to get a word in."

Gerard grinned ruefully. "Your aunt has the right of it, I'm afraid. And as to when, I have not yet seen the invitation, but was told that we'll be receiving one shortly. In a day or so we'll be getting a great many invitations, and I'll go through them with you each morning to help you decide which to accept and which to regretfully decline."

"And I suppose that every Wednesday we will go to Almack's," Leonora said resignedly.

"Perhaps," her husband allowed, "but not necessarily, and we'll rarely stay more than an hour there, but will go on to whatever other engagements we have. It's not unusual to attend three different functions in an evening, you know."

But she didn't know, for she had so rarely gone out of an evening, except for the month they spent in Bath, that to go to three different places the same night seemed a little excessive. However, Leonora was quite prepared to learn a new way of life for the time they were here, and to do whatever Gerard thought best.

"How do I look, darling?" Leonora asked, pirouetting so that Gerard could see all sides of her gown of nile-green net over white satin. The tails of a deeper green velvet bow hung from just below her breasts, almost to the floor, and the hem of the net overskirt and tiny puff sleeves were caught up at intervals with smaller bows of the same color velvet.

"Unbelievably lovely, my dear," he told her, noting the soft flush of excitement on her cheeks. "Despite your caustic remarks, I do believe you are excited at the prospect of attending Almack's and meeting the redoubtable patronesses."

"Excited? I'm terrified, but trying not to show it, for who would not be when those paragons of virtue themselves can either make or mar one's first Season?" she asked. "How would you feel if your wife was ostracized by society for some tiny indiscretion?"

"To be honest, I would feel little concern, for we would return to the country, attend to more serious matters, and start to raise a brood of little Sinclairs," Gerard told her, regarding her tenderly.

He reached for the green velvet cloak that completed the outfit, and as he placed it around her shoulders, he lowered his head and stole a kiss.

"Now, let us go and beard the lionesses in their den. I'm sure your Aunt Charlotte is already downstairs waiting for us," he said.

And, of course, she was, for as they reached the bottom of the stairs, she came out of the drawing room, resplendent in a late-eighteenth-century gown called a polonaise, the overdress in a deep shade of lavender and the underdress or petticoat in a pale lemon. Ostrich-feather plumes attached to a lavender headband waved dangerously atop her powdered wig.

"About time, too," she snapped. "I've been waiting here for you this half-hour and more. Youngsters these days don't know the meaning of punctuality."

"But, Aunt Charlotte, we told you that we would leave at half-past the hour of nine, and it is just that time now," Leonora protested, and as if in confirmation, the hall clock struck the half-hour.

The old lady's face seemed to crumple, and Leonora quickly put an arm around the stooped shoulders and kissed her cheek. "Come along, it doesn't matter, Auntie," she said softly, and the old lady allowed herself to be escorted through the hall, down the steps, and into the carriage. Once inside, she was her old self again.

"Do you have my voucher, young man?" she asked Gerard.

"Yes, Lady Davenport," he said. "I have the vouchers for all of us, and now don't forget, we will leave at about eleven-thirty, drop you off at home, and then go on to the Liverpools' ball. If you wish to leave before we do, just let me know and I'll send for the carriage."

"And what will happen if I don't want to leave at eleven-thirty? I might just be having such a good time that I want to stay later," she said with a roguish smile.

"Then we'll have the carriage take us to the ball and then return here to await your pleasure," Gerard replied with an understanding smile for he, too, had seen her face in the drawing-room doorway, and realized that she was very nervous. She had not been in London for many years, and this evening was probably more important to her than it was to them, so he intended to keep an eye on her and see that she enjoyed herself.

They had been standing in a crush, waiting to enter the ballroom and pass through the line of patronesses, and had finally reached the door. He stepped forward, a lady on each arm.

"Gerard Sinclair, where were you last Season? We missed you," Lady Jersey said with a naughty smile. "And, Lady Daveport, it's a pleasure to see you again after all this time."

She looked at Leonora with eyebrows raised. "And this is . . . ?"

"This is my wife, Sally. May I present the former Lady Leonora Clairmont."

Leonora curtsied low, and Lady Jersey took her hand. "Get up, child, and let me take a look at you," she said kindly. "Why, you're a real beauty, aren't you? Your father's always been a favorite of mine, but I heard he was very ill. And wasn't your brother killed? Shouldn't you still be in mourning?"

The patroness's face had grown stern, and Gerard drew Leonora protectively close as he saw tears threatening to spill.

"Sally," he said grimly, "your information is out-of-date. Geoffrey Clairmont was found and is now in the thick of the fighting once more."

Waving some of the people behind the Sinclairs to pass, Lady Jersey took Leonora into her arms and hugged her. "I'm so happy for you, my dear, and sorry I misunderstood. Enjoy yourself, and if you want to waltz with this handsome husband of yours, you have my permission."

They continued along the line, and the good news had now preceded them, so there were more kisses and hugs from all except Mrs. Drummond-Burrell, who did condescend to smile, however, as she took Leonora's hand.

After settling Aunt Charlotte with a number of her old friends, who were delighted to see her again, Leonora went gladly into her husband's arms for the waltz that was being played, and she was in such a haze of happiness that she did not notice the many people who were watching them.

There were quite a number of disgruntled mamas who had been sure that the very handsome and very eligible Lord Sinclair would be enamored of their daughters. The news that he was waltzing with his bride caused deep disappointment as it traveled quickly around the room.

When the music stopped, Gerard led his wife to where the Torringtons, Sir Timothy and Lady Margaret, stood, and a few minutes later they were joined by several other young people Leonora had met in Bath.

Sir Timothy led Leonora into the next set that was forming. "You look even lovelier than you did in Bath, Leonora. Marriage must agree with you," he told her.

"I'm sure it does, for I feel wonderful, though a little nervous here after what Margaret told me," she said.

"There's no need for that, though there are a lot of young ladies envious of you right now, for the word will have envied everyone that you are Gerard's bride," he said with a twinkle. "They're not only wishing they looked like you, they're wishing they were you."

"My goodness. I know my husband is handsome, but

was he so very much in demand?'' she asked with a laugh.

"He was," Sir Timothy said, "but not for his looks as much as for his prospects, for it's not every young lady can become a marchioness eventually."

Leonora looked a little disbelieving. "They could have the title for all I care," she said, "for it's Gerard I want, and I wouldn't mind if he was a plain mister."

Sir Timothy nodded understandingly, then said, "I see your Aunt Charlotte did come this evening. Perhaps I'll go over and have a word with her instead of dancing the next cotillion."

"Oh, that would be kind of you, Timothy, for I've never seen her nervous before in all my life, but she was tonight. I'm afraid she's getting old, and a lot frailer than we realize," Leonora said with a shake of her head.

"I'm glad to see you and Margaret get along so well together. She has spoken about you constantly ever since you met, for you're the only sensible young woman right now in all of London, to hear her talk," he said.

"We did get along very well, and I'm glad she's to be my friend here, for I recall all too clearly the twins we met in Bath, Julia and Jennifer Dexter, who were sweet, but had not a single brain in either head."

He started to chuckle, then said quietly, "I'm glad you remember them so well, for they're standing on the other side of the room right now, with their mama. They'll no doubt come over to see you before the night's out."

"Then all we need are the Burtons and the Wallaces and it will seem like home," Leonora said gaily.

"Yes," Sir Timothy agreed, "but there's one of the acquaintances from Bath that I hope you manage to avoid. Did you know that Lord Burlington was in town?"

Leonora looked worried. "No, I didn't know, and I hope he does not find out we're here," she said feelingly. She was about to ask where he had seen the man, when the music stopped and he escorted her back to Gerard, who was surrounded by a bevy of young beauties.

Margaret joined her, laughing at the sight, and said, "You must rescue him, Leonora, for there's just one more dance before it's time to go in to supper."

Over the heads of the young ladies, Gerard had seen her, and he made his way toward her to claim the next dance.

"We timed it badly, I'm afraid," he said. "When we go into the supper room I'll get you a plate of stale food, but would not recommend that you eat it. There's bound to be something better at the Liverpools'. How do you feel?"

"I was feeling wonderful until Timothy told me that Lord Burlington has come to town, and now I keep looking to see if he is coming in the door," she said a little nervously.

"He's unlikely to come here, even if he is in town, for the only places I've ever run into him were gaming hells, so you can stop worrying, my love," he told her, with tenderness in his glance. "We'll stay to have just one more dance here after supper, then find out how Lady Davenport is getting along before we leave."

"But you've not danced with anyone else, Gerard," she protested weakly.

"I have. I danced with Margaret Torrington while you got up with her brother," he said, trying not to sound as though it had been a sacrifice, as he was very fond of his friend's sister. "I hadn't realized what fun it would be to get up for every dance with the only one you want for a partner, instead of limiting it to just two dances."

They checked on Lady Davenport, who was having an excellent time reminiscing with her friends, then joined the Torringtons for supper. After one more dance, as Gerard had said, they took the carriage to the Liverpool home and sent it back to wait until Aunt Charlotte was ready to leave.

It was almost two in the morning when they got back to Hill Street, and Leonora was glad she could sleep late for once.

The evening had been so successful that she had very few qualms now about dining with the Percevals. In fact, she was looking forward to it, for she had heard that the Prime Minister was a family man, having six daughters and six sons, and far from being a dashing and flamboyant figure, he was a devout Anglican, puritanical and incorruptible.

He was not yet fifty years of age, and showing himself to be an excellent leader in these troubled times.

The invitation had been received, and Leonora dressed carefully, selecting a gown in a rich royal blue, with which she wore a pearl necklace and had Millie thread pearls through her upswept hair.

She had now formed a habit of going into Gerard's chamber to let him see how she looked once she was dressed for the evening, and tonight was no time to make an exception, for she needed his reassurance.

"You look elegant and lovely, my dear," he said approvingly, "but are you sure you don't want to wear the sapphire necklace? I sent for it and it's now in the safe here."

"Everything I've heard about our host leads me to believe that he is a much more simple man than his contemporaries, and I think the sapphires would be a little ostentatious for what surely will be a business dinner," she said.

Gerard glanced at her with admiration. "How astute you are becoming, my love. I think you are wearing exactly the right thing in those pearls, and you will probably, in fact, make many of the women in jewels appear over-dressed."

He remembered these remarks as they sipped sherry before going in to dinner and he took Leonora around to meet the various politicians and their wives. He felt very proud of her, for she was undoubtedly the loveliest lady there, and she was, of course, the youngest, but she carried herself like the countess she would probably become within a few years.

The dinner was not exceptional. The food was good, well-cooked fare, well-prepared and elegantly served, but the expensive little fancy touches the ladies of the *ton* strove to add to their dinners were not present, and not really missed by most. The wines were, of course, French, and a smile twitched at Gerard's lips as he recalled Leonora's eloquent statement not very long ago regarding smuggling.

He wondered if she remembered it also, and glanced

across the table, but saw she was listening to an oration from an up-and-coming young Tory who had found a patient ear. As though sensing his eyes upon her, she looked up and gave him a lovely, secret smile.

He could not remember now how he had gone on before he met her, for he could not imagine a life without her beside him, without her laughter and her loving, both passionate and tender, and her unusual concern for the welfare of those less fortunate than herself.

The ladies retired to the drawing room, leaving the men to their port, cigars, and the more serious business of the evening, and Leonora found herself sitting beside an older woman, sipping tea and listening to her tell how the country should be run, and would be run if her husband had his way.

She trained herself to listen with only half an ear, and make the required noises occasionally, while she studied the other ladies in the room.

Most of them were like the one beside her, nothing but mouthpieces for the policies and politics of their husbands. Aunt Charlotte had been right, of course, for she had probably been to many such dinners, under another government, and another prime minister, but with the same kind of people, hungry for power.

Only the Percevals seemed different. He was a good man, she felt, and his wife looked gentle and kind, but after having birthed twelve children, she appeared completely worn out, and was probably too tired to spout his policies to any useful purpose.

Leonora allowed her mind to wander to her husband, who was probably as bored right now as she was, but at least he had a glass of wine in front of him rather than this weak tea. When he had looked at her across the dinner table, he had felt so close she could feel him in the tips of her fingers. She loved her family, and Geoffrey, of course, most of all, but the feelings she had for Gerard were something completely different. Without him life would no longer be worth living. She went to sleep each night with his arms around her, and each morning she awoke to find him there, sometimes pressing delicate kisses all over her.

She thought of the child that might be growing inside her, and though she knew she had not gained any weight to notice, she still felt that it was there. There had been no ill effects as yet, and if they came and Gerard saw them, she would have to tell him, but she could not bear his disappointment if she was wrong.

Still thinking of him, while the voice beside her droned on, she looked toward the door and he was suddenly there. She wanted to jump up and run to him, but she did no such thing, and in a moment he was at her side.

"I've sent for the coach, my love," he said, then turned to the ladies. "Your gentlemen have only one more matter to discuss, which is of no concern to me, and they asked me to tell you they would be no more than five minutes. Now, if you will excuse us, we will wish you a good evening."

Leonora slipped her arm in his and walked toward the door, stopping only to say good night to their hostess, and then they were out into the clear air, and the carriage looked most inviting.

Once they were inside and the coach started moving, Gerard drew her into his arms. "The evening must have been scarcely tolerable for you, I'm sure, my love. I am so sorry," he murmured.

"I have spent more boring evenings," she said consolingly, then added, "but not many. Can you believe that those women have not a thought in their heads that has not been spouted by their husbands?"

"Of course I can. And I can also envision the female that young Tory who was seated next to you will marry. I watched him and I don't believe he ever stopped talking except to fork some food into his mouth. It has to rub off onto the wife if she listens to that monologue day in and day out for years."

"They don't want you to go into politics, darling, do they?" she asked rather cautiously.

"Oh, they would like me to, but I have no intentions of doing more than taking my seat in the House when we're a little more settled. I was there tonight to give them a report, and am only sorry that you had to spend such a dreary evening."

"It was enlightening to some extent," Leonora told him as she nibbled on one of his ears. "And I hope you're not as prolific as your Prime Minister, for I have no wish to bear twelve children."

"You won't, love," he murmured, before raising her chin and taking possession of her lips.

It was still as exciting as the first time he had kissed her, and she lay back in his arms, thrilling at the passions sweeping through her and wishing they were home in their chamber and could bring what they had started to a satisfactory conclusion.

When they came up for breath, he still held her close, and said softly, "I'm afraid we have to be up early in the morning, my love."

"Are we going riding?" she asked, for he had promised her they would occasionally ride in the park when no one was around and they could gallop.

"No, but I think it's something you'll like just as much. I have arranged for you to sit for Thomas Lawrence in the morning. He's a member of the Royal Academy, and I also intend to ask him about finding a master for you to study under."

"You do?" Leonora asked. "You shame me, sir, for I thought you had forgotten all about it."

"No, I just wanted to surprise you, that's all," he told her, then allowed himself to be thoroughly kissed once more by a young lady who was fast learning the art.

19

The studio of Thomas Lawrence had large windows to let in the light and smelled delightfully, in Leonora's opinion, of turpentine and oil paint, a medium she was most anxious to try.

Though the hour was early, she had spent considerable time and care on her appearance, and was wearing a gown that Gerard had selected, the one made from the ice-blue lace she had received from Ted. She could not help but wonder if her husband had deliberately selected something that would remind them both of her smuggling days whenever they looked at the portrait.

Her long black hair was loose, and Millie stood close at hand, ready to arrange it in whatever style they should decide upon.

But first came the gown. Mr. Lawrence draped a couch in a cloth of deep blue velvet. "Now, my lady," he said, "I want you to sit down, and then sit up nice and straight."

Leonora complied, and he then told her, "You may wriggle a little now, but maintain those straight shoulders, and make yourself as comfortable as possible, for I will require you to hold the pose for about half an hour at a time."

Leonora did as he asked, smiling a little nervously at Gerard, who lounged against a pillar, watching.

Mr. Lawrence then picked up one of her arms and laid it along the armrest, placing her hand so that it drooped elegantly, and showed off her betrothal ring. The other arm was allowed to rest in her lap, but only after he had skillfully arranged the skirts of her gown to fall elegantly and evenly to the floor.

"Now I need your abigail," he said, and Millie stepped forward, proud of her promotion, though in name only.

"You will disturb nothing but the hair, and I wish to see height of this much." He indicated about three inches with his hands. "Then it must trail over the shoulders on each side, like this, but the ends must be turned into soft, fat ringlets."

Millie went to work, and Mr. Lawrence looked at Gerard. "You have, perhaps, a family necklace you wish her to wear?" he asked.

Gerard nodded. "There is a sapphire-and-diamond necklace which would look well, but I hardly like . . ."

"Quite so, my lord," Mr. Lawrence said with a smile. "As long as I know that something will be there, I need not have it before me until the next-to-last sitting."

He instructed Millie on a couple of details, then stepped back and judged it to be perfect except for one small detail. "I would like to also see a matching coronet atop that magnificent hair," he told Gerard.

Leonora opened her mouth to protest, but Gerard just smiled and nodded as though such pieces of jewelry grew upon trees.

"It will be here on the same day as the necklace, Mr. Lawrence," he assured the artist, "and now I have a favor to ask of you. I know that you do not teach students, but my wife is most talented in watercolors and I would like her to study oils under a master. If you know any Academicians who have openings in a class, I would appreciate their names."

Mr. Lawrence seemed not at all impressed. "I know of many young ladies whose families believe they paint excellent watercolors of flora and fauna," he said dryly, implying that his associates did not like having their time wasted on mediocre talent.

"Turner is lecturing on perspective, but that might be rather difficult for a lady to grasp," he went on vaguely, "but John Constable has an excellent landscape in the Royal Academy entitled *Dedham Vale*, and I believe he has only moderate means as yet and may be taking students.

He would, of course, need to see a sample of Lady Sinclair's talent before agreeing to teach her."

"Do you have his direction, by any chance?" Gerard asked, slightly irritated by the fellow's disdain.

Lawrence nodded. "Yes, I'll let you have it as soon as I have something down," he muttered as he prepared his palette, then took a large brush and made sweeping strokes on canvas.

Gerard waited, a little impatiently, for more than twenty minutes until the artist laid down his brush and allowed Leonora to relax her pose. Then he went over to her while Lawrence walked across to a desk in the corner and started to shuffle through a mass of papers.

"Ah," Lawrence said triumphantly, holding out a slip of paper, "here it is. This is his present residence, only a few minutes from here, so perhaps you would like to pay him a call while Lady Sinclair sits for another half-hour."

Gerard took the paper and placed it in his pocket, then bent over Leonora. "I'll be back by the time you are ready to leave, my love," he said, dropping a kiss on her forehead, then hastening from the room.

Leonora had stretched her arms and moved her body from the position it had stiffened in, but she had deliberately not moved her legs for she knew that her skirts would have taken a long time to rearrange.

After Gerard left, Millie came over to make sure Leonora was all right, and to let the artist, who to her was a rather peculiar kind of man, know that her mistress was being well-guarded.

When she was in her pose once more, and Lawrence was busy at work, Leonora addressed some of her annoyances, keeping her voice well-modulated, however, so that he would not think her anything but a lady.

"I think you should know, Mr. Lawrence, that I do not paint flora and fauna, and watercolor is the only medium I have learned," she told him.

"Then what do you paint, my lady?" Lawrence asked. "Not portraits, I'm sure."

Carefully keeping her head in place, despite her impatience with the man, Leonora said, "I paint portraits, sir."

Lawrence peered around his easel and applied another brushful before asking her, "Who taught you?"

"To paint portraits? No one. As I have no doubt you expected, one of my governesses taught me to paint in watercolor because my needlework left so very much to be desired. It was after she went the way of all the rest that I tried to adapt it to portraits."

"With little success, I imagine," Lawrence said dryly.

"On the contrary, sir, with considerable success, for I adopted a free-flowing style instead of the compact style I had been taught." Leonora's head remained in position, though her expression was a little fierce. However, Mr. Lawrence was not painting in detail today.

"Free-flowing?" Lawrence asked. "But that's not the current watercolor style."

"Maybe not," Leonora replied, "but it is extremely effective, though lacking the precision of oils. Would you happen to have any watercolor paints here?"

"As a matter of fact I do, but it's no good convincing me. The one you have to convince now is Mr. Constable," Mr. Lawrence told her.

It was difficult not to turn her head, but she managed it as she said, "I will convince him, Mr. Lawrence, make no mistake about that, for I have few other feminine accomplishments, but I most certainly paint better than anyone I know."

"That makes me wonder how many people you know, my lady," Lawrence said dryly. "But if Lord Sinclair is not back by the time you need your next rest, I will give you the opportunity to show me."

That was all Leonora needed, and the minute he told her she could relax the pose, she leapt up from the sofa. "Where are the paints?" she asked.

He gave her a pad, water, brushes, and paints, then stood watching how she went about it, noting that when she said free-flowing, she really meant it, for there were no dainty dabs of color as the hand that held the brush swept across the paper.

A few minutes later there was a knock on the door and Gerard entered, but Leonora did not look up as she determined to prove her worth. Then with one final flourish she put down the brush and handed the pad to Mr. Lawrence.

He gazed at it in astonishment, and Gerard came over to see what he was looking at. It was, of couse, quite unfinished, but there was no doubt that it was an excellent sketch in watercolors of Mr. Lawrence.

He handed it to Gerard. "Here. If Mr. Constable wishes to see her work, you may show it to him and tell him she completed it in less than ten minutes. But don't leave it with him, for I want it back."

"Are you finished for today?" Gerard asked.

"Yes, sir. Your wife is an excellent subject, as I am sure you know, and she is also a patient model, so I was able to accomplish much in a short time. Come back at the same time two days hence, and I'll be waiting."

Before they left the house, Millie helped her mistress into a pelisse that completely covered the lace evening gown, and placed a matching bonnet on her head, then left to make her way back to Hill Street. Leonora and Gerard went out to the waiting carriage and drove no more than four or five streets away to a little old house that had seen better days.

"Constable is not yet in the financial position of Lawrence, but I am sure he will be, for I saw some of his work, which is quite exceptional," Gerard said. "You will not learn portraiture from him, but he is an outstanding landscape painter, and is bound to gain in popularity in the years ahead."

"Did he agree to accept me in his class?" Leonora asked.

Gerard pointed to the portrait Lawrence had lent him. "He will, when he sees this. You amazed the imperturbable Thomas Lawrence, and that is quite an achievement."

They mounted the steps and a housekeeper let them in and showed them up to the attic, where the artist had his studio, opening the door and announcing them to her employer.

Mr. Constable was not a young man, but in his middle years, quite close to the age of Mr. Lawrence, Leonora would have guessed, and he took the still-damp watercolor from Gerard and examined it closely.

"You just painted this, Lady Sinclair?" he asked in some surprise.

"Yes," Leonora admitted. "Mr. Lawrence thought I painted flora and fauna, as he put it, and I convinced him otherwise."

"And you've never tried oils?"

"No, sir, for I know it to be an entirely different technique and wanted to learn to do it the right way," she said.

He nodded slowly. "I have a class that meets twice a week on Tuesday and Thursday mornings. Do you think you could get here promptly at nine o'clock after spending the previous evening, no doubt, at Almack's?"

"As long as I am here at nine each day, I hardly think my activities of the night before are any of your concern, sir," Leonora said sharply.

"Then be here on Thursday at nine, and bring this list of supplies." He handed Leonora a slip of paper, which she glanced at, then put into her purse.

"I'll be here, Mr. Constable, complete with everything on this list," she said firmly, then thought of one more question. "Do the ladies in your class wear an apron?"

"There are no females in my class, my lady, and I would advise you to bring something to cover up your gown if you do not wish it to get spattered with paint. Good day to you, my lady, my lord," he said, and closed the door after them.

"What a surly man," Leonora remarked. "He seemed to take an instant dislike to me, and I cannot think why."

"He did not wish to accept a female student, but when Lawrence sent that portrait over, there was no possible way he could refuse without giving himself a bad name," Gerard told her. "Had you brought a painting that had

been done some time ago, I am sure he would have said it
could be anyone's work, but he could not deny that it was
yours when such an eminent artist as Lawrence had
authenticated it," he went on. "Are you sure you want to
work under him?"

"I really don't see why not, unless he makes it very
uncomfortable for me, in which case I will let you know."
Leonora paused. "I tried to get a glimpse of Mr.
Lawrence's work thus far, but he had covered it even
before I rose from the sofa."

"He'll probably do that every time," Gerard said with a
grin. "I can't think why he would not want your criticism
as he goes along, can you?"

Leonora laughed merrily. "Yes, I can, and I really don't
blame the poor man. He's probably wondering now how
he'll ever get through all the necessary sittings, for though
he said otherwise, I must be a much worse model than
anyone he's ever painted before."

"He painted Queen Charlotte's portrait a number of
years ago, and is the official painter to King George, so I
doubt that you can claim distinction as his worst model,
my love," Gerard observed. "I felt you earned his respect,
for he did not like to part with your watercolor of him."

"He is rather free with your purse, Gerard. You may
have a necklace that I can wear, but to practically order
you to buy a coronet is surely going too far," Leonora
suggested.

"I don't have to buy one, love," he said, surprised that
she had thought such a thing. "There is a coronet that
matches the necklace in the safe here in London, so it's just
as easy to use both pieces as one. I'll take them out when
he needs them, and return them the same day."

They had turned into Park Lane and were halfway along
when Gerard asked, "Would you like to go for a drive
through Hyde Park? You haven't been there, and might
enjoy it."

"I'd be delighted, darling, though I'm not dressed as
fashionably as I had intended for my first drive."

Gerard looked at her pelisse and bonnet. "You'll do

nicely, for there are not yet many people in town, and we will probably not see anyone we would stop for.''

He swung the carriage into the park and proceeded at a much slower pace, occasionally nodding or raising his hat to acquaintances, but saw no one to whom he wished to introduce Leonora. He had been right, there were not many members of the *ton* in town as yet, but things would be very different in a few weeks.

After a half-hour they started back and, to their surprise, encountered Sir Henry Wallace and his sister, Genevieve, out for a morning ride.

''I say, my lady,'' Sir Henry said jovially, ''I was very sorry to hear about your brother. Hope your father's in prime twig now, but he must be, I suppose, if you're in town.''

Leonora looked at him strangely, wondering whether he was commiserating with or congratulating her. Then Genevieve came to her rescue.

''We missed you when you did not come for the Season, and then we heard that your brother had been killed in Spain and your father laid low with the shock. Is he feeling better now?'' she asked anxiously.

''He's much better since we heard that my brother is well and back in action,'' Leonora told them. ''In fact, we're hoping that he'll soon be home on leave so that we can see for ourselves how well he is.''

''You're staying in Hill Street?'' Sir Henry asked. ''I'll stop by and take you for a ride one of these days. You never did get that ride I promised you in Bath.''

Gerard's smile did not quite reach his eyes. ''I'm afraid we're still on our honeymoon, old boy,'' he said with sarcastic familiarity. ''And for the time being, when my wife wishes to go for a ride, I take her.''

Genevieve reached over to grasp Leonora's hands. ''Allow me to wish you happy, my dear,'' she said, quite delighted at the news, then turned to Gerard. ''And you, sir, I congratulate for being so astute, for she is a rare find.''

Sir Henry still sat with his mouth open and eyes wide

with surprise until his sister nudged him with her riding crop. "Oh, yes. Yes, of course. Congratulations and all that. Bit sudden, though, wasn't it?" he asked.

"Not really." Leonora decided it was time she entered the conversation. "You see, we are distant cousins," giving the impression that they had known each other for years. "You must come to tea, Genevieve. I shall be at home tomorrow afternoon."

"I'll be there, and Mama will probably come too. Are Lord and Lady Clairmont in town also?" Genevieve asked.

"No, they're waiting until Papa is a little more recovered, and also until my brother comes home on leave," Leonora explained. "But my Aunt Charlotte is with us at Hill Street."

"Bad luck, old fellow," Sir Wallace said gleefully. "Hoped you'd have the place to yourselves, I'm sure. Must get along now if we're to be back for luncheon, but I'll see you tomorrow afternoon."

"What a pity he has to come also," Leonora said when they were out of earshot.

"He is a bit of a bore, isn't he, love? I've yet to hear him make one sensible statement, but I certainly shocked him when I said we were wed."

"I thought he was trying to catch flies, his mouth was open for so long. But we'd best get back now, for Margaret promised to come immediately after luncheon and take me somewhere where I can get oil-painting supplies. You did say you would be out, didn't you?" she asked.

"Of course, but even if I hadn't been, I would never begrudge you time with your friends. You two seemed to take to each other right away."

"Having a woman friend is new to me, and I think I am going to enjoy it. There's so much we can talk about," she said with a mischievous twinkle, "like clothes, curtains, maids, new dishes to serve."

"And much more, I'm sure, love, for Margaret Torrington happens to be one of the brightest young women of my acquaintance. Timothy is bringing her again, so if you're going to be back for tea, we'll make a point of returning also."

20

Between sittings for her own portrait and taking oil-painting classes twice a week, Leonora's mornings were completely taken up now, and she had insisted on Millie accompanying her, instead of wasting Gerard's time.

Afternoons were occupied in what she thought a useless round of entertaining and returning calls, except for the occasional shopping that must be done, and Leonora now found that she saw less of Gerard than she liked.

She was doing what he wanted her to do, however, and if she was bored much of the time, the people she was with never knew, for she had learned to conceal it beneath a big smile and a gay laugh.

And this would not go on forever, for the portrait must soon be finished, and she had a feeling that when she told Gerard of the interesting condition she was in, he would insist on returning to Devon immediately.

She had just come home after paying calls. Margaret had dropped her off in Hill Street, and she was still in the hall when the doorbell rang. Unfortunately, the footman was new, or he would never have opened the door while his mistress was making her escape up the stairs.

"Leonora, I'm glad I caught you home," the familiar voice boomed, and she turned around to see Lord Burlington pushing his way past the servant.

"Show Lord Burlington into the drawing room," she instructed. "I'll be down in a moment, sir, when I have removed my street clothes."

Millie was tidying up her chamber, and helped her off with her pelisse and bonnet.

"You'd best lie down for a half-hour, milady, for you

look worn out. Doesn't 'is lordship know that you're increasing?'' the maid asked.

"Not yet, Millie," Leonora snapped. "When I start being sick, I'll be forced to tell him, but I want my portrait finished before he sends me home." She sighed. "I can't lie down just yet, for Lord Burlington is in the drawing room."

"Didn't you say 'e was to be told you're out if he called, milady?'' Millie asked in surprise.

"Of course, but that new footman is inexperienced and he opened the door while I was still on the stairs. If he shows no improvement, we'll have to get rid of him," she said, unusually irritable.

"Now, just sit down, milady, and I'll fix your hair. Maybe 'is lordship will come back and take care of 'im if you wait up 'ere long enough," the maid said hopefully.

"I don't think he will be back for an hour or more yet, so I'd best go and get it over with," Leonora said. She had faced him alone before, and would do so again, for there was no way in which he could harm her.

But she did keep him waiting for fifteen minutes before pinching her cheeks to give her a little more color and descending the stairs.

He rose as she entered, declined her offer of tea, and seated her in a chair near the fire, taking an adjacent one for himself.

"Married life seems to suit you, Leonora," he growled. "You're looking very well. There are roses in your cheeks, as though you'd just come back from a sail instead of gadding around London."

She raised an eyebrow, not knowing quite how to reply to such a remark, for she could not recall an occasion when he had seen her returning from sailing her sloop.

"Not that sloop of yours you used to take out nearly every day, though," he said with a grunt. Then his voice changed to a slightly more menacing tone. "I heard you'd gone on to bigger and better boats, like a fishing lugger, for instance."

Had he not been watching her face closely, he would

have missed the slight gasp that escaped her lips. He had not known for sure that it was her, but a fisherman he knew to be a smuggler had let something slip after a drink or two too many in the inn one night. The man had mentioned a high-ranking lady going out with them, and he'd put two and two together and come up with Leonora Clairmont, or Sinclair as she was now called, but would not be by the time he'd finished with her.

"I don't know what you're talking about, my lord. Did you come here to see my husband?" Leonora asked sharply.

"No, I came to see you, and if you're sensible, he'll know nothing about our conversation today," he snapped. "I know you took over Geoff's illegal activities when he went into the army, and I have proof, so there's no use in denying it. And if I decided to give information to the authorities, they'll start to question you and apply whatever pressure they need to make you talk, believe me."

"What do you want, my lord?" she asked quietly. "Why did you come here today?"

"That's better. I thought you'd show some sense." He sneered, his beady black eyes gleaming malevolently. "What I want is your companionship, as you might call it, for starters. I have a voucher for Almack's and I want two dances every night you're there. I want you to be seen with me driving in the park, serving tea to me here in this house, and escorting you places."

"I couldn't," Leonora protested. "Lord Sinclair would not understand. Such behavior would break up our marriage."

A gleam of satisfaction showed on his brutish countenance as he nodded. "I always thought you were smarter than your brother, my gal. If you were arrested and tried for smuggling, that would break up your marriage too, wouldn't it? And that's your only alternative.

"You've snubbed me for the last time, you little bitch, daring to call me a liar! Revenge is going to be very sweet indeed. And when Sinclair no longer wants you, perhaps I'll be good to you, do you a favor and let you be my mistress until I grow tired of you."

He rose and looked down at her scornfully. "I'll see you at Almack's," he taunted with an ugly grin, "and you'd better look as if you're enjoying dancing with me, or it will be the last time they'll ever admit you."

Leonora sat there for some time after he left. It might be due to her condition, but at this moment all she wanted to do was retch, as her stomach churned round and round, so she just sat until the feeling passed and she was able to walk up the stairs without the servants noticing anything.

Millie was still in her bedchamber, waiting for her, and when she saw how pale she was she drew her toward the chaise longue and made her sit down with her legs up.

"What happened, milady?" she asked, deeply concerned.

Millie and Gerard were the only ones who knew of her transgressions, and she dared not say anything to Gerard, for she felt sure he would kill him—or Burlington would kill Gerard.

"One of the men has told him about my smuggling activities, Millie," she said flatly.

"Who would have done a thing like that?" the maid asked in disbelief, for she knew they had a strict code that none of them would willingly break.

"I don't know, just one of them who had too much to drink one night, I suppose. He may not have mentioned my name, but he wouldn't have to, for if he said a lady of rank, who else could it be around there?"

She suddenly looked very pale and tired, and all she wanted to do was leave London and the places where that monster wanted to be seen with her, and just go home.

"I couldn't believe my eyes when I saw whom you were dancing with," Gerard said angrily. "I thought we had agreed that you would rebuff him if he made any kind of advances toward you when I was not around. Instead, you looked as though you were having a wonderful time."

"Oh, darling, he's not half as bad as you make him out to be," Leonora said with a tinkling little laugh. "Don't tell me you're jealous, Gerard?"

It was bad enough to feel her skin crawl when Burlington put a hand on her waist, without Gerard getting so cross, she thought.

When they went home in the carriage, Gerard did not attempt to hold her as he had always done before. Instead he sat in an icy silence in his corner of the coach, for even after he had protested, she had danced a second time with Burlington.

That night, for the first time since they had arrived in London, he did not come to her chamber, and Leonora cried herself to sleep.

A few days later, half the *ton* saw her sitting in Burlington's carriage, driving through Hyde Park, with a bright smile pasted on her face and her head held high—and one of his beefy hands around her waist.

The explosion came after dinner that night, when they had planned to go to a musical evening at Lady Wallace's home.

The meal had been consumed in silence, but when Leonora went upstairs to get her wrap, Gerard was waiting.

"If you think I'm going to take you into the company of the very people who saw you in Hyde Park this afternoon, you must be about in the head," he told her. "I've asked you before, and I'm going to ask you again now. You've always loathed the man. Why are you allowing yourself to be seen with someone of his sort in the most public places?" he demanded, catching her wrist and pulling her toward him as she tried to turn away.

Visibly shaking, Leonora said nothing, and he finally released her wrist, noting with disgust the red marks his fingers had left.

"Lawrence has sent word that he will need the jewelry for your sitting tomorrow. I'll go with you and I'll be ready to leave at nine. Just be sure you're down on time," he snarled, then flung out of the room.

Leonora stretched out on her bed, fully clothed, not crying now, for she seemed to have done nothing but that for the last week. She wanted desperately to go home to Clairmont House, and after the next sitting in two days' time, she would be free to do so, for it was the only thing keeping her in town.

She heard the slam of the door, and knew it must be Gerard, for no one else would dare. He must have gone out without her, she thought as she reached for the bell pull, for there was no point in creasing her gown this way. And if she had a good night's sleep, she'd be up bright and early in the morning.

But she slept badly, and when morning came, she did not go down to breakfast; for the first time, she was sick. Millie put a cold cloth on her head and brought her some dry biscuits to nibble on.

"Let me tell 'is lordship that you're not fit to go today," she begged, but Lenora was adamant. The sooner her sittings were over, the sooner she could leave this wretched city and go home.

"I was just about to . . ." Gerard began when he saw her coming down the stairs, and her white face stopped him. "Are you all right?" he asked.

She managed a smile. "I'm fine, just a little tired after such a late night, that's all."

He had inquired if she had left the house, and been told she had not, but now he wondered if she'd sneaked out to meet Burlington. Then he took himself in hand. She was just being sarcastic because he had not taken her to the engagement they had accepted, nor to the place he went to, but that particular gaming hell was no place for a lady.

The morning was a little cold, but she was warm enough, for a pelisse covered her evening dress, which she had begun to weary of.

When they reached Lawrence's studio, Gerard placed the necklace around her throat and he noticed that she trembled at his touch, but he had no way of knowing that it was a shiver of desire and not a shudder of disgust.

"Yesterday Margaret Torrington brought an invitation

to luncheon at their home, and I accepted. I am sure you would be welcome if you would care to join us," she said, and felt relieved when Gerard nodded.

"I'll come with you and return these to the safe later," he told her, then stood back and watched as Lawrence arranged her hands and gown in the original pose.

There was no question but that she did not look well this morning, he thought, feeling disgusted with himself for the way he had treated her last night. But he simply could not understand why she was defying him and seeing a man he knew she had always despised. He had never actually said she must not see the man, for he did not think it would be necessary once he had indicated his disapproval.

He waited until the sitting was at an end, then put away the jewelry and escorted her to the curricle, making sure she was comfortable before setting out for the Torrington residence. It was early for luncheon, but he wanted to see a pistol that Timothy had bought, and he knew Leonora would enjoy Margaret's company.

When he and Timothy were alone, however, his friend brought up the matter of Leonora seeing Burlington.

"Margaret and I have been discussing it, for she cannot get anything out of Leonora when she asks her, except the foolish answer that she enjoys that boor's company," he began. "So we have come to the conclusion that he has some sort of hold on her, perhaps a different form of blackmail."

"I don't know what you mean, Timothy," Gerard said in disgust. "She seems to be seeing him completely of her own free will, for she smilingly accepts his request for a dance, and she could think of many an excuse if she wished. And I've been told that she looked delighted with that ride in the park, certainly not as though she were with him against her wishes."

"That's just it. Don't you see, Gerard, that it's always in the open. He wants as many of the *ton* as possible to see them together. I don't think he wants her, I think he's trying to break up your marriage."

"He'll succeed if it goes on much longer," Gerard

declared, "for I don't appreciate being made to look like a fool in the eyes of all my friends."

"Have you thought of going home?" Timothy asked. "If you went to Bristol, he could hardly see her there in front of your family, could he? And away from him and London, Leonora might tell you what it's all about."

"It's a good idea," Gerard said, thinking about it carefully. "She has only one more sitting for Lawrence, in two days' time, and then the portrait will be finished, and I have a meeting with Perceval that same afternoon. Perhaps, after that, I can persuade her to visit Bristol, and if we go directly from here and take Lady Davenport with us, it might help."

But before mentioning it to Leonora, he needed to invite Lady Davenport, so when they returned home after their luncheon he explained to the old lady his plan to go to Bristol. She looked at him rather strangely.

"Do you think that will bring her to her senses?" she asked dryly.

He saw no reason to prevaricate. "Something has to, my lady, for her behavior has been very strange this last week or more."

"Why don't you confront the man?" she asked. "She can't be seeing him because she wants to, for she's always disliked him intensely, and she looks to me now as though she's in a quake."

"But I've asked her, told her I will help her if she's in some kind of trouble, but she laughs in my face and says he's good company, implying he is better than I am," he said bitterly.

"And before he came on the scene, you were all lovey-dovey, weren't you now?" Lady Davenport said. "If I was in your shoes, I'd pack her off tonight. He'll not expect it when she's probably told him she's still sitting for Lawrence. I'll go with her, but we'll go to Clairmont House, because I think it's the only place where you'll get to the bottom of it. That's where it must have started, and that's where you'll find the reason for it.

"You stay here and keep saying that she's caught a cold

or something and is in bed, and see him if you have to, and tell him so yourself," she said. "Then there's one other thing. Trump up an excuse and get rid of that new footman. He was the one that let him into the house, and Burlington's always bragged that he knows everything that goes on with the Clairmonts, so he probably makes a practice of paying servants for information."

Gerard looked amazed. "How do you know all this, Lady Davenport?" he asked.

She smiled. "It's easy, for when you let people think you're a little deaf, my lord, and liable to doze off in a chair occasionally, it's surprising what you hear."

For the first time in a couple of weeks, Gerard enjoyed a good laugh.

"I'll go and see her right away, and unless I'm not mistaken, you'll be on your way to Devon tonight," he said.

21

Leonora was resting on the chaise longue when she heard someone go into Gerard's room. A moment later there was a light tap on the door, and he entered her chamber.

"I don't know exactly what is going on, my love," he said gently as he approached and sat down at the foot of the chaise, "but I'm sure something is, and I'm only sorry that you don't feel you can trust me." He put a finger to her lips as she started to say something. "Don't bother to deny it, for it is really of no consequence now. I came to tell you that you're leaving tonight, after dark, for Clairmont House."

She put her hands to her face and he distinctly heard her say, "Thank God," before she asked, "But you're not coming with me?"

He shook his head. "I cannot yet, for a couple of days, so I'm sending you back with Millie and Lady Davenport, and I want no one in the house except them to know you are leaving. When I finish here, I'm going to have a long talk with the footman we recently hired, for I think he may have been collecting information and passing it along to your newfound friend."

"Are you separating from me?" Leonora asked, thinking that Burlington had got part of what he wanted by breaking up the marriage.

There was much sadness in her eyes that Gerard took her into his arms, holding her so close that she could feel his warm breath on her cheek. "Of course not, love. We'll be apart for no more than a week at the most, for I'll stay here only a few days and set a rumor around that you are ill with a putrid throat. Then I'll follow you on horseback and may even catch up with you before you reach Clair-mont House.''

"Can't I say good-bye to Margaret?" she asked.

"I'm sending them a note explaining a change of plan, for they felt you should go to Bristol, but your Aunt Charlotte had a better idea. Timothy and Margaret will probably come by for tea this afternoon, and we'll see them in the drawing room, but after that you will have officially taken to your bed."

He went over to the bell pull and gave it a tug. "I want to talk to Millie myself, to be sure she understands the need for secrecy," he said, "and to see if she knows anything about that footman."

"Why can you not come with us instead of staying here and concealing my departure?" she asked.

"Because I have to meet with the Prime Minister the day after tomorrow," he said, "and I'd rather not delay your leaving for one more hour than I can help." Millie knocked on the door and entered, then appeared surprised when she saw Gerard. She gave a little bob and waited.

"I've just told your mistress that you and she are leaving with Lady Davenport this evening, Millie. You will be going back to Clairmont House and I want no one to know until you are well out of the way. Everyone here will believe that Lady Sinclair is abed with a putrid throat. Is that clear?" he asked.

"Then you told 'im, milady. Thank the Lord for that," Millie said with relief, but was surprised when Leonora shook her head.

Gerard looked at his wife reproachfully. "Start packing no more than you'll both need for the journey, Millie. I'll leave orders, when I finally follow you, for everything else to be packed and forwarded to us," he said, watching Leonora's unhappy face.

"Now I'll go and have a talk with that footman, and send word to Margaret and Timothy," he told her. "I'll be back in about a half-hour."

The maid started to pull out bags and put into them the clothes Leonora would need for the journey, laying out on

the bed the garments she would travel in, and when Gerard
returned, she was just folding the last garment.

She hurried off when she saw Gerard, and he resumed
his seat on the chaise. "Do you really mean to leave me in
the dark as to what is wrong, and yet you have confided in
your maid?" he asked with a reproachful smile.

"I don't want you to get hurt," Leonora said, "for he's
a vicious man—and I've said too much already," she
concluded. "It was one thing for you to go and fight Ted,
but this is different."

"How different?"

"He knows I was a smuggler, and he's going to turn me
in to the authorities unless I do what he wants," she told
him.

"I had considered that possibility but discounted it, for I
would swear that Ted and his men would never give you
away," he said, looking worried.

She shrugged. "I think one of them got drunk one night,
Burlington probably put something in his drink, and he
told him a fine lady went out with them."

"But he could never prove it, love," Gerard said.

"He says he has proof, and in any case, do you think I
could stand up to the kind of questioning they might put
me through? He implied that they would torture me," she
said quietly.

"They would never even touch you, love," he said
softly. "He reported Geoffrey one time, and all they did
was watch his movements, and they told me they never saw
him go near a fishing boat of any sort, so they never even
questioned him. The only way they could touch you would
be if the crew all gave evidence, and you know they'd never
do that."

"Then I went through this awful time for nothing?" she
asked.

"I don't think it was for nothing. I fear he has something more in mind than just being seen with you and
destroying our marriage," Gerard told her. "He must be
getting back at you for refusing to marry him, scorning
him, and calling him a liar. There's no knowing what

lengths he'll go to, so the sooner you are away from here and safely back in Clairmont House, the better I will feel."

"Did you question the footman?"

He nodded, and said briefly, "He'll not give us any further trouble, and I should think Margaret and Timothy will be arriving very shortly. In fact that may be they now." He rose as a tap sounded on the door.

"Why don't you ask them to come up here?" Leonora suggested. "We could have a tea tray brought up."

Gerard nodded, then gave the instructions, for it was a good idea both for privacy and to hint at Leonora's indisposition.

"Who is accompanying the ladies, if you cannot leave yet?" Timothy asked as soon as they were settled comfortably and had heard the change of plan.

"I was hoping I might prevail on you, unless you have something pressing to attend to," Gerard said. "I will follow and catch them up, but will not be able to do so for a day or two."

"Think no more about it, Gerard," Timothy told him. "I know where I can hire three reliable outriders, and I'll make a fourth myself. Then we'll be sure they're well-protected."

Lady Margaret had been sitting talking to Leonora, but had one ear on the men's conversation. "In that case, I'm coming along also," she declared. "I will be company for Leonora, and will enjoy a visit to the Devonshire coast."

Gerard looked over to Leonora with raised eyebrows. He thought it an excellent idea, but it was, after all, her decision.

"I'd love to have your company, Margaret, but I'm afraid it would be imposing on you at such short notice. I do thank you, though."

"If that's your only argument, Leonora, you just lost," Margaret said with a grin. "Decide where we'll meet, and I'll go home and pack a few things and break the news to Mama and Papa. They've heard what has been going on and will, I know, maintain silence as to our whereabouts," she assured them.

Timothy smiled indulgently at his sister, then told the others, "You may as well let her come, for she's a quiet little thing most of the time, but when she makes up her mind, there's no changing her."

The two men discussed the best place for them to meet the carriage with the outriders, and decided on a spot just to the west side of the Hyde Park turnpike. Then, after a brief discussion as to the best inns to stay at, the Torringtons left.

The inn at Dartmouth brought back many happy memories for Leonora. It had been a tedious journey, lightened considerably by Margaret's lively chatter, and they had hoped to reach Clairmont House that night. The weather had, however, deteriorated rapidly in the afternoon, and it was decided not to push on, but to stay at the inn and make an early start in the morning. Gerard had caught up with the party the night before, but there had been no rooms left, for the ladies were sharing a large one and he and Timothy had had to use a smaller one.

Tonight he and Leonora were to share a quite narrow bed, but they looked forward to being alone together and cared little for their surroundings.

Once they were all at supper in the private dining room, Millie slipped into the town, seeking the house where her sister worked. Her note to Ted was not perhaps in the best script or the best English, but he would understand it, she was sure. Her sister's friend was glad of the coin he earned, and knew where Ted lived. Satisfied, she hurried back to the inn and peeked into the dining room to see if she had been missed.

"Do you suppose Burlington will have passed us on the way?" Leonora was asking as they all sipped hot mulled wine at the end of the meal.

"It's more than possible," Gerard told her, "for had I not met up with you, I would have been there a day ago. He travels fastest who travels alone."

He saw Millie in the doorway and waved for her to come in. "Do you have Ted's direction, Millie?" he asked. "I'd like to pay him a visit in the morning if he's ashore."

"Yes, milord. I'll give it to you before we start out tomorrow," she said, smiling to herself.

"Don't wait up for me, Millie," Leonora said. "Just get yourself into bed when you're ready, and Lord Sinclair will help me."

"Thank you, milady," she said with a little bob, and was about to leave the room when Lady Davenport waylaid her.

"I don't have a Lord Sinclair to help me, Millie," she said with a twinkle, "so would you find out where that gal of mine has got to, for I'm sore in need of my rest. These old bones aren't used to sitting in cramped coaches for days on end."

She grumbled but, in fact, was happier than she'd been in years, for she felt useful again. If it had not been for her, they wouldn't be here now, so close to the safety of home.

"I'll find her for you, milady, and send her to your room. How about Lady Margaret?" Millie asked as she reached the door.

"Lady Davenport's maid will help me also, Millie, thank you," Margaret told her, then turned to Leonora. "What a jewel that girl is. I've never known a maid so thoughtful."

Leonora smiled. Her life would not be the same if Millie were not there to look after her, she thought.

"I believe we should all go up now," Gerard suggested, "for we want to make an early start in the morning. What a surprise they will have when we arrive."

He helped Leonora up the narrow stairs and into their small room, and as soon as the door was closed behind them, he took her in his arms and held her close.

"He came looking for you every day," Gerard whispered, his breath warm on her ear. "And there was a look about him on that third day that made me very sure he would leave right away."

"What do you think he will do?" she asked.

"I think the first thing will be a threatening letter. In fact, there may even be one waiting for you when we get there tomorrow. But let's not worry about that now, my love. Do you need me tonight as much as I need you?"

"More, much more," she answered lovingly. "For I've missed you so very much. In fact we've both missed you very much." She placed her hand on her stomach as she spoke.

"You mean . . . ?" he breathed, finding it difficult to believe, and when she nodded, he asked, "How long have you known?"

"I've been sure about it a little over a month," she said, "but I didn't tell you because I knew you'd not want me to travel."

"Oh, my idiotic darling," he murmured, and then, still holding her in his arms, he lifted her off her feet and carried her to the bed, laying her down almost reverently, then just holding her close for a long time.

Finally he became aware that something was tickling his ear and reached up to find that Leonora was playfully beating him with one of her curls.

"Take that, you varmint," she said, "and here's another one, and another one."

"What has that ear done to deserve such a thrashing?" he asked laughingly.

"It wasn't listening properly when I was crying out for help and understanding," she whispered.

"And there I thought I was being very patient and tolerant until that last night when I grabbed you so hard that I left my finger marks on your wrist. Did it leave a bruise?" he asked, lifting the hand but seeing no sign of any mark.

She shook her head, for it didn't matter anymore.

"Do you recall that we were the ones who were going to talk about all problems as they arose, so that they couldn't grow from something small to something too big to cope with?" he asked.

She nodded. "We failed miserably, didn't we?"

"I know something that we will not fail miserably with if we start right now," Gerard suggested.

"Now, I wonder what that could be?" she teased. "Let me guess. Could it—?"

"Never mind the questions, love. I think I'd better show

you instead of telling you this time," he said as he slid his body sensually down hers, and took one tender bud into his mouth.

Some time later they lay exhausted but happy, wrapped in each other's arms, and they were still in that same position the next morning when Millie knocked on the door, then unlocked it and put her head around. She closed it again quickly and knocked hard on the outside of the door until she heard his lordship's voice telling her to come back in ten minutes.

When the carriage arrived at Clairmont House in time for a late luncheon, its occupants were surprised to find that they were expected, though they had sent no advance message. Chambers had been dusted, fires lit, and beds aired for the Sinclairs and Aunt Charlotte, and now maids hurried to prepare rooms for the Torringtons.

Gerard felt most uneasy in this regard, having a grave suspicion as to who had informed Adele of their imminent arrival. When the others went upstairs to wash off the dirt of the road, he stayed behind to speak privately with her.

She led him into the study and handed him a sealed envelope that he saw was addressed to Lady Leonora Sinclair.

Without hesitating for even a second, he opened it and slid out the single sheet, which he read, then slipped back into its envelope and tucked into his pocket.

"Did he deliver this himself?" he asked Adele.

"He did, and he was most rude and officious, telling me that you were on your way and would, in fact, be here last night," she told him.

"We would have been had the storm not delayed us," he said. "However, under no circumstances must you let him into this house again, my dear, for I believe he might do serious injury to Leonora."

Adele showed none of the alarm he had expected; in fact she looked rather pleased with herself as she told him, "He won't injure anyone anymore, Gerard. His body was found an hour ago at the bottom of the cliffs beneath his estate. It is presumed that he took a walk early this morning along the clifftop, slipped, and fell to his death.''

"How very convenient, and what a relief," Gerard remarked, and Adele inclined her head in agreement. "I assume Lord Clairmont knows nothing about this," he said, tapping the pocket where he had placed the envelope. "How is he, by the way?"

"Very well indeed, and he's going to be even better when he wakes from his nap and finds you have all returned. I did not, of course, tell him of Burlington's visit," she said.

"Did you see Timothy Torrington and meet his sister, Margaret?" he asked. "She came all this way at only a few hours' notice, just to keep her friend Leonora company on the journey."

"Yes, I did meet her, and I was so pleased to find that Leonora finally has a woman friend of her own age. She seems to be a lovely girl," Adele remarked. "Do you think Lord Burlington really did meet with an accident, Gerard?"

"You mean did he fall or was he pushed?" He sighed. "Who knows? There must be many others besides us who will not mourn for him. I'll go now and break the good news to Leonora; then we'll come back and tell you all about London."

He had gone no more than a few steps past the door, however, when he spied Millie talking to her mistress on the landing above.

"I'm coming down in a moment, darling," Leonora called.

"Come now and bring Millie with you," he said.

When they reached him, he steered them back into the study, where Adele was still standing looking very thoughtful.

"Why don't you ladies take a seat while I ask Millie a question," he suggested, and when they were seated, he turned to the maid.

"Now, young lady. Did you by any chance send a message to your boyfriend when we were in Dartmouth? As I recall, you have a sister there, don't you?" he asked pleasantly.

"Yes, milord," she said, looking him straight in the eye. "And I did send Ted a message last night. Do you still need his direction?"

"No, thank you. I don't need it now. I'm sure you're looking forward to seeing him after all this time. Why don't you take the afternoon off, go down to the village, and make sure he's all right," he suggested. "And you might tell him, in case he has not heard, that Lord Burlington met with an accident early this morning. He must have slipped when walking along the clifftops near his home, for his body was found at the bottom of them a short time ago."

Millie beamed, presumably happy to have the afternoon off. "I'll tell him, and thank you, milord," she said, making for the door.

"And thank you, Millie," he said. "Enjoy your afternoon."

Epilogue

"Where's Elizabeth, my love? When I rode in a few minutes ago, Jean and Dorothy were playing with her on the lawn, but now they're nowhere to be seen," Gerard said anxiously.

"It was time for her nap, and Nanny went out to collect her charge. You know, if we're not careful she'll grow into a very spoiled little girl, for between your mother and your sisters, not to mention the two of us, she is petted and pampered all day long," Leonora told him, smiling but shaking her head.

"It's very different from your upbringing, love, isn't it?" he said, bending to place a kiss on that smiling mouth. "It will do her no harm, and she'll have competition when our son comes along."

She put a finger to his lips. "Hush, darling. Don't tell anyone yet, or they'll start to fuss over me from morning to night as they did when we came home just twelve months since."

He held her hand to his face, placing a kiss in its palm. "I'm glad to hear you call it home, for I was afraid your love of Clairmont House would make it difficult for you to live elsewhere."

She looked around the drawing room, the blazing logs on the fire reflecting on shining copper and brass. Bowls were filled with flowers and leaves from the garden, a basket of needlework was beside a comfortable chair, a well-used book on a table next to a man's pipe. Like the rest of the old manor, it had a friendly, comfortable feeling.

"I'd never seen this warm, inviting house then. Nor had

I met such a wonderful family who made me a part of them the moment I stepped through the door. Besides, Clairmont House is Geoffrey's, not mine," she said, "and, speaking of my brother, where do you suppose he has got to? His betrothal party is only two days away."

"He's probably over at the Torringtons', for he's hardly let Margaret out of his sight since the day he arrived at Clairmont House and found her wearing his old clothes and learning to sail your sloop," he said with a grin, then heard the sound of a familiar voice in the hall. "And, talk of the devil, here he comes."

The black-haired young man who walked into the drawing room a few minutes later was very different from the thoughtless boy who had gone eagerly to fight in Spain almost two years before, leaving his sister a dangerous legacy.

The resemblance between brother and sister was strong, as was the bond of affection. He smiled at Gerard and tweaked one of Leonora's curls. Gerard excused himself to go and change from his riding clothes, leaving them together.

"When are Papa and Adele expected, Geoff?" she asked him.

"This afternoon. I'll ride out after luncheon to meet them, for this place is not the easiest to find," he said thoughtfully, "and though Papa has made a remarkable recovery, I'd feel better if I were there to help him if needed."

"You mustn't continue to blame yourself for his seizures," Leonora gently scolded. "The doctor said the main cause was the life he had led, you know. His illness would have started even if you had not been thought killed in action."

"Yes, I suppose it would, Leo. But had he known what you were doing at my behest, he would never have survived the shock." He shook his head. "Before you left Clairmont House, Gerard told me what Burlington was trying to do to you."

"That was much more frightening than the smuggling

runs themselves," Leonora admitted. "And though I have a good idea what happened to him, I don't want to ever put it into words or hear anyone else do so, so let's not talk about him. Is Margaret getting nervous about her party?"

"A little, for there's a great deal of planning to do, but the Torringtons are a very sensible, calm lot on the whole. I can't believe my luck," he said feelingly.

Leonora smiled. "Believe in it, Geoff, for that's how Gerard and I still feel about each other, and we don't intend to lose it, for it's very precious." She heard some commotion and glanced toward the open door. "It would seem Papa has saved you some trouble, for I think they're here already."

"I must go and help," Geoffrey said, jumping up and heading for the hall, almost knocking over Nanny, who was bringing a gurgling baby Elizabeth to her mama.

"Where's my granddaughter?" Lord Clairmont roared as he came through the door. "My, how she's grown since her christening. Let me have her."

Lord and Lady Sinclair came in, and then Gerard returned, caught Leonora's eye, and walked around the group to where she stood watching the adults making willing fools of themselves as they clucked and cooed, vying for the attention of the tiny baby.

He placed an arm around her and looked down at her softly smiling face. "Happy, love, with all your family around you?" he asked.

She nodded. "As long as you're here, darling, I'm always happy," she told him, "for you made all this possible."

He bent his head, putting his lips close to her ear. "With quite a bit of help from my partner, love," he whispered as his lips found what they were seeking.